Just Say When

ELIZABETH BRIGHT

Paperback ISBN: 979-8-9916602-1-1

Cover Design by Yummy Book Covers

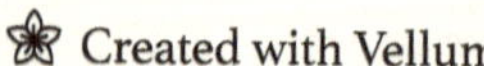 Created with Vellum

You were never too much.
They just weren't enough.

ESSIE

I f there was one thing Braxton Hale excelled at, it was ruining a good time.

Specifically, *my* good time.

I took a casual sip of my club soda with lime and pretended I didn't see Brax glaring at my reflection in the oily mirror from two barstools down. He'd probably already tattled to my twin brother, Jack. Later tonight I'd get an email from somewhere in the world—Jack rarely gave me an exact location, preferring to keep it vague, like "the Middle East" or "Africa"—demanding to know why I was at the Painted Cat, flirting with Alan Gaffney, a man a decade older who had a reputation for being a mean drunk.

Because of course Brax thought I was flirting. That was what I wanted him to think—the *him* being Alan Gaffney, of course. I didn't give a hot damn in hell what

Brax thought, so long as he didn't think I was here to get the man good and drunk so I could steal his horse.

Which was exactly what I was there to do.

A good time if ever there was one, and I was not about to let Brax Hale ruin it for me.

Pretending Brax didn't exist, I angled my body toward Alan and swung my leg, letting the short skirt I was wearing creep up my thigh another inch, because I wasn't above such things.

Alan was whining about something because, in addition to being a mean drunk, he was a man-baby.

I cupped my chin in my hands and stared at him like I found it all super fascinating. "Tell me more about that."

It was something I'd heard my friend, Chloe Adams, say and it never failed to get someone talking. Of course, Chloe was working on her doctorate in psychology in addition to being a barista at the local coffee shop, and she actually cared about the answer. Whereas I only cared about hearing whether Alan was slurring his words yet.

"It's like this," he said, each syllable perfectly crisp.

I sighed and rubbed my temple. That was the problem with getting a drunk drunk. It took a lot more alcohol to get them there. Reluctantly, I pushed my empty glass across the bar toward Janie, who took it with a raised eyebrow.

"Another round?" she asked.

I nodded. I was drinking a gin gimlet, hold the gin, but that was a secret between me and Janie. She hadn't asked why and I liked that about her. A splash of something stronger to get me through this tedious conversation with Alan would have been nice, but that wasn't a good idea. Rule Number One of horse rustling was don't get drunk on the job. Probably, anyway. This was my first go at it, but I already suspected I was a natural.

"And another beer for my friend," I added as Alan tipped the last of his ale down his throat.

His grin was lascivious as he swayed toward me. "Thank you, *friend*."

I didn't like anything about that, but I managed to swallow my vomit and smile back. "How about a shot of whiskey to wash it down?" I suggested to speed things along. "You could use it after such a rough day."

"Top shelf." His eyes glinted.

The audacity. What, exactly, did he think he was offering me in return? Sloppy sex? He couldn't honestly believe he was worth top shelf. I could do better for myself with both hands tied behind my back.

Janie looked at me, waiting. Masking my wince, I nodded. "Top shelf."

Goddamn, stealing a horse was an expensive thing. Paying in liquor might cost me more than paying in cash —which I had already tried, to no avail. If there was one universal truth of abusers, it was that they liked to keep the object of their abuse close, whether they were beating a woman or beating an animal.

Alan had been guilty of both at one time or another. His wife had had the good sense to leave his sorry ass years ago, but Pirate never had that option. Alan had won him as a leggy yearling in a poker game with a rich kid who had more money than sense. In the two years since, he'd kept him locked in his backyard that was barely big enough for a dog, forgetting to feed him more often than not.

I might never have known about it, but Alan liked to brag. There wasn't a single person in Aspen Springs, Colorado, who hadn't heard how Alan Gaffney had won Gee Whizz's colt with a straight flush and someday he'd be rich from stud fees.

Unlikely, considering Pirate spent every day standing cannon deep in his own shit, thrush evident in both hind hooves.

It made my blood boil thinking about it now. Boiled my blood and steeled my resolve.

Getting Pirate out of there was worth every cent of that whiskey. More. Not because the blood of a champion ran through his veins, but because the heart of a champion beat in his chest. I had taken one look at his mismatched eyes—one blue, one brown—and promptly fallen in love.

I had to save him.

"Hellion."

The word was a breeze against my bare neck, causing a riot of goosebumps on my arms. I spun slowly on my barstool and tilted my chin up to meet Brax's disapproving gaze. "Prig."

It was our standing greeting, at least for the last fifteen years or so—that is, when we bothered to greet each other at all. Mostly we ignored each other or let our glares do the talking.

With a narrow glance at Alan, he gripped my elbow with one large hand, hauled me off my stool and into a corner at the far side of the bar, and proceeded to loom over me in a way that made me wish for a few extra inches on my five-nine height.

"What the fuck do you think you're doing, Essie?" he demanded, his voice barely more than a low rumble.

I gave a toss of my ponytail and batted my eyes, knowing it would piss him off even more. "Having fun."

He glowered. "That's what I was afraid of."

You used to like my idea of fun. That was the kind of thing I would never say out loud, due to the high risk of it coming out wistful. And honestly? Death first. I would never give him the satisfaction.

Brax had always been a stickler for rules when we were kids. My brother Jack was even worse. Still, the three of us—Brax, Jack, and me—had been a tight trio. We had done everything together, right up to the day in our junior year of high school when Brax almost died. That had changed things—between me and Brax, anyway. He was still close with my brother. He *liked* Jack, the way he used to like me. Nothing had changed for them, not even when Jack joined the Army.

It was me he took umbrage with.

Umbrage. That was a good word. Too bad I so rarely had a reason to use it. I almost never took umbrage, aside from animal abusers. Unlike Brax, who took umbrage against every single thing about me.

"What are you up to, Essie?" He released my elbow and crossed his arms over his chest, legs akimbo, blocking my ability to get up to anything at all.

That annoyed me. Not that he was in my way; Brax wasn't prone to violence, and I knew his ticklish spots, so getting around him wouldn't be much of a challenge. No, I was annoyed that I had stood there for a solid minute and hadn't once thought to remove his hand from my elbow. He'd let go first, like my elbow had served its purpose and was no longer of any interest to him.

Galling, really.

I almost took umbrage with it.

But I had the feeling he would like that, so I simply smiled, knowing he wouldn't like that at all. "Can't a girl have a couple drinks and some laughs on a Friday night without people jumping down her throat?"

"Sure. But you're not having some laughs, Essie. You haven't laughed once. Alan Gaffney has never said a single interesting thing in his life, even by accident, and you rubbed your temple a moment ago. That means you're bored. Boring people give you a headache. The fact that you're still here talking to that jackass means you're up to something. Tell me what it is."

Damn our thirteen years of friendship.

"You know," I said coolly, "it's customary to forget all those intimate little details you learned about a person when the friendship no longer exists."

The corner of his mouth kicked up. "That so?"

"A gentleman would. It's the polite thing to do."

"See, that's the problem, right there." He leaned forward, his gaze hot as it seared into mine. "I've never felt like much of a gentleman where you're concerned."

My pulse jumped at the base of my throat as I swallowed hard. If Brax pushed me against the wall right now and put his hand up my skirt, I would be slow to stop him. I blamed his forearms and broad shoulders. It should be illegal to look that hot on the outside and be that irritating on the inside. False advertising, that's what it was.

I gave him a good, hard shove that failed to move him even a little bit. "You've been a gentleman every goddamn day of your life, Brax, because that's how your mama raised you, so don't try acting all tough with me. Even when you're asshole, you're a gentleman about it."

Which was exactly why I was going to win this little game. Brax was a gentleman to his core. Fortunately for Pirate, I was no lady.

"Get out of my way. I need to piss." I pushed past him, my shoulder hitting him somewhere in the bicep.

He let me pass like I knew he would. *Sucker*. I glanced over my shoulder to see him settle in next to my empty barstool and then jerked my chin at Janie. She followed me to the bathroom.

I handed her a wad of cash. "For Alan's next four drinks."

I almost felt bad about it, but the truth was, he was going to drink those drinks regardless of whether I was paying for them. Around ten, he'd pass out in his truck in the parking lot, too drunk to drive home. It was his Friday night routine. Me paying for it was for my own peace of mind, to make sure he stayed where I needed him to, for as long as I needed him to.

Janie nodded and tucked the money into her pocket. "And Brax?"

I heaved a long-suffering sigh. "Not much anyone can do about him," I groused. "Try to stall him, I guess."

"I'll do my best. Go out the back door, okay?"

"Thanks." I paused. "You know, we have a sewing club. Saturdays at the library, ten a.m. You should come."

"A sewing club?" She wrinkled her nose.

I laughed at her unenthusiastic response. "It's fun," I promised. "You get to stab things."

"Huh." She tilted her head, looking interested.

The sun was low in the sky when I slipped out the

back door of the bar. There was just enough daylight left for me to pick up Pirate and get him settled for the night. But first I had to slow Brax down. I grabbed the rapid tire deflator from my SUV—a nifty little device that had come in handy on more than one occasion— and squatted next to Brax's truck, adrenaline making my heart race as the air whooshed out with a hiss.

And then, even though I knew I shouldn't, I pressed my lips against the windshield. I wanted to leave no doubt in his mind that it was me. That I had won.

In my rearview mirror, I caught sight of him bursting out of the bar as I tore out of the parking lot, the empty horse trailer rattling behind me. I grinned. He was too late to stop me.

"Toodle-oo, mother fucker," I muttered, and hit the gas.

2

BRAX

Well, shit.

I eyeballed the deflated tire, then squatted low to get a closer look. There were no signs of treachery—other than the obvious one, anyway. I ran my fingers over the grooved rubber and found nothing. She hadn't made use of the pocket knife she always kept handy. I'd have to put on the spare, but at least I wouldn't need to shell out for a new tire. Real neighborly of her.

Still, I reached inside the driver's side to pop the hood, just to make sure she hadn't fucked around with anything else. I wouldn't put it past her, lulling me into a false sense of security with the deflated tire, only to cut the brakes.

That's when I saw it, the bright red mark on my windshield. Essie's kiss. I'd recognize that mouth anywhere. A cupid's bow with sharp peaks and a slightly fuller bottom lip.

I stared at the mark, rubbing my chest absently, while I considered my next move. She didn't want me following her, that much was clear. What was she up to? It only took a second for the puzzle pieces to click into place. The empty trailer bouncing over the gravel parking lot. Her sudden interest in the biggest loser alive. The lack of alcohol on her breath despite the empty glasses.

God*damm*it. I thumped my palm angrily on the steering wheel, then smacked it again for good measure, wishing it was Essie's ass. The little hellion deserved a spanking for this. She had always been wild and reckless, following her heart instead of her head. Straight into trouble, more often than not. Like the day she'd almost died—she hadn't learned one fucking thing from that, either.

The tire would have to wait. There was no way I could beat her to Gaffney's house. Even without the flat tire, she had a head start. If I couldn't stop her from taking the dipshit's horse, then I would simply have to change the stakes. A little jailtime might be exactly what Essie needed to get her head on straight, but Jack would tear mine right off if I ever let that happen to his twin sister.

I had made a promise. To him. To their mom. And

more importantly, to myself. Fuck if I was going to break that promise.

I shoved through the ancient oak door with enough force that it bounced off the wall. Janie's head jerked up and she eyed me warily as I approached the bar.

"Forget something?" she chirped, twirling a red lock of hair around one finger, her brown eyes wide with feigned innocence.

Like she was fooling anyone. We both knew her whole deal with the credit card machine giving her problems had been a stall tactic to help Essie. The woman had balls, I'd give her that.

Then again, it was the rare person who could say no to Essie Price. Her smile was wide, her laugh loud, her spirit bright. She was fun. Exciting. She was a rainbow in a gray world, and the thing was, if you stood next to her long enough, you got the crazy idea that maybe you could be a rainbow, too. I couldn't blame Janie for risking her job to be a rainbow.

I settled onto the stool Essie had vacated and gave Janie a baleful look. "You got a pen and notepad back there?"

She tilted her head, suspicion etched on her face like she was trying to figure out if giving me what I asked for was going to bite her on the ass. "Yeah."

"I'll take that and a water."

"You got it."

I turned to Alan. "How much for the horse?"

Since he only owned the one, he didn't ask for clarification. Just squinted at me with a greedy gleam in his dim-witted eyes. "Pirate's not for sale."

"Everything has a price."

"Not Pirate. He's special." He drained his beer, then nudged the empty glass to Janie. "Another one, sweetheart."

Janie reached for it, but I gave a quick, subtle shake of my head and she paused, then moved down the bar to cut limes, taking his glass with her.

I wondered what made Pirate special to a man like Alan Gaffney. Most people would point to the colt's bloodlines. Sired by Gee Whizz, a World Champion reiner several times over who had already earned his owners a cool million in stud fees, his dam being Pretty Gal, another winner, he had the potential to earn thousands in the ring.

He was pretty to look at, too. Of course, it was hard to tell lately, what with all that mud covering him. But underneath the filth, he was a flashy black-and-white paint quarter horse with a bald face. The white mark covered one blue eye, while his other eye was brown. Hence his name.

But I would hazard a guess that none of that mattered to Alan. If it had, Pirate would have been stabled at Lodestar, my family's quarter horse ranch, where the head trainer, James, could make a winner out of him. Instead, Alan had left him to rot in his backyard like a lawn ornament. Alan talked a good game, but making Pirate's sperm worth anything more than bragging rights would require capital and effort, two things he was never going to find at the bottom of an empty pint glass.

Bragging rights was all he gave a shit about, and the only thing he had worth bragging on was that damn horse. Hard to put a price on that.

"Five thousand," I offered, even though I knew better.

Essie wasn't stupid. She wouldn't have woken up one day and thought, *golly gee, I do believe I'll steal a horse today.* No, she would have gone the legal route first. Maybe Alan's price was too steep for her. For most people, that would have been the end of it. Not Essie. She didn't quit. She *finished.*

Alan hooted and slapped his knee. "His sire earned that in stud fees last month. Hell, no."

"His sire has a wall covered with blue ribbons and a proven record of producing winners," I pointed out. "What does Pirate have?"

The question didn't phase Alan even a little bit. He grinned sloppily. "Did ya hear how I won him? Poker. It was down to me and the kid. Everyone else had folded. But I was no coward and I know how to read a person, you know. So I looked him dead in the eye and raised him."

Alan droned on. I allowed it, taking a deep swig of

tepid water to keep my eyes from glazing over while I reconsidered my strategy. Letting him keep Pirate wasn't an option and drunk though he was, if I kept raising my offer, he was going to figure that out. I made a good living as the only attorney in Aspen Springs, Colorado, and had plenty of investments to show for it, but hell if I was going to let this rat bastard drain me dry.

Fucking Essie. She would laugh her ass off if I let Alan get the better of me, just to save a horse she had already saved. It would never occur to her that the only thing I cared about saving was her. And that was exactly how I wanted it. She'd tunnel her sweet ass right under enemy fire to give her brother a piece of her mind if she knew the truth.

"Where's my drink?" Alan whined.

Because the only thing Alan loved more than bragging was beer. As the only bar in Aspen Springs, the Painted Cat was the one place he could have both at the same time. This little dive bar was his happy place.

Now, *that* was something I could work with.

I jerked my chin at Janie. She put aside the limes, filled Alan's glass, and brought it over.

"'Bout time," Alan grumbled.

I clicked the pen and pulled the notepad toward me. "Here's the deal. Five grand for the colt. You keep a one percent ownership interest. You have no say in Pirate's care or career, but you get one percent of any earnings and you get to call yourself an owner." The pen scratched against the paper as I wrote and I shuddered. Fuck, how I hated a scratchy pen. "You sign here."

"I'm not signing that," Alan said, which was what I expected.

"Then enjoy the beer, because it will be your last at the Painted Cat."

Alan laughed like he thought I was joking. "Says who? This ain't your granddaddy's whorehouse no more, boy. Your name don't mean shit here."

Boy. I was thirty-two, for fuck's sake. The piece of shit next to me might have a decade on that, but he hadn't been a man for a single day of it. I was going to enjoy this.

"Give him the good news, Janie," I said. "Who signs your paychecks?"

She grinned. "You do."

"That's right. I do."

Back when Aspen Springs had been nothing but a mining camp for gold prospectors, my great-great-great grandfather had figured he could make a lot more money—and for a lot less work—selling booze and women to lonely miners than digging for gold. He had been right, and the money from the Painted Cat was enough to buy a nice chunk of land that had been passed down through generations of Hale men as a cattle ranch. My dad had swapped cattle for horses, and now Lodestar Ranch—named for my mother—was slowly building a strong reputation for breeding and training some of the best quarter horses around.

The Painted Cat, on the other hand, hadn't been in the Hale family for at least a hundred years. But I'd always been fascinated with the history of it, so six months ago when the opportunity arose to buy it back, I took it.

A fact I still hadn't shared with my brothers, Adam and Zack. I didn't need those assholes thinking they could drink for free on my dime.

Alan grunted. "Take the damn horse, then. He costs too much to keep, anyway."

He scribbled his signature next to mine. I stood, tossing a couple bills on the bar for Janie. "I'll have a copy of the contract and a money order to you tomorrow."

Alan grunted again.

I was barely out the door when I remembered I still had to change out my busted tire.

Fucking Essie.

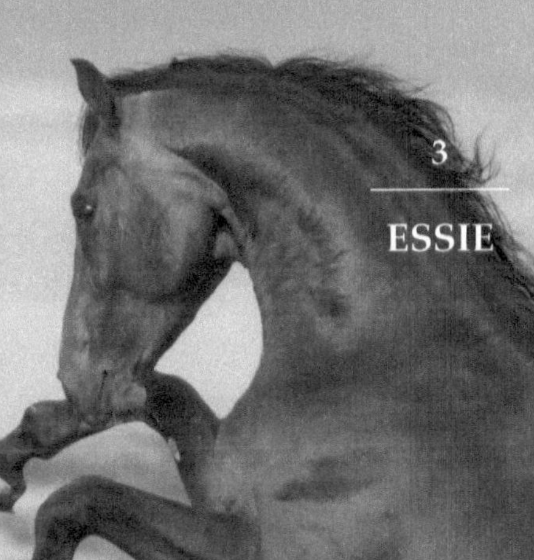

3

———

ESSIE

ESSIE
Hey, remember that time when we were eleven and you couldn't find your bike and Brax said he didn't know where it was, but actually he did? You can't trust people like that.

JACK
...
What did you do, Essie?

ESSIE
I'm just saying, once a liar, always a liar.

JACK
You stole my bike and crashed it. He only knew where it was because he was fixing what you broke.

When I thought about it, I remembered that Brax hadn't actually lied. Not directly, anyway. *Your bike is around here somewhere. It'll turn up eventually.* That was what he'd said, and of course it had been true. Brax hated lying. Deep down, he was as dishonest as the rest of us mortals, but he preferred the method of withholding information. Easier to defend in court, or some shit like that.

"Mom?" I called as I stepped through the front door of the bungalow we shared. Pirate was still in the trailer, but I wanted to give Mom a head's up before I settled him into his new home.

"In the kitchen!" she hollered back.

I found her making a pitcher of iced tea, still in her work clothes. "Need help with dinner?" I asked.

She shook her head. "I brought home a potpie. We had an extra, so it was half off, plus my discount. I can pop it in the oven when you're ready to eat."

Mom had been working at Sweetie Pie, a bakery on First Street that specialized in pies of all kinds except pizza, for as long as I could remember. Back when I had rodeos every weekend, she pulled ten-hour shifts, four days a week, so she could have Friday through Sunday free to haul me and Buckley to barrel racing competitions all over the South and Midwest. My travel schedule had slowed considerably this past year, but somehow Mom's schedule hadn't lessened a bit.

Barrel racing was an almost entirely female sport—with the exception of the horses—and leaned young. By the time they turned thirty, most professional racers had hung up their spurs, married a cowboy, and were hard at work popping out the next generation. I had hung on a little longer, not retiring until last summer. Not because I wanted to settle down. No fucking thank you to *that*.

I retired because I was bored. I wanted a new challenge. Now I was halfway through an apprenticeship with James Campos at Lodestar Ranch, learning how to train reining horses, which was a hell of a lot different than the fast and furious rides of barrel racing.

I had hoped that with a less-demanding travel schedule, Mom would have changed her work hours to something more manageable. But nope. She was still working the grueling 5 a.m. to 5 p.m. shift, the only change being that now she often went in on Fridays and Saturdays, too.

"You hungry, honey?" she asked. When I nodded, she turned the dial to preheat the oven. "Good. So am I. You're home later than I expected."

"Oh. Right." I cleared my throat. "You know how Buckley has been a little sad since Atticus died?" Atticus was our goat, who served no purpose on this earth other than to terrorize chickens and keep Buckley company in his retirement.

Mom nodded slowly, her lips pursed like she knew what was coming.

"I found him a new friend," I said brightly. "So he won't be lonely anymore."

"Another goat?"

"A horse."

Mom's eyes narrowed. Then she sighed. "You have the biggest heart in the world, Essie."

I knew she figured I had picked up a rescue from the auction pen, one of the poor animals intended for slaughter in Canada or Mexico, and I didn't disabuse her of that notion. Brax wasn't the only one who knew how to withhold.

But I had a good reason. It was one thing to steal a man's horse. It was another thing altogether to make my mother, the woman who had birthed twins when she was still a kid herself and sacrificed her own dreams to support mine, an accessory to a felony. Hell, no.

"I'll go get him settled and give Buckley his hay. Give me forty minutes?" I asked. "You should relax a little before dinner. Sit down, have a glass of wine."

"Maybe I will." She patted my arm. "Go take care of your boys."

Maybe it was odd for a thirty-two-year-old to still live at home with her mother, but it worked out well for us.

Mom liked having me home, and she had tagged along to rodeos and shows to help out right up until the end. With both of us on the road together so much, it didn't make sense for me to move out and waste all that money on rent or a mortgage for a place I rarely slept in.

Now that I had retired, maybe it was time to find a place of my own. But I wasn't in any hurry. I didn't mind living with Mom and, anyway, my horse was here.

Coaxing Pirate into the trailer had been a piece of cake and backing him out again was just as smooth. For a three-year-old still in possession of his balls, he was surprisingly well-mannered. Of course, that might have been because he was weak and malnourished from his years of neglect with Gaffney. He didn't have any fight left in him.

But he had heart.

I saw it in the way he lifted his head as I introduced him to his new home and the flare of his nostrils as he caught Buckley's scent. He was still interested in the world around him.

I gave Pirate and Buckley a moment to sniff each other before I put Pirate in crossties and got to work. He needed a thorough grooming, but that would take at least an hour of hard labor that neither of us were up for tonight. It would have to wait until tomorrow morning. Tonight, I needed to get a better understanding of his feet.

His front hoofs were in decent shape. Overgrown

and unshod, but sound. When I propped his left hind between my knees, however, my suspicions were confirmed. A black, smelly, tar-like substance oozed from his frog. Thrush.

Luckily, I was prepared. I had been planning Pirate's arrival for a week now, so the empty stall was clean and ready for him. Thrush was a common enough problem in horses that the medication was available at any feed store, and I had some on hand. It was absolutely fixable, but if left untreated, it could cause permanent lameness. After cleaning off the mud and ooze, I doused both hind feet with medicine.

"Colorado State Code title thirty-five, section forty-three," a deep voice rumbled behind me.

I damn near jumped out of my skin. Whirling around, my hand on my throat, I found Brax leaning in the doorway. That flat tire hadn't slowed him down as much as I'd hoped. Damn his competent ass.

"Any person who commits theft of, or knowingly kills, sells, drives, leads, transports, or rides away, or in any manner deprives the owner of the immediate possession of any horses, commits a class four felony and shall be punished." He smirked, like he relished the thought of it. "Do you know what the punishment is, hellion?"

"Brax," I gritted out.

"Yes?"

"Shut the fuck up."

He did not. "Two to four years imprisonment and a two thousand dollar fine," he supplied. "That's the punishment for horse theft. Plus return of the horse to the owner, of course."

I growled.

"Fortunately for you, I don't think the owner intends to press charges. Maybe he's as crazy as you are." His hard blue gaze latched onto mine like a tractor pull. "What the hell were you thinking with this goddamn Gadarene quest? Did you stop to think for even a second what you were going to do with Pirate once you had him? You can't show a stolen horse."

Gadarene. I didn't know that one. I tugged my phone out of my back pocket and typed it in.

"It means disastrous." Brax knew exactly what I was up to. "Fucking foolish. Like in the Bible, where the pigs of Gadara run themselves off a cliff."

"I hate you," I said, but there was no heat in my tone.

The truth was I loved his big words and lawyer vocabulary. Got a nice little spark every time he gave me a new one. A quick hit of adrenaline. You spent your whole life hearing the same words over and over again. Him, her, apple, no, because. It got boring. I had never been a big reader, which meant the opportunities were few and far between, but damn, did I love being hit with an unfamiliar word when I wasn't expecting it. The strange sound of it jerking me to attention. And then the thrill of using it myself for the first time, of making it mine.

It made his lectures almost tolerable.

Almost.

"What's the plan, Essie?" he pushed. "What are you going to do with Pirate?"

I shrugged. "Haven't really thought past saving his life and getting him healthy and sound again."

Brax's gaze cut to the colt and he frowned. Pirate shifted his weight between his hind legs, giving each hoof a break in turn, clearly uncomfortable as he munched his hay. Brax didn't live and breathe horses like I did, but he had a fondness for the animals and hated any kind of cruelty and suffering.

"What's the damage?" he asked gruffly.

"Bad case of thrush, in both hind feet. He's too sore for bleach and water, but I have medication for him." Like he knew we were talking about him, Pirate lifted his head. I raised my hand to rub his white face, then retreated slowly when he flinched. I didn't take his reaction personally. My beautiful boy hadn't been treated well.

Brax's frown deepened. He wrapped his large hand around the wood beam above his head, like he was checking its sturdiness. "It's a good barn, but we didn't build it with a stallion in mind. What if he doesn't get on with Buckley when he regains his strength? He needs more space."

I didn't particularly enjoy the reminder that my backyard barn existed thanks to my ex-best friend. Back when we were thirteen and I was just starting to get attention at rodeos, Brax had wrangled his brothers, his dad, and Jack into building me a two-stall barn. I might never have been able to afford to keep a horse of my own if he hadn't done that.

"He's a sweet baby," I protested, even though I knew as well as he did that that was likely to change.

"He's three. If Pirate needs to be gelded, it has to happen soon. The decision needs to be made one way or the other."

Brax was right. Bloodlines alone didn't make a horse worthy of keeping his balls. Pirate's sperm would be downright useless if he couldn't prove himself in the ring, and *that* came down to training and temperament. He needed discipline and an eagerness to please. And stallions? More often than not, they were assholes. A stallion that had been abused for most of his life?

Well.

The odds were not in his favor.

Prevailing wisdom was to lop off the balls before a colt showed stallion-ish behavior because once that behavior was there, it often didn't go away again, even when the testosterone did. That behavior generally reared its head somewhere between ages two and four. Pirate had just turned three.

But just because Brax was right didn't mean I had to tell him so.

"I don't see how that's any of your business," I said. "I literally stole this horse, Brax. The only person who has any right to voice an opinion about Pirate's balls is his owner, and I don't see him standing here, do you?"

His grin was a slow, dangerous thing that had my stomach flip-flopping before he said a single word. He leaned in, the muscles of his forearm tensing as he gripped the beam overhead.

"You're looking right at him, hellion."

4

ESSIE

"Someone give me a needle," I said as I stormed into the library Saturday morning. "I'm in a stabbing mood."

Hannah Bell, the Aspen Springs librarian and the organizer of our little sewing club, grabbed my embroidery project from the metal cabinet that also housed a hodge-podge of holiday decorations and signage from past library events.

"What's going on?" she asked as she handed over my half-completed cowgirl flipping the bird under a Dolly Parton quote: *Don't be a lady. Be a legend.*

"Braxton Hale." I practically spat his name like it tasted bad.

James Campos, the head trainer at Lodestar Ranch and very likely to soon be Brax's sister-in-law, judging from the way his older brother, Adam, lit up every time she was near, exchanged a knowing glance with Chloe Adams, the fourth member of our club, who was generally very smart, but was under the misguided impression that Brax was nice simply because he was polite and tipped her generously at the coffee shop every morning.

Frankly, I didn't care for it.

I threw myself onto one of the empty chairs and split a glare between the two of them. "He's a jerk," I announced in a tone that dared them to contradict me.

"He does seem to rub you the wrong way," James said diplomatically.

It wasn't a contradiction, but it wasn't agreement either. She wasn't one to talk shit about someone behind their back, and she actually got along with Brax. Of course, most people in Aspen Springs would argue that Brax was a goddamn delight compared to his grumpy older brother, Adam. I wasn't one of them.

Chloe smirked at the butterfly she was embroidering. "Sometimes when people rub each other the wrong way, it's because they want to tear each other's clothes off and rub each other the *right* way."

"Chloe!" James snorted as she tried to hold back her laugh.

"Just a thought."

"Well, it's a disgusting, vile thought," I grumbled,

even as my brain—unhelpfully!—supplied me with a mental image that made me push my thighs together. Hate, unfortunately, was a very arousing emotion.

James poked her needle through the linen fabric, a funny little smile hovering on her lips. "Hmm."

"What?" I asked.

"Nothing. Just...Adam once told me something about Brax that—" She bit her lip, her eyes sparkling. "I probably shouldn't repeat it, though."

"You should definitely repeat it," Chloe encouraged.

"Let's just say that according to Adam, he's the smallest of the Hale brothers." She leaned in. "And he isn't small at all."

My needle slipped and poked the end of my index finger. I sucked the pain, glaring at the fabric. I really wished she hadn't told me that. I didn't need to know my ex-best friend had attributes below the belt that matched his ego.

Hannah furrowed her brow. "Isn't Adam taller than Brax? Not by much, though. I don't see how an inch more matters at all."

Chloe, James, and I stared at Hannah in baffled surprise. Then Chloe tipped her head back on a loud bark of laughter. "Trust me, Hannah. An extra inch matters."

"Not height," James explained gently. "We're talking about..." She made a gesture to her lap.

"Dicks," I supplied.

"Oh." Hannah pushed her glasses up the bridge of her nose, blinking her blue eyes like an owl. She considered that for a moment, then shrugged. "No, I stand by my original statement. Size doesn't matter. An extra inch isn't going to improve the outcome."

"What outcome is that?" Chloe asked.

Hannah shrugged again. "Disappointment."

I sniggered. I couldn't help it. Disappointment summed up the majority of my sexual encounters, too. Sure, there were outliers. And I was fortunate that none of them were necessarily *bad*. Just...meh.

"Maybe your expectations are too high," Chloe said. "It's those romance books you're always reading. They give you unrealistic expectations."

Hannah sniffed. "I hardly think an orgasm is an unrealistic expectation. If I can get myself there in three minutes, he should at least be able to accomplish it in thirty. Basic care and consideration for the person you are literally *inside of* should not be too high a bar to scale. It's a foregone conclusion that men will have an orgasm from every sexual encounter. The same should be true for every woman who wants it to be." She stabbed the fabric with her needle. "The bar is so low it's a tripping hazard in hell," she muttered.

That shut us all up.

Hannah was something of an enigma and despite

the fact that she had called Aspen Springs home for nearly three years, I knew her only slightly better now than I had the day she moved here. She looked the part of a librarian, with her blonde hair pulled into a bun and those long skirts she liked to wear. Prairie chic. She was reserved and a little mousy, but I wouldn't call her shy. When she had something to say, she said it. Firmly.

I cleared my throat. "I'm going to need to borrow one of those books." Might as well indulge in a fictional man since the real thing was taking its precious time showing up.

Hannah eyeballed me speculatively, lips pursed in thought. I got the feeling she was reading my soul. Then she brightened and snapped her fingers. "I have just the thing. I'll bring it for you next time."

"Great." I wrinkled my nose. "Not one of those Bridgerton books, though. I don't care about balls and society rules. Give me something interesting."

Hannah laughed. "I *love* those books, but don't worry. I know *exactly* what you need."

I opened my mouth to ask for the title so I could look it up and see what I was in for but stopped when I caught sight of Janie hovering in the doorway. "Hey, you came!" I turned to the group. "You all know Janie, right? She bartends at the Painted Cat. I invited her last night, or I would have given you a heads up."

"No worries. I have supplies." Hannah bustled over to the cabinet. "Have you ever embroidered before?"

Janie shook her head. "Never."

"I'll get you started with a sampler, then. It's the easiest way to learn stitches."

Hannah pulled Janie into a corner to teach her the basics.

"Hey, Essie," James said. "You never told us what Brax did that made you so mad."

Janie's head jerked up. She looked interested but, like last night, she didn't ask questions.

"Oh." I frowned at the thread that had somehow tangled itself in a knot. "He bought a horse I rightfully stole, that's what."

Silence.

I looked up and saw everyone staring at me, mouths agape.

James recovered first. "Say that again?"

I pushed my project aside, frustrated. Hannah silently picked it up and got to work on the knot. "You know how Alan Gaffney is always bragging how he won Gee Whizz's colt in a poker game? Well, Brax bought him."

James sucked in a sharp breath. "Pirate?" she gasped. "Brax really bought Pirate?"

I nodded. "He really fucking did. Must have cost him a small fortune, too, because I made Gaffney an offer several times and he always said no."

"Oh my god!" James let out an excited squeal, shimmying a little in her seat. "What's the plan? Is he going to keep him at Lodestar? Pirate will need training—"

"James," Chloe cut in with an incredulous look. She shook her head. "Horse girls, I swear. Essie, go back to the important part. You know, where you committed a felony."

I waved her aside. "Probably better that you don't know the details. My point was that I had everything under control, and then Brax swept in and took over." I growled at the memory of his smug face informing me that he was Pirate's new owner. "But I don't want to talk about it. I want to stab something."

"Almost done," Hannah said. "This thread is really tangled."

Chloe tilted her head, then pushed her project across the table to me. "You can do my French knots. I always mess them up." She watched as I twisted the thread around the needle. "It must have been frustrating for you to deal with that."

With my attention focused on making a rosebud-shaped knot, I nodded. "*So* frustrating. Maybe my way wasn't perfect, but it would have worked. I had a plan. He acts like I'm a kid he needs to rescue or something."

Chloe propped her chin on her palm. "What do you think he wants to save you from?"

"Anything he doesn't approve of, probably." I heaved a sigh. "We used to be friends, you know. In high school. He wasn't like this back then. He wasn't overbearing and so damn bossy. Now that we're not friends, this is *all* he is."

Honestly, it wasn't even only him. People sure did love to save me from my nonexistent problems. My mom. Jack. Fucking Brax, most of all. Like everyone thought I was too damn incompetent to be left to my own devices. Or worse, too fragile to face even the smallest inconvenience without having a breakdown.

It was infuriating when it came from my mother or Jack.

It was downright unbearable when it came from Brax.

"Tell me more about that," Chloe said.

"Uh-uh." I pointed the needle in her direction. "Don't you go psychoanalyzing me. I'm onto you, Dr. Adams."

Chloe laughed. "I have a ways to go before I'm doctor anything. Anyway, I'm not psychoanalyzing you, I promise. We're just talking."

Yeah. I didn't believe that for a second. Chloe didn't like to slap labels on things, and especially not people, so I knew she wasn't sitting there, silently thinking *daddy issues*, even though we both knew damn well that's exactly what I had. But she loved to *understand*. To figure someone out.

But right now, I didn't want her to figure me out. Because if she did, she might discover that Brax was right. Maybe I was incompetent, wild, and fragile. I didn't feel that way about myself, but when three of the smartest people I knew said otherwise, well…It gave me pause. Maybe I *had* fucked up. Maybe I had gone too far this time and needed someone to swoop in and save me from myself.

But I would be damned if I allowed Brax to be the one to do it.

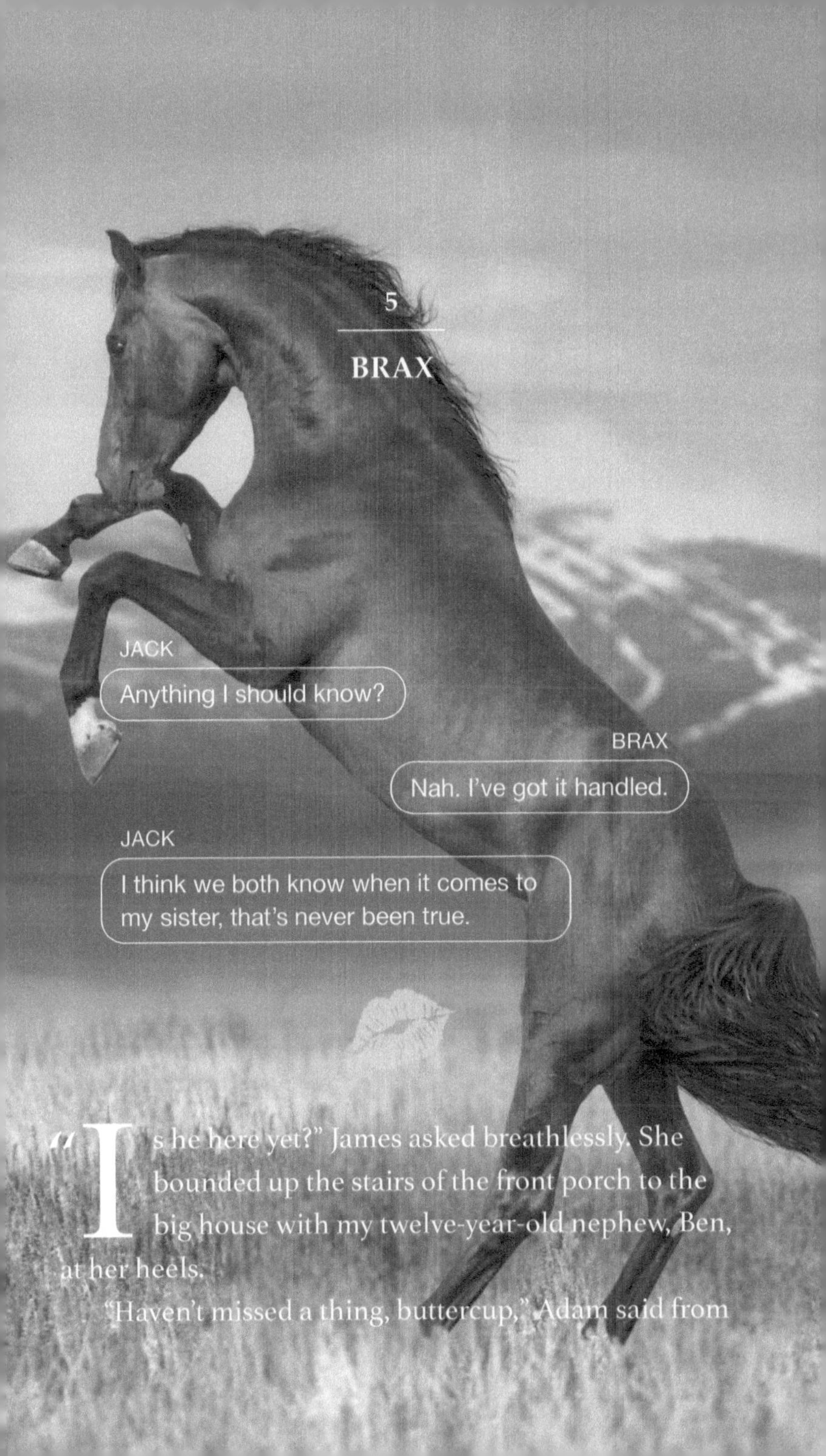

5

BRAX

JACK

Anything I should know?

BRAX

Nah. I've got it handled.

JACK

I think we both know when it comes to my sister, that's never been true.

"Is he here yet?" James asked breathlessly. She bounded up the stairs of the front porch to the big house with my twelve-year-old nephew, Ben, at her heels.

"Haven't missed a thing, buttercup," Adam said from

his rocking chair next to mine. "Come have a seat." He patted his thighs in invitation.

"Dad!" Ben protested, looking as appalled as only a twelve-year-old boy faced with public displays of affection could look. "No one wants to see that."

"Give it another year," Zack, my younger brother, said. He was in another rocking chair to my right, which meant I was sandwiched between them, the three of us lined up according to age and the alphabet. "You'll be singing a different tune."

Now it was Adam's turn to look appalled. "Don't listen to him, Ben. You have plenty of time before that happens." His eyes were full of affection as he looked at his son.

My dad chuckled. "It goes quick. That's a fact."

My heart twinged in my chest. Hale men tended to fall hard, fast, and young. There were stories that my great-great-great grandfather Thomas—founder of the Painted Cat—had taken one look at my great-great-great grandmother Celine and refused to let her rent out her bed to another man. My mom and dad had been high school sweethearts, and to hear my dad tell the story, they had been meant for each other from the first moment they clapped eyes on each other. Adam had followed that same trajectory, marrying his high school sweetheart as soon as she graduated from college.

Of course, it wasn't long before she'd left him for another man. So maybe that wasn't the best example.

Still, I always figured I'd do the same sooner rather than later. Get married, start a family while I was still young enough to chase kids around. At this rate, Adam would be well into his second marriage before I had started my first.

Most days that didn't bother me. Hell, most days I was grateful for it. As Aspen Springs's only lawyer, I saw firsthand how nasty people could be when love turned to hate and marriage ended in divorce.

But sometimes, like now, when I watched my brother wrap an arm around James's waist and pull her, laughing and fake protesting, onto his lap, I wasn't all that grateful. Adam had had more than his fair share of misery, and I was glad he had found love with James. I didn't begrudge him his happiness but staring it full in the face like that felt fucking unnecessary.

James only stayed in Adam's lap for a moment before she was back on her feet again, bouncing on her toes with excitement. "Blaine and Jesse have a stall ready for Pirate in the birthing barn, since it's not being used right now," she said, referring to two of the ranch hands. "We'll keep him quarantined until he gets a full vet check. Who knows what he could have picked up in that asshole's yard. Probably nothing communicable, but better safe than sorry."

"Remind me. What time did Essie say she'd be here, again?" Zack asked, tipping his bottle of beer to his mouth.

I glanced to where the sun was dipping below the mountain ridgeline. "She'll be here soon."

We hadn't specified an exact time. *You have until sundown*, I'd told her.

Or what? she'd challenged. *You gonna meet me outside the saloon at high noon? I'm a better shot than you.*

Or I'll take your mom up on her dinner invitation, I'd said. *Not sure what I'll say if she asks me a direct question. You know I can't lie to Cat.*

She'd glared something fierce, but we both knew it was game over. Risking jailtime for herself was one thing. Disappointing her mother was a bridge too far. Maybe it was wrong of me to play that card, but what the hell else was I supposed to do? Let her keep *my* horse in her backyard?

"And remind me, how is it that Essie is bringing Pirate instead of Gaffney?" Adam asked. "How did she get involved?"

James spun on her toes to face us. Her big brown eyes were almost comically wide with faux innocence. "How *did* Essie get involved, Brax? I would love to hear about it."

I narrowed my gaze on her, wondering how much Essie had shared. "It's not that interesting. She picked up Pirate last night so she could take care of his feet. Gave him a good grooming and dose of medicine." Strictly true. Did it matter if she had taken Pirate without permission? That was no one's business but hers and mine now.

"Huh." James slowly blinked her long eyelashes. "That was so nice of her to help you out like that. She must have spent her whole day off taking care of your horse for you. I hope you thanked her properly."

This earned snorts of laughter from my idiot brothers.

"Yeah, Brax," Zack taunted in a sing-song voice. "Did you thank Essie *properly*?"

"Shut the hell up," I muttered.

"Hey, man," Adam said. "Watch the language." He jerked his chin toward Ben, who rolled his eyes.

"I already know that word, Dad. And lots worse," he added. "I'm *twelve*."

"Well, just because you know the word doesn't mean you should use it," Adam said.

Ben nodded. "James says there's a time and place for everything, especially swear words."

"Did she, now?" Adam's gaze shot to James, who grinned unrepentantly.

"I figure she's right," Ben said. "I've heard you say pretty bad words in the barn, but you never say those words in church."

Adam laughed and squeezed James's hip. "Can't argue with that, I guess."

"Here's what I don't get," Zack said suddenly. "Why the he—*heck* did you buy Pirate anyway? Gaffney's had dozens of offers but he turned them all down. Must have cost you a hefty wad of cash to convince him to sell. What do you think, Adam? Isn't that odd?"

"Come to think of it, that is odd." Adam made a show of scratching his chin. "Brax has never shown much interest in horses as anything other than pets or transportation. What would make him interested in owning a colt like Pirate? It's out of character, that's what it is."

They were talking past me like I wasn't sitting right there between them. "You're both idiots," I said. "But unlike you, I know a good investment when I see one. Pirate's bloodlines make him a good investment."

"I have a theory," Zack said, ignoring me. "Do you want to hear it?"

"Absolutely, I do," Adam said, raising his bottle of beer like a toast.

Zack leaned over me. "The specifics are cloudy, but the gist of it is Miss Essie Price."

"The same Miss Price who is on her way here with Pirate right now?" Adam asked with fake surprise.

"The very same."

"That's a damn good theory."

"Dumbasses, both of you," I muttered.

"I know that word, too," Ben chimed in earnestly. "Dad says it a *lot*. Mostly about Uncle Zack."

Zack's hoot of laughter was echoed by Adam, Dad, and James. I might have joined in if I hadn't been distracted by the sight of a cherry red SUV kicking up dust as it came down our unpaved road, just as the sun disappeared behind a mountain peak.

Essie was here, right on time.

The kick of anticipation in my chest told me my brothers were right. Buying Pirate had everything to do with Essie Price. More than my promise to Jack. More than simply wanting to keep her out of jail.

Because I could have kept my mouth shut. I could have bought Pirate and figured out a way to keep her from ever finding out. Hell, I could have just given her the fucking horse and washed my hands of the whole damn thing.

But I hadn't done any of that.

No, instead I'd demanded she bring Pirate here to Lodestar, the ranch my family owned, where she was currently doing a trainer apprenticeship.

I wasn't a liar. I didn't lie to other people, and I sure as fuck didn't lie to myself. I knew exactly why I did it. Essie was here. Wherever Essie was, that's where I wanted to be, too.

I just needed a reason.

Fifteen Years Ago

.   .   .

If I could save only one thing in a fire, it would be Esther Louise Price. Odds were she was the one who started the fire to begin with, but I'd still toss her over my shoulder without a second thought, and give her ass a good, hard smack every time she reached for a flame on our way out.

Because she would. She definitely would.

There were a lot of things wrong with this hypothetical scenario posed by Mrs. Dunphy, our eleventh-grade English teacher at Aspen Springs High School. The first being that if Essie was there to save, then so was Jack, her twin brother and my best friend, because the two of them were a package deal. He might have something to say about being left to burn. Of course, if Jack were there, he would have saved us all, put out the fire with superhuman spit or something, and I wouldn't have gotten anywhere near his sister and her spankable ass. So.

I didn't write about any of that. Mrs. Dunphy said it had to be an inanimate object, which was the opposite of Essie Price. Mrs. Dunphy didn't want to make us choose between parents and ruin our home life, she said.

"What did you write about?" Essie asked, falling into step with me as we exited the classroom.

"My cellphone, of course. It's the most useful thing I own. Did anyone *not* say they would save their cellphone?"

She looked up at me. As ever, it was a sucker punch. Cornflower blue eyes and that cherry red lipstick she always wore. Looking at her face was like looking directly at the sun. It burned. The shape of that red mouth was branded onto the back of my eyelids even after I looked away.

"I didn't," she said.

We paused at her locker to deposit our books. She grabbed her brown bag lunch, which I knew would contain a baloney sandwich and an apple, like always. Essie hated baloney, but it was cheap, so that's what they got. She usually ended up giving her sandwich to Jack, whose stomach was a bottomless pit. It all worked out, since my lunch was always more than I needed and I could share with her.

"What did you save?" I asked.

"The matchbooks. From my dad."

She didn't have to explain. Essie's dad was some rich kid who knocked up Cat Price when he was in Aspen Springs during a family vacation. They had both been sixteen, so maybe I couldn't blame him for being a little shit back then and running away from his responsibilities. But instead of growing the fuck up, he had become an even bigger shit. He dropped in every year or so and brought Essie and Jack a matchbook—a souvenir from his travels that he seemed to think made him more interesting than anyone else in the room.

He was a dick.

And Essie knew that. She'd said it herself multiple times. But still, that was the thing she'd save. I couldn't make sense of that.

I shook my head. "The house is on fire and you're running around with matches? Smart."

"It's *hypothetical*." She rolled her eyes. "It's not about proving how smart you are. It's about who you are deep down. What is the most important thing in the world to you, the one thing you would risk your life for?"

I pulled my phone from my pocket and caressed it lovingly. "Shhh, baby. Don't listen to her. You're the love of my life. Smart *and* beautiful."

Essie smirked and slapped her locker shut with a loud bang. "That's where you stash your porn, isn't it."

"Don't be ridiculous," I deadpanned. "That's what my laptop is for."

She punched me lightly in the ribs and I laughed. Essie's affection was always a little violent. I didn't mind it.

Her quick pace slowed as we approached the cafeteria. Her gaze darted left and then right and I knew—I fucking *knew*—she was looking for teachers. Essie hated school. For one thing, it was inside. For another, there were no horses. If Jack were here with us, she wouldn't even try to escape. But it was Tuesday, and Jack had JROTC on Tuesdays. Which meant that the only thing standing between Essie and freedom was me, which was pretty much the same thing as nothing at all.

She knew I was a sucker.

"Let's ditch." She tugged my elbow.

I stood stock still, putting up a fight as if we didn't both already know how this would end. "I promised your brother."

Her eyes narrowed. "You promised Jack what?"

"I promised him I'd make sure you got to all your classes."

"Well, that was dumb, Brax. Because it wasn't your promise to make. You're not the boss of me." That was unfortunately true. "And also because you shouldn't make promises you know you won't keep."

"I'm keeping my promise right now," I protested, hoping that she wouldn't make a liar out of me. That for once in her life, she'd cave first.

Instead, she leaned into my side, rubbing her temple against my shoulder like a cat. "But it's never just the two of us. You're *my* best friend, too, right? Not just Jack's?"

Jesus fucking Christ, this girl. I never stood a chance.

"Of course I'm your friend—"

"Best friend," she insisted.

"Best friend," I grunted. I felt some kind of way about that, but I wasn't going to examine it. This was how it had to be. We were friends. Best friends. Like I was with Jack. Even if it felt a little different when we were all hanging out at the lake, with her in a bikini.

I looked down at her and found her staring back at

me with pleading blue eyes from underneath that dark fringe of lashes. Fuck.

"We could go for a hike," she offered.

It was a bribe. Hiking was my thing, not hers. She preferred to be on horseback. But she also probably knew that we'd be more likely to get caught if we went back to Lodestar Ranch and saddled up a couple of horses. My parents weren't dumb.

"Okay," I grumbled. "But only because it's the last week of school and we're not doing anything anyway."

"Yippee!" She grinned. "I knew you couldn't say no to a hike."

I shook my head. The only thing I couldn't say no to was Essie Price.

6

ESSIE

Two weeks after Pirate joined Lodestar Ranch, the thrush in his hooves had been vanquished and he was fully sound. He had also put on enough weight that he was no longer a sack of dirty bones. And that spark in his eyes that had told me his spirit hadn't been entirely broken had brightened to full mischief. I was nearly vibrating with excitement, because today would be his first lesson under saddle—if I could catch him, that was.

Pirate, it turned out, was a goddamn clown.

I stood in the small pasture near the gate, a carrot in one hand and a lead rope in my other. Pirate stood in the center of the field. We stared each other down, each waiting for the other to make the first move. We'd been through this three times already. He'd trot toward me, amiable as you please, only to pull out of reach before I could clip the rope to his halter. Then he'd bolt around the fence line, kicking up his heels like a fool, so damn proud of himself.

I had the feeling he didn't actually hate the idea of coming with me, even though he had no clue what was in store for him today. It was more like he thought this was a game, and he was winning.

Which he was.

Damn his pretty hide.

I wasn't fool enough to chase after him. There was no way my two legs could outrun his four. Dogs, fathers, horses—they were all the same. You chased them, they'd run. So I responded the only way I knew how: I turned my back and pretended I didn't care.

And found myself staring straight into Braxton's amused face.

"Is the sweet baby giving you problems, hellion?" he drawled.

Lord, deliver me from this smug man. I did not have time for assault charges today.

"This isn't stallion behavior," I informed him, my tone dripping with false patience, like he hadn't spent his life around the animals. "He's not dropping dick or vocalizing. He's just got high energy now that he has food in his belly and hasn't figured out how to manage it yet."

Brax's gaze flicked behind me and his lips tilted up before he met my eyes again. "Is that so?"

I resisted rolling my eyes. If he thought I didn't know Pirate was sneaking up behind me, he was mistaken, and so was Pirate. A nine-hundred-pound animal wasn't exactly subtle. "Yes, that's so," I snapped.

I listened to the muffled clomp of hooves against the damp ground. Pirate was almost close enough. When I heard his soft snuffle, I pivoted slowly, opening my hand to offer the carrot on my flat palm. He lipped it up and I cautiously lifted my other hand to his halter. "Easy, baby," I murmured.

But before I made contact, he snorted and pressed his forehead to my chest, and with a big nod sent me reeling. I took a step back to regain my balance, but the water trough hit me behind the knee and my leg buckled. I went down, splashing ass-first into the cool water.

"Brat!" I shrieked.

Pirate was already halfway across the field, pleased as fuck with himself. Judging from Brax's loud laughter, he wasn't the only one.

Ever the gentleman, Brax extended a hand. "Here, let me help you."

"I've got it." I glared and hoisted myself out. It wasn't pretty and involved a bit of twisting and sloshing, but I got the job done. Soaked from my knees to my armpits, I said, "See? I'm fine."

His gaze raked down my body, taking in my wet clothing. My yellow tee shirt had probably gone fully transparent, and he could likely see my nipples, rock hard from cold, poking through my sports bra, but I kept my chin up, refusing to verify this for myself. What I didn't know couldn't humiliate me.

He jerked his face away, a muscle ticking in his jaw. "You always were too proud to accept help."

His words infuriated me. I wasn't too proud to accept help. I just hated help being foisted on me against my will.

"Am I? Because I could use a little help drying off."

"Wha—" His eyes widened as I lunged for him.

Even though it was exactly what I intended, I still felt a bolt of surprise when my body made contact with his. Brax had never been slow on his feet and I had half expected him to dodge. But instead, he caught me instinctively, his arms banding around my waist. I wiggled my dripping torso against his broad chest and firm abs, making him as wet as possible, using his body like he was my own personal towel.

"Jesus, hellion. You trying to kill me?" he muttered against my forehead.

"Just accepting your help, that's all," I said, my voice dripping with sugar.

I had meant to piss him off, nothing more, but I had miscalculated how good it would feel to be wrapped up in all that hard-bodied warmth. An embarrassing sound of contentment escaped me and I rolled my lips together to keep it from happening again.

"Cold?" he asked gruffly. He didn't wait for me to

answer—my peaked nipples pressing against his ribcage probably told him everything he needed to know— before he briskly rubbed his large hands up and down my back.

A memory surfaced of the last time we had held each other like this. The day he almost died, fifteen years ago. It had been adrenaline then rather than cold that had made my body shake, and I had pressed my ear to his chest and let the sound of his heartbeat calm me. His arms had wrapped me up so tightly, like he was afraid I would disappear if he let go.

But he did let go.

I remembered that, too.

"I'm good now." I pushed away from him, then smirked like my mind wasn't all tangled in the past as I took in his gray shirt. Soaked. "Thanks for the help."

He rubbed his chest, like something bothered him there. Maybe we had collided a little too hard. "I'll get Pirate and give you time to change. You can't ride like that. Your thighs will chafe in those wet jeans."

"I'm not riding."

"You're not? Isn't today supposed to be Pirate's first lesson under saddle?"

"Yeah, but not with me. James is doing it." I hoped he didn't hear the sour note in my voice.

That was because James was taking the lead on Pirate's training. I tried not to feel some kind of way about that. When it came to training horses for reining and fence work, she was one of the best there was, and there was no doubt in my mind that in a few more years, she would be *the* best. Hell, I'd even hired her last year to work with a horse of mine before I retired from barrel racing. Pirate was in good hands with her.

But I wanted it to be me.

It was better for Pirate this way. I knew that. I was two years older than James, but I didn't have her decades of experience training horses. I had been riding since I was five and competing since I was eight, and my junior world championship barrel racing record still stood—in fact, I had broken James's record to get it, and I had been younger than her when I did it. As a barrel racer, there were maybe three women in the whole wide world who could claim to be better than me on a bad day. But as a trainer? I was just an apprentice.

Still. There was a little voice in my heart whispering that the bond between me and Pirate was special, and by working together we could push each other to great- ness. Was that silly? Sentimental? I wanted it to be me. It *would* have been me if Brax hadn't stolen Pirate out from under me.

I knew I should be grateful that he had found a legal way to keep Pirate safe and healthy, and I was. It was just that my gratitude ran a little feral around the edges.

"Right." Brax frowned. "You okay with that?"

I didn't want to admit how childish I was feeling

about the whole thing. Not to anyone, really, but especially not to him. "Why wouldn't I be?" I challenged.

"Well, if I had to guess, I'd say you have strong feelings about this horse and how things should be done with him, and you'd like to be the one to have final say in his training and care." He moved to the fence, picked up the length of rope draped over the top rail, and studied it. Ben must have been out here earlier practicing his roping tricks. "But I also know that you want what's best for Pirate and you also know, even if it stings your pride a little, that James has a skill set you haven't mastered yet. I figure that means you'll tell people you're okay with it until you find a way to actually *be* okay with it. You'll push aside whatever jealousy you feel to do what's best for Pirate."

I hated that he could still read me so well, all these years later. "Well, I'd say that's about right."

He cocked a brow. "Of course I'm right. That's who you are. You allow yourself to feel your feelings. What you don't allow is for your feelings to run you."

That almost sounded like a compliment. I swallowed hard and looked away, occupying myself with wringing as much of the water from the hem of my tee shirt as I could. The bright Colorado sunshine would do the rest.

"What are you doing here, anyway?" I asked. "Shouldn't you be in a windowless office, gussied up in a suit and tie and confusing people out of their money?"

He snickered. "I don't wear a suit, and if people are

confused when I'm done with them, then I didn't do my job right. I'm my own damn boss and I decide how I spend my time. Today, there wasn't anything more important than seeing Pirate's first lesson under saddle."

"Yeah, well, you should call first." It couldn't be denied that I sounded a little sulky about it. That might have something to do with the fact that he had witnessed my interactions with Pirate.

I doubted he was surprised at all. Falling into a water trough was probably exactly what he expected from me. Incompetence.

"Who would I call?" He cocked a brow. "It's my horse and my family's ranch. I'll come and go as I please."

Me. So I can leave.

"I'm just saying, a heads up would be nice. So we can have Pirate ready for you. Otherwise..." I gestured to the colt, who appeared to have lost all interest in us and was moseying through the pasture, nibbling grass. He'd be easy to get now.

Brax squinted. "Hm. I might be able to do something about that."

With the rope in hand, he walked toward Pirate, coming at him from an angle to avoid arousing the horse's suspicions. As he got closer, he twirled the rope above his head, faster and faster, opening the large loop at the end. I held my breath as I watched. Brax was ridiculously good with a lasso—maybe even better than Zack, and Zack was a professional.

At the exact moment Pirate gave into his curiosity and lifted his head, Brax sent the loop sailing. It fell neatly over Pirate's head. With a quick tug, the lasso tightened around his neck. Pirate was caught.

Brax clucked his tongue and Pirate ambled forward without a fuss. He seemed to have forgotten all about his earlier game.

I bit back an annoyed groan. Once again, Brax had swept in to save my ass. Fucking cowboy. There would be no living with him after this.

But holy hell, was it hot.

7

BRAX

"**B**raxton! How are you, honey?"

It was a familiar voice, one I didn't get to hear as often as I would've liked, that had the simultaneous effect of my lips tilting up in a grin and my balls ascending for cover. I turned and found Essie's mom with a pie balanced on each strong, slender fore-arm. Essie was next to her carrying the same.

As friendly as Cat Price had been to me over the years—even after her daughter wanted nothing to do with me—there was still a part of me that was terrified of the woman. Cat might look like Essie's older sister, but she was a mama bear through and through. Fiercely protective of her daughter against threats both real and imagined—including myself. Once upon a time, Cat had sat me down at the kitchen table, a pile of unshelled walnuts and a hammer laid out in front of her, and gave me her version of the sex talk.

You're a good kid, Braxton, but teenage emotions are powerful stuff. I know you're just friends now, but it's easy to be overwhelmed by hormones and think with what's in your pants instead of what's in your skull. You understand what I'm saying? she'd asked while looking me dead in the eyeballs.

A cold bead of sweat had rolled down my spine. It was like she had seen into my brain and discovered the image of her daughter in a bikini branded there. *Yes, ma'am.*

Good. Because when boys think with what's in their pants, it's the girls who suffer for it. Girls are the ones who bear the consequences. But I'll tell you this. My girl won't bear them alone.

And then she'd brought the hammer down onto a walnut, cracking it clean in half.

My balls shrank at the memory.

At fifteen, I had thought that whatever threat I posed Essie was one hundred percent a figment of her mother's overactive imagination. We were friends, that was all. Until the day she almost died. Then I realized how much of a threat I truly was.

"Ms. Price, I'm glad you could make it," I said as I relieved her of the pies. "I'm doing well. How about yourself? These peach?" I asked with an appreciative sniff.

"You know to call me Cat," she scolded. She took one of the pies Essie carried, easing her daughter's burden. "Ms. Price makes me sound like an unmarried librarian with a million cats."

She happened to say this right as a vaguely familiar looking woman approached bearing a large bowl of potato salad. The woman wrinkled her nose like she was trying to shift her glasses with the movement and shot Essie an amused look.

"Mom!" Essie groaned.

Cat blinked her big blue eyes. "What?"

"I'm Hannah Bell," the woman said. "Unmarried librarian who happens to share her home with a delightful glaring of five cats." Her lips tilted wryly. "That's well under a million, so I'm not offended in the least."

I turned just in time to catch Essie shape the word silently with her lips, like she was learning the feel of it. *Glaring.* Her eyes lit up. And I knew exactly what was happening in that brain of hers. She knew the word, but not in this context. It was unexpected. She was considering how well one context translated to another, the spirit of the verb and the spirit of cats. Watching her find a new word was like watching the sunrise crest a mountain. She fucking glowed from it.

"Where should I put this?" Hannah asked, raising the bowl higher.

It was Lodestar Ranch's second annual summer

barbecue. The tradition had kicked off last year as a way to eat all the watermelon Ben had grown in Mom's old garden, which had gone to weeds a couple years ago when she died of cancer. This year was even bigger, as Ben had expanded his farming skills to cucumbers, tomatoes, and various peppers and beans.

My answer to Hannah's question got stuck on the sudden lump in my throat.

Shit, Mom would have loved this.

Before it could get awkward, Essie piped up with, "Those tables over there look like the right spot." She wasn't looking at me when she spoke, but I knew she'd seen me choke up just the same.

That was the thing about Essie. She wasn't nice, but she was kind. Even to an asshole like me who probably didn't deserve her kindness. Mom had loved her, too.

With the pie balanced on one palm, Essie lifted her other hand to wave to James, who was organizing the various bowls and dishes of food on the red-checked tablecloth. James waved back. "This way—"

"I'll take that." My dad hefted the pie from Essie's palm. He aimed a grin at Cat that I hadn't seen in a long, long time. "Cat Price, as I live and breathe. It's been too long, darlin'. Why don't we leave the young people to themselves and catch up?"

I blinked. Was Dad *flirting* with Essie's mom? I hadn't seen him flirt with anyone, ever, other than Mom, so I couldn't be sure that was what I was witnessing. It was probably nothing. Essie and I were the same age, but Dad had a good fifteen years on Cat. They headed for the picnic tables, chatting like the old friends they were.

Hannah sighed and stepped after them. "I've never been young a day in my life, so why would I start now," she muttered. "Have fun, *young people*."

Essie laughed. "I'll come with you."

There was a flash of color as her ponytail swished in my face. Instinctively, I wrapped it in my fist, halting her mid-stride. Hannah kept going, not realizing Essie wasn't with her.

"What is this?" I asked, examining the rainbow glimmering underneath her natural brown.

"The last thing you'll ever see if you don't let the fuck go," she snapped.

But she stepped closer to loosen the tension on her scalp and that gave me incentive to hold on a little longer. She hadn't stood this close to me since she'd rubbed her wet body all over me a month ago. In fact, I'd say she'd gone out of her way to avoid me. And when she couldn't avoid me, she'd made sure to keep a horse or a human between us at all times.

I tugged again and she stepped even closer.

"Pretty," I remarked like she hadn't threatened my life.

I ran my thumb over the colors in order. Red, orange, yellow, green, blue, purple. Essie had always liked to experiment with hair color, both natural and unnatural, trying on blonde and blue the way other people tried on clothes. But for the past year or so, she had stuck to her god-given brunette shade. This rainbow on the underside of her hair was a lot more subtle than what she used to go for. It was like a game of peekaboo, trying to find the colors.

"Stop petting me, jackass." She swatted my hand away. "It's not for you."

I grinned and let her hair tumble free. "You did it for your mama, didn't you."

Essie's hair color was another one of those imaginary threats that kept Cat up at night. Her mom had never expressly *forbade* Essie from dying her hair, but there had been a lot of head shaking, lip pursing, and dire warnings every time Cat came home to find Essie sporting a brand-new color.

Essie tossed her ponytail and folded her arms under her chest, testing my resolve to keep my eyes up where they belonged. Fucking sundress. That paired with worn-in cowboy boots was my kryptonite. And the woman wearing them? Kryptonite didn't begin to describe it. I was the tide and she was the moon, pushing and pulling me however she wanted. I wasn't even mad about it.

"As a grown-ass woman, I don't consult my mother on my style choices," she said. "I told her the same thing I always tell her. It doesn't matter whether other people take me seriously. *I* take myself seriously. What other people think of me is none of my business."

"I bet that went down as well today as it did fifteen years ago." I tweaked her ponytail. "Like it or not, you'll always be her baby, Essie."

Her grimace told me exactly what she thought about that and I laughed again.

"I know she only wants what's best for me." Essie's gaze was on her mom and my dad as she spoke, like she was thinking out loud and not to me specifically. "I know she's scared I'm too much like her. But I'm thirty-two. It's not even possible for me to be a teen mom at this point."

"You can ruin your life at any age," I pointed out. Lord knew I had seen plenty of adults do exactly that.

"That's the problem, I guess. People are so goddamned afraid of ruining their lives that they created all these asinine rules to prevent that. But it won't work, because no one ever ruined their life by dying their hair blue or pivoting to a new career path. Life isn't that serious."

Now, that was interesting. This was about more than just rainbow hair, then. Had Cat disagreed with Essie's retirement from barrel racing?

"Stupid rules," she muttered. "People too scared of living their own lives so they have to come take all the fun out of mine. Why should I have to live my life in a way that makes them feel better about how they live theirs? That can't possibly be my responsibility."

"That's what I like about you, hellion. You don't follow anyone's rules."

She pivoted slowly on her toes to face me, her dark brows drawn together in a deep scowl. "Don't even think about it, Braxton Hale. I am not your manic pixie dream girl." She jabbed me hard on the shoulder with her index finger. "Absolutely not."

"What the hell is a manic pixie dream girl?" I asked.

"You know, the delightfully quirky side character who shows up in a male protagonist's story for the sole purpose of making him interesting. And I'll tell you right now, I'm too old for that shit. There's no such thing as a manic pixie dream *woman*." She poked my shoulder again. "And do you know why?"

I barely knew what the fuck we were talking about, much less the why of it all. I shook my head.

"Because they *die*, Brax. They die young so the boy can become a man with depth and an interesting back story. You'll just have to find some other way to grow a personality. I'm not dying."

She laughed like there was anything funny about her fucking *dying*, when there sure as hell was not. Fifteen years after the day she almost had, and I still hadn't fully recovered. I doubted I ever would.

I grabbed her wrist before she could assault me

again. "Damn right, you're not. Don't even fucking joke about that."

Her laughter caught in her throat and she stared at me with wide eyes. Then she blinked and her expression twisted into something angry. She wrenched her wrist from my grasp. "Don't pretend you care," she spat.

She stalked off, her spine rigid with rage, and I was glad because it kept me from telling her the truth. I had never pretended to care. The only thing I had ever pretended with Essie was that I didn't.

"WHAT ARE YOU DOING?" JAMES ASKED.

I looked up from my paper plate, piled high with food. A hamburger with all the fixins', buttery corn on the cob, and a heap of watermelon salad. "What does it look like I'm doing?"

"I already know what *I* think you're doing." She threw a short, muscular leg over the picnic table bench, straddling it to face me. "*I* think you've forgotten how to communicate like an adult, so you've reverted to kindergarten antics to get a girl's attention. What I want to know is what *you* think you're doing."

That was the problem with James. She didn't miss a damn thing. My brother apparently liked that about her.

I did, too. Mostly. Right now, it wasn't my favorite trait of hers.

"I think I'm eating a burger," I deadpanned. I took a large bite to prove my point.

"I'm talking about you and Essie," she clarified, like I didn't know. "You literally pulled her hair."

"Well," I said, after swallowing my food, "in my defense, it was shiny."

She rolled her big brown eyes at me. "Mature."

I thought that was the end of it, but I could feel her eyes on me while I steadily ignored her in favor of shoveling delicious food into my mouth. She was thinking things, I fucking knew it. That was how James was. Curious, thoughtful, patient. Again, mostly attributes I considered positive, until this very moment.

Finally, I couldn't take it anymore. I wiped my mouth with a napkin and gave her my full attention. "Say it," I commanded.

She didn't hesitate. "Essie is my friend, but besides that, we have a professional relationship. She's an apprentice here at Lodestar Ranch. I'm her mentor. That is a huge responsibility, one I take very seriously."

James paused like she was waiting for me to respond. I waved a hand at her to get on with it.

"At the same time, I also have a relationship with you that is both personal and professional," James continued. "On the personal side, you're Adam's brother, and also—I hope—my friend. On a professional level, your dad is my boss. And now you've hired me to train Pirate."

"What's your point, James?" I asked.

She leaned forward. "My point is that none of this matters until it does, and then it matters a whole lot. If Essie has a problem with you, then I have a problem, too, because we're all tangled up together, personally and professionally. So I'm asking you, are you going to make this a problem for me?"

Her words sank in and I wrinkled my forehead. "You think I'd ever ask you to fire Essie or take Pirate's training and care away from her? Hell, no. Jesus, James. I'm not that guy."

She blinked, pulling back in surprise. Then she snorted. "You sweet summer child. No." She patted my hand. "And it wouldn't matter even if you did. Essie has so much potential and, as I said, I take my position as her mentor very seriously. What I'm saying is that if you're harassing my apprentice, you're not welcome here. Training Pirate is the opportunity of a lifetime, but it's one I'll pass on if you can't behave yourself."

"You'd fire me as a client?" I demanded incredulously. "You can't fire me. I'm the owner's son."

"Not only would I fire you, I'd leave it to you to tell your dad why."

I winced, picturing his reaction. He had known Essie

since kindergarten. Hell, when her dad bailed on our middle school's father-daughter dance, my dad was the one who had escorted her, since he didn't have a daughter of his own. He'd straight up kill me if he thought I was treating Essie with anything less than the respect she deserved.

"Damn, James. You play dirty." I tipped my beer can at her. "Can't say that I don't admire that about you." Beneath those freckles and big cow eyes of hers was a spine of steel. She was the perfect mentor for Essie in a business that tended to be rough on women.

"Of course you do." She flashed me a cheeky grin. "But you didn't answer the question. Do we have a problem?"

"Did Essie *say* we have a problem?" I countered.

She tilted her head, considering. "No. She said you were an asshole. A prig. She says that a lot, actually. Sanctimonious—"

"I get it," I grumbled, holding up a hand to stop her from rambling through what I was sure was a very long list of faults, as told by Essie.

"But she's never come to me with a specific complaint of harassment," James finished.

I shrugged. "We've known each other since kinder-garten. There's a lot of history there. We like to rile each other up."

"Like brother and sister?" she asked innocently.

I narrowed my eyes at her over the rim of my beer can. "Not quite."

I expected her to give me shit about that, but she only nodded briskly, her mind clearly on more important matters.

"I'm glad we don't have a problem, because Pirate is special," she said, cracking open a can of lemon-flavored sparkling water. "That's what I wanted to talk to you about, actually. Pirate is showing amazing aptitude for reining. His natural talent is truly incredible."

I nodded. "He has the genes for it. It's a miracle the last two years didn't break his body or his spirit."

"We should discuss taking his training to the next level and what that would entail," James said. "The way I see it, we have two paths forward. The first is status quo. We would start showing him now, nothing too big. See how he does on the local circuit. Then we would push hard next year and aim for a national championship."

"Sounds reasonable. What's the second path?"

"We go aggressive." James took a swig of water. "We do a couple shows here and maybe Texas. Use the next three months as a warm-up for the real thing. Then we take Pirate to the futurity championship in November in Oklahoma."

I blinked. The National Reining Horse Association Futurity Championship was a three-day competition to showcase the best up-and-comers in the industry. It was only open to three-year-old horses, so for Pirate, it was now or never.

"That's a purse of one hundred grand. Pirate would be competing against three-year-olds that have been training all year for this. He's barely had two months under saddle. Seems risky to me. If we're keeping him for stud, we need him to win as many blue ribbons as possible in the next two years. A poor showing at the futurity will make him less valuable as a stud."

"Sure, but *winning* the futurity would make his value skyrocket," James argued. "Essie reminded me that the non-pro division, while still competitive, could give us a better shot at a ribbon."

I rubbed my jaw. The non-pro division required that riders be owners of the horse, rather than a professional rider or trainer. Professional riders were relegated to the open division.

The problem was that I was Pirate's owner. Pirate might be ready for competition, but I sure as hell wasn't. I rode horses for fun or to do a job. I didn't know how to do anything fancy like spins or sliding stops.

"Gotta be honest, James, I think Pirate deserves better than me weighing him down. If I ride him in the non-pro division, we'd be stuck in level one or two with the baby riders. The purse is much smaller."

James smirked. "That's what I said. But Essie reminded me that you have a brother, and under the rules, brothers count as immediate family and can ride as the owner."

I scrunched my forehead. "Adam? He trains horses. Aren't trainers considered professionals?"

"She was talking about Zack," James clarified. "Under the rules, he's a non-pro. In reining competitions, he's only ever entered on Lodestar Ranch horses in the non-pro division. At rodeos, he does the bronc riding—which doesn't count for reining competition."

"Zack, huh?" I looked around and found him pouring Essie a watermelon margarita. Their heads were closer together than necessary and both were laughing. I couldn't say it warmed my heart to see my brother and my ex-best friend so chummy together. More like it curdled my gut. "This was Essie's idea?"

"Sure was. She has so much faith in Pirate and really wants him to have this opportunity. And I agree with her. He can do this. It's a big risk, but so is the reward. We could retire him from competition after one year instead of two. Imagine breeding him with Belle. How gorgeous and talented would their babies be?" She clasped her hands under her chin, her eyes wide and sparkling.

I laughed. James loved Belle, a feisty palomino who was currently a rising star on the reining circuit. She planned to breed her in the next two years and restart Lodestar Ranch's breeding program.

"Slow your roll, darlin'. Pirate hasn't even competed in his first show yet. For all we know, he'll hate crowds."

"The only way to find out is to try." She raised her eyebrows. "So what do you say?"

I looked at Essie again. She wanted this. I knew that much. I turned back to James and clinked my beer to her water. "Let's do it."

8

ESSIE

There wasn't a single part of my body that didn't ache. A good ache, the kind that came from a long day spent on horseback in the autumn sunshine. A satisfying ache, the kind that came from fully focusing my mind and body on learning something new.

And it *was* new, that was the crazy thing about it. I had spent my whole life around horses. First as a barn rat, latching on to the Hale family, helping with ranch chores because they were nice enough to let me ride their horses whenever I wanted. Then as a horse owner myself and professional barrel racer.

That all helped, but the actual business of horse training was entirely new to me. I had only ever been on the client side of things. I'd had no clue what it took to turn a horse and rider into a winning team. The nuance of it all. As a barrel racer, I had focused on how a horse performed for and with only me. Now the thing I cared most about was getting the horse ready for someone else—and since riders had their own quirks the same way horses had their own quirks, this was no easy task.

But damn, it was *interesting*.

It was something I could see doing a good long while. Maybe not forever. Forever wasn't something I could wrap my brain around. But a decade, at least.

I wasn't interested in planning out the rest of my life. Right now, the only thing I wanted to plan was dinner.

With both Mom and I working long hours most days of the week, we usually made do with whatever she brought home from Sweetie Pie. That didn't mean I *couldn't* cook. I actually loved cooking, when the mood struck me. I had a whole Instagram account dedicated to chefs and recipes so I never had to make the same recipe twice. I loved scrolling through, discovering food I would otherwise never know existed. Aspen Springs was my favorite place in the whole world, but good luck finding a restaurant that served anything other than burgers or pizza.

Tonight I was making red lentil curry, if I could reach that can of coconut milk. Normally grabbing things off the top shelf wasn't an issue for me, since I was on the tall side, but my shoulders were still burning from this afternoon's ranch chores.

I groaned as I lifted my arm. And then suddenly

there was another arm stretched over my head, swiping the can of coconut milk in front of my face. I knew who that fucking arm belonged to before I even turned around. Brax had chosen his aftershave and deodorant in high school and never wavered from it. I would recognize that spicy clove scent anywhere.

He was frowning when I turned to face him. "What's wrong with you?" he demanded, looking me up and down like he was searching for injuries.

"Why are you literally everywhere?" I grumbled as I reached for the can. "Give me that."

"I can't be *literally* everywhere," he reasoned. "It's *literally* impossible. But if what you mean is we seem to run into each other a lot, well, the explanation is simple, really. You work at my family's ranch. My house is a block from yours. There's only one grocery store in this town and, being human, we both have to eat, so here we are."

"Gee, thanks so much for explaining the obvious. You just can't help yourself, can you?" I shook my head. "This is why people don't like you, Brax. In case you were wondering." I moved to get past him, but he angled his cart to block my path.

"The only thing I'm wondering is why you're rubbing your shoulder like that. What's wrong with you?" he asked again.

I immediately dropped my hand and glared. "It's nothing you need to worry about. Aches and pains are part of ranch work. I guess it's been a while since you did anything but sit at a desk and get soft."

"Honey, there's nothing soft about me, I promise you that." His lips quirked.

I gave him a skeptical look and took my time with it, my gaze lingering where it would hurt the most. But the joke was on me because that only served to remind me of what James had said about Adam being the *small* brother. My cheeks felt hot as I pushed past him.

This time, I was successful in outmaneuvering him. I had almost made it out of the aisle when his hand clamped down on my shoulder, his fingers splayed across my collar bone above my breast. "Hey!"

"I can fix this."

"It won't work," I said. "You're too irritating. It makes my muscles even more tense. My body will reject you."

But his thumb found the knot where my shoulder met my neck and I whimpered. He laughed softly. "There you go," he soothed, like I was a high-strung filly.

I wanted to stiffen up again just to spite him, but instead my eyes drifted closed and my head lolled to the side, giving him more room to work. His hand slid under the collar of my shirt. The knot didn't stand a chance against the gentle, relentless pressure. It melted away. Fucking traitor.

Brax leaned down, his five o'clock shadow scraping the shell of my ear. "I think your body likes me just fine," he whispered.

"Yeah, well, my body likes a lot of things that aren't good for it," I muttered. "Tequila, bacon, Bobby Waters." That last one happened to be a bull rider with more charisma than brains, and a mistake I'd embarrassingly made more than once, usually after too much tequila.

His thumb dug in with sudden force and my eyes popped open. "Do not *ever* say his name when my hands are on you," his voice growled in my ear.

I twisted to stare up at him in disbelief. "Are you serious right now? I'm not—" The words evaporated in my throat at the fury in his eyes.

I had never seen him like this before. Annoyed, sure. Irritated, most definitely. But this was something else. Something that made every cell in my body shiver with sudden awareness.

And still, I couldn't resist taunting him, just a little. "Take your hands off me, then, because I'll say whatever name I want."

He didn't move, just kept staring at me. Waiting me out.

Well, he could wait forever. I wasn't giving in.

Except...the look in his eyes was doing uncomfortable things to my insides and I was aggravatingly damp between my thighs. Plus he hadn't done my other shoulder yet and it was every bit as knotty.

"Fine," I huffed, turning back around. "Not that it matters, since you will never have your hands on me again, but I promise I won't say his name." His name wasn't worth saying, anyway, so no loss there.

The pressure immediately lessened. He rubbed in gentle circles, easing the tension he had put there himself. "There, was that so hard?" he murmured.

"Shut up and do my other side."

He chuckled. "Yes, ma'am."

"What's your deal with him, anyway?" I asked. "I didn't know you'd ever met before."

"The deal with who?"

I had the feeling he was testing me. There was a mocking note in his voice. "You know who," I sassed back pertly. "I'm not allowed to say his name, remember?" When his other hand joined the first, it felt like a reward. "Is it because of Zack?" Zack didn't ride bulls, but they both competed in the steer wrestling event at rodeos.

"No, he and Zack are good, as far as I know. Zack's never said anything to the contrary. I fucking hate that guy, is all."

"Oh." I didn't press, mostly because I didn't care. The man had magic hands. I leaned into his touch and moaned. "Mmm."

Mrs. Gottlieb, reaching for a can of stewed tomatoes, stared at us with her mouth agape.

"Mind your business, Mrs. Gottlieb," I said, but my tone lacked its usual snap due to my muscles melting into puddles. It was a lost cause, anyway. Mrs. Gottlieb was a farmer's wife and president of the Aspen Springs Beautification Society, and she had never minded her own business a day in her life.

"It's indecent, that's what it is," she muttered, hurrying away, eyes averted like she was afraid we might start fornicating right there in the grocery store.

Brax's chest rumbled with a low laugh. "She has six kids. You'd think she'd know what indecent looked like."

I moaned again. "Don't stop."

There was a pause as his hands spasmed on my skin. "I'm beginning to see her point."

"Harder," I said, because I could never resist putting on a show and also because, good golly god, it felt like I had died and gone to heaven when Brax kneaded the knot.

"Behave, hellion," he warned.

"You know Mrs. Gottlieb is still listening, even if she can't see us. Might as well make it worth her time."

"Yeah, but so is my dick and if you keep it up, I'm going to have trouble walking out of here."

The words stunned me into silence. I didn't shock easily and had a policy of having the last word, but this was *Brax*. Accusing *me* of making his dick hard. I couldn't have been more surprised by a parade of talking elephants.

Brax *despised* me.

Then again, maybe that was the point. After all, he was far from my favorite person, but that never stopped my dumb body from reacting to him with inconvenient lust.

"I've always said that hate makes people horny," I said. "Good to know it's true even for uptight prigs like yourself."

I heard his sharp inhale, felt the slow release of his breath. I was glad I couldn't see his face. I had the feeling it might hurt me somehow, and I had been hurt enough by this man who used to be my closest friend.

He squeezed my shoulders, then took his hands away from me altogether. "Pirate's first show is next weekend. I doubt I'll make it, but it should be a good time."

The abrupt change in conversation nearly gave me whiplash. His detached tone was like a door shutting politely but firmly in my face.

And that hurt, too. But it was a hurt I was familiar with.

Our friendship hadn't ended with a big fight. Everything changed the day he almost died, and I didn't even realize it in the moment. We still talked. He still gave me a ride home from school when Jack stayed for ROTC. A week into it, I knew *something* was wrong, but I couldn't pinpoint exactly what it was.

Our easy way with each other was just...gone. He didn't tell me dirty jokes anymore. If I touched him, he moved away. We didn't laugh or goof off together. And when I tried to talk to him about it, that tone right there was what he gave me. Polite. Distant.

Back then, I got mad. I yelled. And when that didn't work, I finally understood. Because I had been there before, standing outside a glass wall with the person I loved on the other side, begging him to love me back. I could see him through the glass, but I couldn't reach him.

If you don't stop crying when I leave, I'm not going to come see you anymore. My dad said that when I was seven, during one of his infrequent visits. It had worked. I stopped crying. But his visits remained as sporadic as ever.

I learned from that, too.

I cried a lot when I realized Brax and I would never go back to the way we used to be. It had broken my heart. But I never let him see that. I knew it wouldn't do any good, anyway.

So I just...stopped. Stopped asking for his attention. Stopped expecting him to care. Eventually, I stopped talking to him altogether, other than forced civilities. Somewhere along the way that civility turned into purposeful antagonization. In my defense, he started it.

But I couldn't resist egging him on.

Even though, deep down, I knew it was because I still craved his attention, however I could get it.

Fifteen years ago

I propped my socked feet on the dash, making myself comfortable for the forty-minute drive to the trailhead. I had kicked off my Chucks the second I had slid into the passenger side of Brax's old Ford pickup. One hand floated out the window—Brax's truck pre-dated air conditioning—catching the hot breeze on my fingertips, while the other rested on the bench seat between us.

Perfect.

Not just because the red brick school building was in the rearview mirror, although that didn't hurt. I preferred to think of myself as running toward something rather than running away from anything. It was something my dad liked to say. *If you spend your life running away, your past will always be chasing you, dictating every move you make. Run toward your future, baby girl, and you'll make yourself a life worth living.*

Dad was always running toward something. Not me. Or my brother. Or my mom. We were the things he saw in his rearview mirror as he ran toward whatever exciting thing caught his attention. There was always something.

It was shitty of him. I knew it was shitty. But, *damn.* What a way to live. Pure freedom. That was what I wanted for myself. Minus the whole teen pregnancy and subsequent abandonment of offspring, of course.

So right now, I wasn't running *away* from school. I was running *toward* an afternoon of fun with my favorite person in the world.

"Aren't you happy we did this?" I asked, unable to keep the smile off my face.

Brax paused for a beat. "Yes."

I studied his profile, wondering what internal calculation had made him hesitate before coming to, in my humble opinion, the only correct response. It couldn't be the school part. Final grades had already been turned in. I was once again looking at a B- average. Brax had straight A's. He was the top student in our class, and I had no doubt that next year, he'd be the valedictorian. It wasn't even close.

He just didn't like breaking a promise to Jack. That was my guess. Fortunately, the pleasure of my company outweighed such pesky details. I hoped.

I loved Jack. Next to Brax, he was my best friend. But despite sharing a womb for nine months, we didn't have a lot in common. We didn't have the same taste in food, or music, or hobbies. Brax was the only thing we shared.

Most of the time that was fine. Despite our lack of common interests, we got along great. The three of us were always together. Whatever trouble I was quick to get us into, Brax and Jack were just as quick to get us out of. I felt good having them both with me. Safe. Indestructible.

But honestly, sometimes I wasn't in a sharing mood. Like now.

Between school and chores at his family's ranch, Brax had always been busy, but now that he'd taken a part-time job with the only lawyer in Aspen Springs, it felt like I never saw him anymore. And when I *did* see him, Jack was right there, too.

That never used to bother me. But lately...lately it did.

Like he felt the weight of my thoughts, Brax found my hand on the seat between us and tapped my knuckles with his index finger, his eyes never leaving the road. "What?"

"What do you mean, what?" I asked.

"You're staring at me. And you haven't spoken a single word for five minutes. It gives me a spooky feeling, like the calm before a storm."

I laughed. "You can relax. There's no storm brewing. I was just thinking, that's all. Summer's coming."

His left hand twisted on the wheel. His right hand was still on the bench, not actually touching mine, but so close I could swear the tiny hairs on our fingers brushed each other's like an electric current.

"You got the rodeos planned out?" he asked.

"Hell, yeah, I do." I grinned.

This summer would kick off my last rodeo season as

a junior barrel racer. I was at the top of my game. The championship title was mine to defend, and I intended to do exactly that. There would hardly be a weekend I was at home while I traveled to rodeos from Oklahoma and Tennessee to Nevada and Texas. It was exhausting, but it was also exhilarating. A taste of the real life waiting for me.

"One more year," I promised myself softly.

"And then?" he asked, like he didn't know.

That was one of the things I loved about Brax. He gave me space to ramble on about my hopes and dreams for my future, no matter how crazy it all sounded. He never tried to temper my enthusiasm with bummer advice like *be realistic*, the way Jack would.

"And then world domination, silly. Make a million dollars on the barrel racing circuit. I'll be the next Charmayne James."

He glanced at me quickly before returning his eyes to the road. "You're not going to be the next anyone. You're going to be the first Essie Price. Little girls will pretend they're you when they trot their ponies around barrels."

I meant to say thank you, but the words came out a strangled clump of sounds I doubted he could decipher. If I were the crying sort, my mascara would be black streaks on my cheeks right now. Fortunately, I wasn't.

I punched him on the shoulder. "Damn straight."

"Ow!" He rubbed his shoulder, and I immediately

regretted it because it meant his right hand took the wheel from his left. "You trying to run us off the road, hellion?"

I rolled my eyes. "I didn't hurt you."

Inside, I glowed at the nickname he had given me. It wasn't the kind of thing a boyfriend would call a girlfriend, like baby or sweetheart, and I liked that about it. It meant he wasn't going to give it to someone else someday. It was all mine.

He grinned. "Nah, you didn't hurt me. Just wanted to offer you a little encouragement. It's tough throwing punches when your hands are so little," he teased. He placed his right hand on top of my left, engulfing it in his.

I stared at our hands. My hands were a perfectly normal size, thank you very much, but I couldn't deny they were a lot smaller than his. And even though they were calloused from years of riding, they didn't have his strength, either.

"Jerk," I said.

But I left our hands where they were.

BRAX

ADAM

James said she's heading out to celebrate Pirate's win. You're going too, right?

BRAX

Wasn't planning on it. Zack and Essie will be there, though.

ADAM

Yeah, that's the part that worries me. They need adult supervision.

BRAX

Goddammit.

I'm too old for this crap.

Mistakes had been made.

The first mistake was making the drive to Pueblo for Pirate's first show to begin with. I should have sat this one out like I'd told Essie I would. But dammit, that horse had loped his way into my affection. I wanted to be there in case anything went wrong—even though I knew he was in good hands with Essie and James.

Maybe if I had considered that being there for Pirate meant spending hours at a time within arm's length of Essie, I would have reconsidered. Maybe if I had understood that every sound she made would remind me of the way she moaned as I touched her in the grocery store, I would have stayed the fuck home.

But I really wanted to see Pirate win.

Which he had, and that blue ribbon led to mistake number two: letting Adam talk me into going out to celebrate instead of driving straight back to Aspen Springs. Because goddammit, Essie was wearing those light wash Wranglers that cupped her sweet ass to perfection, and a tee shirt that hung off one shoulder to reveal a red lacy strap of something. A camisole? Her bra? I would have given my right pinky finger to find out.

And all of those mistakes culminated with the

biggest one of all: not throwing Essie over my shoulder and getting her the hell out of there the second I realized the bar had a mechanical bull. Because I knew without a shadow of a doubt that Essie was going to ride that fucker before the night was over.

And I was going to have to watch her do it.

Worse, I couldn't even numb myself to her effect with whiskey because I was the designated driver. Instead, I was slowly sipping my way down a bottle of shitty beer, the only drink I was allowing myself for the night.

"You're going to crack that bottle in half if you don't lighten up." Zack smirked at me across the high-top table and took a sip from his own shitty beer, eyes alight with speculation. "What the hell are you glaring at everyone for? We're here to celebrate. I got you a shiny blue ribbon, man."

I didn't say anything as I rolled the bottle between my hands, letting the chilled glass cool me down. The room was overheated, packed with bodies, and every time I glanced at the bar where Essie and James were making each other laugh, another one of those bodies was standing too close to them, and usually that body was male. The girls seemed to have no trouble fending off unwanted advances. Neither one of them had signaled for help. That would likely continue for James, but I figured it was only a matter of time before Essie saw something she liked.

My gaze slid to the bar again just as Essie leaned forward across the counter to get the bar tender's attention, giving me an excellent view of her ass in those fucking jeans. Unfortunately, I wasn't the only one to get an eyeful. A guy tapped her shoulder. She turned, he said something I couldn't hear over the hum of voices and country music, and at her nod, he flagged the bartender.

Fucking great.

I took another sip of my shitty beer. Unsurprisingly, it did not improve my mood.

"You're coming to the rodeo tomorrow, right?" Zack asked, pulling my attention back to him. "I'm entered in the bronc riding."

I shrugged. "Might as well."

"Gee, thanks. Way to be a supportive big brother. It's almost like you don't care that I'm doing you a huge fucking favor right now."

"With Pirate, you mean?" I raised my eyebrows. "Can we really call it a favor when you get to keep half the winnings?"

Zack grinned, his eyes flicking over my shoulder and then back to me again. "Nah, I'm not talking about Pirate. I'm talking about how I'm keeping you distracted while Essie is on that bull."

"What?" I whipped around so fast I nearly tumbled off the stool.

Sure enough, Essie was astride the mechanical bull,

her long legs wrapped tightly around the barrel. Christ. The bull was surrounded by foam mats to cushion her body when—not *if*—she fell. Falling was inevitable. No one was allowed to dismount on their own, because where was the fun in that?

A crowd had gathered around the low barrier around the bull. I could barely make out James's short frame front and center. I would have missed her entirely if she hadn't cupped her hands to her mouth like a foghorn and hollered, "Ride, you sexy thing!"

Fucking James.

Essie grinned widely in response. Zack let out a piercing whistle, which earned him a sharp glare from me. Essie looked up, her gaze searching until she found us, and she lifted her hand in a wave. Then she wrapped her hand around the grip, her top teeth digging into her bottom lip.

That fucking mouth.

I rubbed my chest. She looked so happy. She always did, when I wasn't going out of my way to piss her off.

The bull started up and her hips immediately caught the rhythm. I should have looked away, saved myself from the torture, but my eyes refused to budge. My cock thickened with every rock of her hips.

"Damn, that girl can ride," Zack said, admiration loud in his voice.

Of course she could ride. She was one of the top barrel racers in the country. Riding a horse, riding a

mechanical bull, riding a man...I had no doubt Essie
Price knew what she was doing.

"She's not for you," I warned, in case Zack had
similar thoughts.

"Yeah, you've made that abundantly clear. You've
been pissing circles around that girl since you first laid
eyes on her." Zack snorted. "What I don't get is why you
think she's not for *you*."

I shook my head. "It's not like that with us. She was
never for me."

And that was the fucking truth. One I reminded
myself of every damn day. Essie Price was meant for
greatness. She didn't need any man tying her to a small
Colorado town. Like her dad, she craved freedom. But
unlike her dad, she wasn't willing to sever ties to have it.
Her heart was too big and too loyal.

More than eight seconds had passed, but Essie hung
on. The crowd started counting down, starting at ten. I
had the feeling her ride would end when they got to one
and, sure enough, the operator jerked her from one
direction to the other, making her lose her seat. The
crowd cheered good-naturedly.

I slid off my stool as Essie rolled over and pushed
to her feet, laughing. She took a swaying step and then
stopped and braced her hands on her knees, clearly
dizzy. I sliced through the crowd, already halfway
there when James climbed over the guardrail to help
her. But tiny James was no match for Essie's height,

and they tumbled together into a pile, giggling hysterically.

"Jesus Christ," I muttered. I pushed aside two guys overeager to help and hauled James to her feet. "You good?"

She nodded, smiling widely. "I'm not the one who was spinning in circles."

I didn't need the reminder. I was already squatting low so I could scoop Essie into my arms. "I've got you."

"No," she said, sounding genuinely horrified.

"Yes," I said, and strode off the mats with her.

The crowd parted for us, people calling out compliments on her riding skills as we went. I headed for the table with Zack, but she tugged at my collar. I looked down at her, the question in my eyes.

"Air," she said. "I need air."

I nodded. "James—"

"I'll get Zack." She dropped a bottle of water into Essie's lap. "We can head back to the hotel."

"No," Essie protested. "I just need a minute. It's so hot in here, but I don't want to leave yet. It's still early."

James looked at me and then back to Essie. "Okay, but if you change your mind, it's fine. I don't mind getting some rest."

I kicked the door open with my boot and carried Essie out into the crisp night air. She sucked in an audible deep breath.

"Whew. You can put me down now."

I set her on her feet, watching her carefully in the fluorescent lamplight as she uncapped the water and took a long swallow.

"Go back inside. I'll follow in a couple minutes." When I gave her a look, she smirked a little. "Yeah, I knew you weren't going to go for that."

"Sit down." I gestured to the graying wood-planked bench against the wall, but she shook her head.

"I'm fine. Really. It actually feels good to stand. Wow, it's been a really good day, huh? Pirate won his first competition. How amazing is that?" Her words tumbled over each other.

I cocked my head, studying her. "Are you drunk?"

"No." She laughed and then flashed me an impish grin. "Well, maybe a little bit. Can you be a little bit drunk? Or is it like being pregnant? Once you're in, you're all in. I'm not pregnant, either, by the way. I haven't had sex in...oh...nine months? That's too long. Don't you think it's too long?"

I stared at her.

Oh, no.

I had never seen Essie drunk, to my recollection, but I had seen her sober plenty of times and this wasn't it.

Sober Essie hated me. But drunk Essie was looking at me with an offer in her eyes that I might not be strong enough to refuse.

She swayed toward me a step, and then another. Not in a drunk, unsteady on her feet kind of way. In a hips swinging, seductive kind of way. When there wasn't space to fit a Bible between us, she tilted her face up and licked her bottom lip. I bit back a groan.

Whatever the fuck was happening right now, she was going to hate me more than ever in the morning. I couldn't do it. I wouldn't do it. Unless she put her lips on mine right now, because in that case—

"You used to be my best friend," she whispered. "Why did you stop?"

She could have slid a knife right into my gut and it would have surprised me less. Hurt less, too, probably. The ache of it filled my lungs instead of oxygen. I couldn't breathe around it.

"I told you everything. My hopes, my fears, all of it. I even talked to you about Jack, the good and the bad, even though you were his friend, too, because I knew you would never breathe a word of it to him. I knew you wouldn't betray me. You were mine in a way that you were never his, weren't you? I don't know how else to explain it, but that's how it felt."

That's how it was.

But I didn't say a damn word.

"I told you everything," she said again. "Well, almost everything. I used to think about what it would be like if we were more than friends. I never told you that. But it's true. I used to wonder about what it would be like to kiss you." She looked up at me, her blue eyes as luminous as the stars overhead. "Did you ever wonder that?"

She moved like she meant to put her wondering to rest once and for all, but I moved faster. I caught her jaw with my hand, her chin snug in the curve between my thumb and index finger, and held her back.

"No," I roughed out. "I never wondered what it would be like to kiss you. I didn't have to wonder." I slid my hand from her jaw down the smooth column of her throat where I could feel her pulse thrum. She stared at me with wide eyes, her mouth falling slightly open. "Because I knew how it would be. The way it always is with us. Too much, and not enough."

With a gentle squeeze, I released her throat. "Let's go."

I took her hand and pulled her into the safety inside.

10

ESSIE

Too much, and not enough.

What the hell did that even mean?

I didn't know. I was probably never going to know, either, because I would rather pull out every one of my toenails than ask.

Last night was in the past. And today? Well, today I was going to pretend last night never happened.

My god, I loved the rodeo. The sound of country music blasting over stereos. The smell of hay and animals, sweat and corndogs. The shine of sequins, leather, and silver belt buckles. I loved it all. I twirled slowly, my arms outstretched, like I could wrap it all up in a big ole hug. *This used to be my playground…*

"What's that you're humming?" James asked. "It's the song from *A League of Our Own*, isn't it?"

"Yeah, the Madonna song." I grinned, feeling at one

with the universe. Even though the universe included Brax, who was right behind James with Adam and Ben. "It's a good movie, James."

She laughed. "I don't disagree."

Nothing could ruin my good mood. Not Brax. Not the hazy memory of things better left unsaid. Not his answer, twisting inside of me. Did I cringe every time I heard the echo of my voice asking that goddamn question? Yes. Did I want to demand he explain his words? Also yes. Was I going to do that? Fuck no. I was going to claim alcohol-induced amnesia. Because I had a little thing called self-respect, last night's nonsense to the contrary.

Yesterday I had been too focused on Pirate to truly enjoy myself. It had been Pirate's first competition. We had chosen a Colorado rodeo only a two-hour drive from Lodestar Ranch. It was more of a test of his attitude than his skill. We wanted to see how Pirate behaved under pressure. Would he hate to travel? Would sleeping in a strange stall mess with his stomach? Would the loud noises make him nervous?

Pirate passed with flying colors. I was giddy with excitement. And today, I could relax and enjoy the rodeo. Zack was competing in bronc riding. Should be a good time.

Our group made our way to the stands. We moved in a line, with me, James, and Ben in the middle bracketed by Adam and Brax.

Brax walked a half-step behind me, one hand hovering near my lower back without actually making contact, his other arm outstretched by his side. Protecting me from random strangers bumping into my space. The gesture was so familiar. We had walked like this a thousand times when we were teenagers. I doubted he even realized what he was doing.

We settled into our seats and I was once again between Brax and James. I angled my body slightly away from him and leaned forward, resting my elbows on my knees. The sweet scent of kettle corn mingled with horses and hay. I breathed deeply.

"Dad, ice cream?" Ben, who was sitting between James and Adam, tugged at his dad's sleeve and pointed to the ice cream stand.

"Sure. Anyone else want a cone?" Adam asked, standing.

James and I both requested a cone. Chocolate for her, vanilla for me. Brax shook his head. I took that as a character flaw.

"Do you ever miss it? Barrel racing, I mean," James asked.

I considered. "Well, sure, I miss it. I miss it the way I miss fifth grade recess or—" A sudden awareness made me glance up to find Brax's gaze on me. *You. The way I miss you.*

So much that I ached with it, sometimes. The memories between us felt palpable.

But I sure as fuck wasn't going to say that out loud. I had done enough of that last night.

"Like the way I miss an old friend," I finished, wrenching my attention back to James. "Barrel racing is like that. It was such an amazing time in my life, and I'll always cherish the memories. No hard feelings about any of it, but I'm ready for something new."

"I get that," James said, nodding. She smiled up at Adam as he handed her the chocolate cone. "I loved racing in high school. But I love what I do now, too."

I was aware that Brax was eavesdropping. He wasn't even being subtle about it. After accepting my vanilla cone from Adam with a quick thank you, I turned to him with bugged out eyes and brows up to my hairline. "Can I help you?"

"No need to snap at me when I'm just sitting here, minding my own business." He grinned. "What's the matter, you need an aspirin for that hangover?"

As it happened, I didn't have a hangover because I hadn't actually been drunk last night. Alcohol and I had an interesting relationship. Nothing less than five drinks could give me a hangover. Four drinks in, and I was asleep, so hangovers almost never happened. Three drinks made me horny. Two drinks? That was the danger zone, when when the alcohol loosened my tongue.

Not for kissing. For talking.

Two drinks turned me into a chatty sweetheart completely unphased by my own vulnerability.

I was *emotionally* slutty.

Disgustingly so.

And two, unfortunately, was the precise number of drinks I'd had when I decided to ride that damn bull. Those gin and tonics were still wreaking havoc in my bloodstream when Brax carried me outside.

"I'm fine," I said.

"Are you?"

I stuck my tongue out at him and blew a raspberry.

"Careful, hellion," he murmured. "The next time you show me your tongue, I might take it as an invitation."

Feeling the need to prove something, I locked my gaze to his and dragged my tongue from the base of the ice cream to the very tip, then closed my lips around the swirl and pulled it into my mouth.

A flush bloomed high on his cheekbones, his eyes darkening as he watched. I took the opportunity to sink my teeth into the crisp cone and rip off a chunk. He winced. I laughed so hard I nearly spewed crumbs at him. Men were too easy.

"Sorry." I clapped a hand over my mouth, still giggling.

"Are you five?" he grumbled.

"Shhh, the event is starting."

We turned our attention to the arena, where the first rider exited the bucking chute to a loud cheer. Like bull riding, bronc riding was an eight-second ride. Zack did both bareback and saddle bronc events, but today it was bareback, where the rider held on with one hand to a rigging attached to the girth, keeping the other hand in the air. The goal was to stay on through the full eight seconds of bucking without touching the horse with the free hand.

The first rider was bucked off in heartbreaking 7.8 seconds. The second rider stayed on for the full eight seconds, hand in the air where it belonged, but only earned tepid applause on account of the bronc being less nasty with his bucks. In bronc riding, both the rider and the horse earned scores on a scale of zero to fifty, for a combined score up to one hundred. The rider earned points for control and technique, while the horse earned points for bad behavior. The meaner the bronc, the higher the score.

Which meant Zack was thrilled when he got a nasty one. I could see the devilish grin on his face as he waited in the chute. The grin became a mask of focused concentration as they entered the arena in a fury of bucks and twists.

It felt like so much longer than eight seconds before the bell rang, but when it did, Zack was still astride the bronc. We whooped and hollered as the pickup men rode into the ring to extract him.

And then suddenly everything went wrong. Horses

tangled, men shouted, Zack tumbled from the horse and disappeared beneath the frantic cluster of limbs.

I jumped to my feet, my hands over my mouth to muffle my scream. Next to me, James had turned Ben into her, covering his eyes. Brax and Adam were pushing through the crowd to get to their brother.

Zack lay crumpled on the sand floor, unmoving.

11

BRAX

Lying in the hospital bed, Zack was damn near unrecognizable. A deep purple bruise bloomed along his cheekbone. His mouth was pale except for an ugly red split down the middle. One shoulder was in a sling, dislocated from when he hit the ground. His right leg was in a cast.

I had seen him banged up before, but never like this. Zack had always been the one with a glint of mischief in his eyes and a teasing smirk on his lips. He was the first one to tell a joke and the last one to leave a party. But now? He looked gray. Lifeless.

My baby brother.

"You look like shit," he said.

I damn near jumped out of my skin. "Your eyes aren't even open. How the hell would you know how I looked?"

"Took a wild guess." He cracked open one lid and eyed me up and down. "Whaddya know. I was right."

Ah. There he was.

"I look better than you," I said, my relief outweighing my annoyance.

"Debatable. Women love a roughed-up cowboy. They'll be beating down the hospital door for the chance to take care of me. I'm thinking about holding interviews. Make them work for it."

"Funny," I said. "I don't see any women."

"You just missed Essie, actually. She went to get coffee." Zack smirked and then winced, lifting his good arm to his mouth.

It shouldn't bother me that Essie had made a bee line for the hospital the moment Zack was allowed visitors. They were friends. Only an asshole would be jealous when his brother was stuck in a hospital bed with a broken leg, for fuck's sake.

But as Essie had told me time and again, I was an asshole.

"If you think Essie's going to give you a sponge bath or rub salve on your wounds, you've got another thing coming," I said, claiming the absurdly small plastic chair under the TV. "She's not exactly the sweet nurse type. She's the smack you on the ass and tell you to stop whining type."

"Shows how much you know," Zack said. "She

happened to be very tender when she called me a jackass."

"Why'd she call you a jackass?"

Zack sighed, his eyes drifting shut again. "Something about scaring the living beejezus out of her by getting bucked off like that, why the hell didn't I roll the other way instead of getting tangled under the horse's legs, she thought I was dead, blah blah blah."

"She has a point," I said gruffly. "You scared the hell out of all of us."

"Everyone gets bucked off," Zack reminded me. "That's the whole point of bronc riding. It's only fun if it's impossible."

I shook my head. "You're getting too old for this shit."

"Yeah, maybe." He sighed again. "Fuck, I'm sorry, man. I should never have been on that bronc to begin with."

"You're a rodeo rider. That's what you do."

"I knew it was too risky, with the futurity championships coming up. But I was so fucking close to taking the lead. I really thought I could have it all. A National Champion rodeo buckle and the futurity championship for reining. I fucked it all up."

"You were doing us a favor. We never expected you to put your own goals on hold to help us with ours. So we'll have to rethink our strategy with Pirate. It's not like he's the one with a broken leg. He can still compete."

"You gonna move him to the open division? Pirate and James would make one hell of a team to beat."

"Maybe," I said. "But not with James riding. She's already riding in the pro division for another client. Besides, competition is a lot stiffer in the open division. Either way, Pirate will be up against horses who have been training for this all year, instead of hanging out underfed, unworked, and unshod in some asshole's backyard. James thinks he can take a ribbon in the open division, but we both know his odds of taking the top spot are better in the non-pro division."

"And that top spot means a world of difference in breeding value," Zack conceded.

"Yes, it does. Not to mention the hundred grand in prize money."

"You could ride yourself."

I snorted. "Let's hope it doesn't come to that."

"You're a damn good rider, Brax. For a lawyer, anyway. I could see you and Pirate taking a Level Two ribbon. Might get beat out by a nineteen-year-old, but you'd make him work for it."

"Gee, thanks."

"Money isn't as good for Level Two, though," Zack pointed out.

"That's true. It's not."

We both fell silent, the only sound the steady *beep, beep, beep* of the machines, monitoring Zack's vital signs while the IV dripped pain medication into his veins. I started to stand, figuring he was drifting back to a much-needed sleep, when suddenly his eyes popped back open.

"You need a wife," he said.

I nearly fell out of my chair. "Come again?"

"A wife who rides horses but isn't a professional reiner. The NRHA rulebook defines non-pro as the owner or owner's immediate family. A wife is immediate family." He locked his bloodshot blue eyes on mine. "You should marry Essie."

My heart did something stupid in my chest and I pressed my palm to it. *She's not for you, dumbass.*

I hooted like it was the funniest thing I'd ever heard. "Damn, kid. What the hell kind of drugs are they giving you? I'm not going to marry Essie just for the chance to win a hundred thousand dollars and earn my horse a shiny blue ribbon. Have you lost your damn mind?"

He raised an eyebrow, his gaze never wavering. "I didn't say you'd marry her for a hundred grand. But I do think a hundred grand might convince her to marry *you.*"

"Convince who to marry who?" Essie asked, stepping through the door with a paper cup of steaming coffee. She paused when she saw me. "Oh, Brax. I didn't know you were here. You'll have to get your own coffee."

And my heart did that thing again, that stupid, stupid thing.

My wife, it whispered.

"Why are you looking at me like that?" My gaze swept from Brax to Zack and back again. Both of them were sizing me up like Zack needed an organ transplant and mine might be the right fit. "I don't think I like it."

"Oh, honey. You're gonna *hate* it." Zack flashed a mischievous grin and then immediately slapped a hand to his split lip. "Ow. Goddammit."

Despite the fact that he was clearly plotting my demise with my enemy, I took pity on him. I dug into my bag and pulled out a small pot of coconut oil and a tube of Aquaphor. "Move your hand," I instructed.

I sat next to him on the edge of the bed, careful not to jostle his leg, and scooped out a smidge of coconut oil. I rubbed it between my fingers until the cream became a liquid and then dabbed it gently on his lips. I followed that with a dollop of Aquaphor. It was my own personal remedy for cuts, burns, and the cracked lips that came with living in a dry-ass climate.

"The coconut oil is for healing, and the Aquaphor is for protecting," I explained. "How does it feel?"

He smacked his lips together a few times, testing it. "Better. I can move my mouth without crying now. Thanks."

"I'll make a kit for you."

"If you two are done playing sexy nurse, can we please have a serious conversation about Pirate?" Brax asked, sounding annoyed.

Zack gave me a knowing smirk. I knew what he was thinking. Last year, Zack and I had indulged in a little flirtation. Not a big deal, because truthfully, Zack had a little flirtation with every woman he came in contact with between the ages of twenty-one and sixty-one. I had it on good authority that Zack was a fun way to spend a night, but he had nipped my advances in the bud, on account of the man currently glowering at us like he wouldn't mind pulling us apart with his bare hands.

But Zack had it all wrong, both then and now. Brax didn't care who I fucked. He just didn't think I was good enough for his little brother, that was all. Hell, he didn't think I was good enough for anyone.

I twisted my torso to bat my eyelashes at Brax over

my shoulder. "Ohhh, you think I'm sexy?" I asked in a sing-song voice.

Brax scowled. "If you think a snotty nose is sexy, then sure, because that's exactly what's going to happen to my brother if you keep sharing beauty products with him. He doesn't need a virus on top of a broken leg."

"Stop being such a prig. I'm not going to get Zack sick. I haven't had so much as a cold since Thanksgiving, and I always replace my stuff when I get sick. Anyway, I used the hand sanitizer right outside the door before I came in. So there." I almost stuck out my tongue at him, but I remembered what he said about that and kept my tongue safely tucked inside.

His gaze dropped to my mouth like he was remembering, too. When he licked his lower lip, I swallowed hard. I was *this close* to showing him mine, just to see what he would do about it.

"Jesus Christopher Christ," Zack grumbled. "If you two could stop eye fucking each other when I'm a trapped audience on account of this fucking leg, I'd be much obliged. I'm a human being, dammit. I have inalienable rights to not see this shit."

"It's not eye fucking," I said. "It's eye loathing."

"Loathing, huh?" Zack rubbed the three-day growth of stubble on his chin. "Well, that's gonna make this conversation real awkward, then."

"What conversation is that?" I asked warily, looking

between the two brothers again. Something was definitely up.

"The one where we talk about Pirate's future." Brax folded his large body into the small red plastic chair, looking only slightly ridiculous. He rested his elbows on his knees, which were drawn up almost to his chest, and leaned forward.

My brows pushed together in a frown. Now I was good and worried. Had something happened to Pirate while we were all preoccupied with Zack? "What about it?"

"We're eight weeks from the competition. There's no way Zack's leg will heal by then. Without a rider, we'll have to pull Pirate from the show."

I let out a breath. Pirate's career had obviously taken a backseat to my concern for Zack. As much as I loved that fucking horse, I had grown up with the Hale brothers. In that terrible moment when I had heard the bone snap, I had known what it meant for Pirate's future, but all I cared about was that Zack was okay.

"Shit, is that all?" I asked. "Jesus, Brax, you nearly gave me a heart attack. Of course we'll have to pull him from the show. It's not ideal for Pirate, but it's not career-ending, either. And hopefully it won't be career-ending for Zack, either."

"Thanks," Zack said drily. He leaned back on the pillow and closed his eyes. "Damn, I'm tired. These pain meds are crazy."

"It's not career-ending for Pirate, but it's a pretty big setback," Brax said. "You know as well as I do that there's a difference between competition stallions and breeding stallions, and horses don't work like light switches. You can't turn it on and off."

I knew what he was referring to. Stallions had a limited window to prove themselves in the competition ring, if the owner intended to use him for breeding down the road. The behavior expectations for showing were different than breeding. Stallions were supposed to keep their sex drive locked down in the ring. Mares would be present, and a stallion couldn't go dropping dick, vocalizing, or trying to mount other horses. It wouldn't be safe for the horses or their riders.

That didn't mean it was impossible to show a stallion in the ring, and in some ways, it mimicked the behavior of wild horses. Horses were pack animals by nature. They hated being alone—a good thing, too, because there was safety in numbers. But harems—groups of mares and their foals—were led by one stallion and one stallion only. Males were run off the herd when they weaned. These males either stole a harem of their own from another stallion or formed bachelor herds with other males.

The thing about these bachelor herds was that eventually, without a way to procreate, they became sterile. It was a use-it-or-lose-it scenario. And the same was true of a stallion that had spent years behaving a certain way for competition. Eventually, they weren't good for anything else. Most stallions intended for breeding only spent two or three years in competition first, so it was important to make the most of those years.

"The futurity is a big deal," Brax said like I didn't already know. "There's no bigger payout for three-year-olds. Next year, he won't be eligible."

"Okay," I said slowly. "So we pull him from the non-pro and enter him in the open class, with Adam riding." I knew James wasn't an option, since she'd already be riding for a client.

"That's one possibility. We could enter him in the open class, but he'd be competing against horses who have a solid year of training under their saddles instead of a couple months. I'm not saying he doesn't have what it takes to win, but it's a bigger risk. Don't you want him to have the best possible start?"

I blinked at him, baffled. Why the hell was he asking me that? I wasn't purposefully holding Pirate back from success. It wasn't *my* fault Zack got bucked off and stomped. "Of course I want that. We all want that. But what are we supposed to do about it? The only person who can ride in the non-pro category is the owner or immediate family of the owner. Your dad's not in competition shape, and Ben's not ready for that yet. Are you going to ride?"

"I think we both know that's not the best idea. I'm a decent rider, but I'm not a competitor. I'll do it as a last resort, but honestly, putting him in open competition with Adam riding would be a better option."

"Then we're back to that," I said bluntly, annoyed that the conversation had circled right back to where we had started. "You're out of relatives, Brax. There's no way around it."

Zack cracked one eyelid open and smirked, courtesy of my lip balm. "There might be a way around it."

I eyed him suspiciously. "What do you mean?"

"It's right there in the definition of immediate family. Spouse, parent, spouse's parent, partner's parent, stepparent, legal guardian, child, stepchild, sibling, sibling's spouse, sibling's partner, half sibling, stepsibling, aunt, uncle, grandmother, and grandfather." Zack rattled off the list like he had been waiting for that question. "We just need to find a spouse. A woman who happens to be a damn fine rider would be ideal. Know anyone?"

I wrinkled my nose. Surely Zack couldn't be suggesting what I thought he was suggesting. I turned to Brax for confirmation. Or better yet, for him to unequivocally refute it. "You...you want me to marry Zack?"

The expression on Brax's face reminded me of a thunderstorm moving over the mountains, dark and lethal. "You'll marry Zack over his dead body."

"Hey!" Zack protested. "What the fuck, man? Why do I have to be the one to die?"

Brax's icy blue gaze cut to his brother. "You're already

battered and broken. I'm still all in one piece. I have too much to live for."

"It doesn't even make sense," Zack muttered. "How can she marry me if I'm dead?"

"She can't," Brax said. "That's the point."

"No one's dying," I cut in, exasperated. "And no one's getting married, either."

Brax exchanged a long look with Zack. My heartbeat skittered like a nervous foal. If they weren't talking about Zack, then that meant...*No*. Absolutely fucking not.

"Tell him, Brax." My voice was an octave past shrill. "Tell him what a ridiculous idea this is."

He paused for a beat, then shrugged. "It might be worth considering."

I choked on a shocked laugh. "It is *not* worth considering. Have you lost your damn mind?"

"It makes sense, if you think about it. Do you have a better idea?"

"Giving up horses and moving to Antarctica to train polar bears to do flying lead changes and sliding stops would be a better idea," I snapped.

"Penguins," Brax said.

"Now, even I know that doesn't make a lick of sense. How you gonna ride a penguin?" Zack asked.

"Penguins live in the Antarctica. Polar bears live at the North Pole," Brax explained. "So either you need to train penguins in Antarctica, or you need to train polar bears in the North Pole. You can't mix and match."

I stared at him.

He stared back.

"I hate you," I said with feeling.

He looked the tiniest bit regretful. "I know, hellion."

"Whatever." I grabbed my bag and made for the door. "I'm going to get Zack coconut oil and Aquaphor. The next time I see you two clowns, you better have come to your senses." I paused half out the door and leveled Brax with my best disappointed look. I'd seen it often enough on Mom to know how. "Zack is on pain killers, so I'm willing to give him a pass. But there's no excuse for you."

"Think it over," was all he said.

I shook my head. The fuck I would.

13

BRAX

ZACK

I'm bored. Come hang out with me.

BRAX

Hey, Adam. Painted Cat tonight?

ADAM

Hell yeah.

James says she's in, too. She's calling her friends.

ZACK

Um, hello??

BRAX

8 pm?

ADAM

Sounds good. We'll eat dinner with Ben
first and then he can watch a movie
with Grandpa.

ZACK

Wtf, you're hanging out without me?

BRAX

Thank god Zack is still busted up. He
ruins everything.

ZACK

I hate you both.

ADAM

Open the door. We brought beer and
pizza.

Two days after his surgery to put a metal rod in his leg, Zack came home from the hospital. Despite Adam's offer to recuperate at the big house, he insisted on moving into his old cabin on the Lodestar Ranch property. Adam and I had swung by last night to keep him company and make sure he had everything he needed within reach and ended up staying later than we'd planned, laughing and talking like old times.

Better than old times. Adam was still a grumpy son

of a bitch, but he was a lot more fun now than he had been in over a decade. James was good for him.

But I was paying for our late night now. I had a bankruptcy to file, my least favorite part of my job, and I could barely keep my eyes open. I needed more coffee. I dragged my hands down my face, shoved my rolling chair back from my desk, and pushed to my feet.

Right as Essie walked through the door.

Suddenly I was wide awake.

It had been a week since I asked her to marry me and she told me she'd rather move to Antarctica. I had figured that was the end of it.

But here she was. And I could think of only one reason for it.

Her gaze circled my office, taking note of everything in that curious way she had, before she did the same to me. "You said you don't wear a suit."

That wasn't what I expected her to start with, but okay. I glanced down at my standard work attire: a decent button-down shirt, a blue tie patterned with silver horse shoes, jeans, and cowboy boots. "I don't wear a suit. I'm wearing jeans. Pairing that with a tie doesn't make it a suit."

"Hm." Her head tilted. "Jeans and cowboy boots on the bottom. Button down and tie on top." She air circled the items with her fingertip. "It's the clothing equivalent of a mullet. Business up top. Party on the bottom."

I cocked an eyebrow. "Are you implying there's a party in my pants, hellion?"

She gave an uppity sniff. "I'm sure I have no idea what's in your pants, prig. But I'd hazard a guess it's nothing interesting."

"I'd be happy to issue you a personal invitation and let you find out for yourself." I braced my hands on the desk and leaned forward. "Just say when."

Her gaze dipped and the oddest expression crossed her face. Like she was actually imagining the possibility, and didn't entirely hate it. Aroused and perplexed all at once.

"Don't be ridiculous," she said. But she still looked like she was considering it.

I grinned. "Why are you here, hellion?"

"Oh. Right." She cleared her throat, then gestured to the chair behind me. "Sit down, please. I don't want to have this conversation standing up."

"Sounds serious." I hooked the chair leg with my ankle and rolled it closer to me, watching her as she took the chair opposite the desk.

"Well, marriage is serious. So people tell me anyway."

My ass was halfway to the seat and I nearly fell the rest of the way. Even though I had expected that was what she was here for, it still came as a shock. "What?"

"It doesn't have to be, though, right? I mean, you and me. It doesn't have to be a big deal."

I wasn't going to lie to her. Not about this. "A marriage is only as serious as the people in the marriage take it to be," I said carefully.

She nodded eagerly and leaned forward across the desk. "Exactly. This marriage for love thing, that's a pretty recent development, when you consider, like, the history of the human race. People married for money, power, and kids. There's nothing *wrong* with getting married so we can enter Pirate in a competition. Horse doping, now *that's* wrong."

"Very wrong," I agreed.

"And if we get divorced a month later, who cares?" she continued. "Sometimes marriages don't work out. People get divorced all the time."

I'd care. "You could file for divorce any time," I said, with the faintest stress on *you*. It sure as hell wouldn't be me.

"You're a lawyer. You could write up one of those prenup things."

"Sure," I said. "But you'll need to hire your own lawyer to look over it before you sign. Make sure it protects your interests."

Her eyes narrowed suspiciously. "Why?"

"Because, Essie, it's a legally binding contract," I said, exasperated. "You can't just trust someone to look out for your interests, especially at the expense of their own. There's a power imbalance here. I'm a lawyer. I could write a prenup that screws you and you wouldn't know it until it was too late."

She leaned back and dismissed my words with a wave of her hand. "You wouldn't do that."

"Of course I wouldn't," I grumbled. "Get a lawyer anyway."

"Fine, fine. Whatever." She crossed her arms and stared blankly out the window, nibbling her plump bottom lip.

Jesus Christ. Was she actually considering it?

For fuck's sake, *why*?

"What about the prize money, if Pirate ribbons? How would that work?" She kept her face averted when she asked that and the twist in my gut told me I had the answer to my question. "Fifty-fifty split?"

I frowned. Not because I disapproved of her mercenary instincts. But if she needed money, I'd help her. I sure as hell wouldn't force her to marry me. "Are you in some kind of trouble?"

"Well, see, there's this Russian…" She broke off with a laugh when I growled. "I'm *kidding*. Geez. No, I'm not in trouble. You were going to split the winnings with Zack, right? It's a lot of money at stake, and I would like my fair share of it, that's all. Is that a problem?"

I didn't buy her bullshit for a second. I stared her down silently, eyebrows raised, and waited for her to give me the truth.

She sighed. "Fine. The owner of Sweetie Pie is

moving to Texas to be closer to her family and grand-kids. She offered to let Mom buy the place, but Mom doesn't have that kind of money. I could help—I saved a lot of money living at home, even considering the costs of hauling to shows and keeping the horses—but she won't let me. It would wipe out half my savings. I told her I don't care. I can earn more money. But she says it's too risky."

Frustration seeped into her voice. I understood the feeling. Cat was a proud woman with a fierce independent streak. Despite Essie's dad's family being loaded, she'd stubbornly refused to file for child support until Essie was in high school, when it became clear that if she wanted to take barrel racing to the next level, she would need a horse of her own. Horses were expensive.

Even then, Cat couldn't afford the attorney fees. Fortunately, my boss, who happened to be the only attorney in Aspen Springs at the time, took her case pro bono. If she suspected I was the reason, she never said. There was nothing she wouldn't do for Essie and Jack.

And there was nothing Essie wouldn't do for her mom.

"We'll split the purse fifty-fifty. Hell, I'd be happy to offer up my half as an investor. Cat deserves it."

"That's not necessary. I can take care of my mom myself."

Of course she'd say that. God forbid she let me help. I made a mental note to reach out to Cat directly. She wouldn't take charity, but I was a businessman. She'd understand it was an investment. "You really think if you win on Pirate, she'll be okay with taking your winnings?" I asked.

"Well." Essie rolled her eyes and let out a huff of a laugh. "I might have played hardball on that one. Winning would be great for the career path I'm on now. If I could show clients I know my stuff in more than just barrel racing? Yeah. That would be great. Even winning the non-pro division is a big deal. You know as well as I do that those level four riders are every bit as competitive as professionals. So I told Mom the only way I'll ride is if she agrees to take the money. And I reminded her that this way, I won't have to touch my savings."

"You...you told your mom we'd have to get married?" Shit. I'd better invest in a steel jockstrap. Cat was not going to like that idea at all.

"Oh. No. I...left that part out. I figured it was better to tell her after we nailed down the details."

I studied her. Essie was close to her mom. I doubted she told her everything—Essie's short stint as a horse thief, for example—but if she hadn't told her this, it meant she still had doubts.

"What details are you concerned about?" I asked.

"Like, do we have to live together? Do we tell people why we're getting married, or do we keep it a secret?" She pushed to her feet and paced to the window, then back again. "How can we keep it a secret if I'm entering a competition for owners only, but everyone knows I'm not the owner?"

"The way I see it, the only way this works is if everyone believes it's a real marriage. We can tell our families the truth—"

"They'd never believe us if we said we were marrying for love, anyway," she cut in.

"But everyone else needs to believe it's real. That means we'd live together, at least until after the show. You could move in with me." My insides engaged in a whole lot of unnecessary silliness. My heart picked up speed. My stomach flipped around. *She's not going to agree to this.*

"Do you have an extra room?" she asked.

I nodded slowly. My heart got even sillier. "I have a guestroom."

"Do you know how to clean a bathroom? Like, scrub toilets? Do you rinse your beard hair out of the sink every day?"

I stared at her unblinking. "What do you think?"

"I think I've heard horror stories about what it's like to live with a man, that's what I think." She crossed her arms. "I think I remember sharing a bathroom with my brother for most of my life."

"I keep my bathroom clean." I enunciated every word slowly and distinctly.

She eyed me doubtfully. "We'll see."

I swallowed a laugh.

"You won't be able to date other women, you know. Not that I care what you do or who you do it with, honestly, but I'm not going to have people pitying me behind my back, whispering about my husband stepping out on me. I'd have to set your truck on fire just for appearance's sake. No hard feelings."

"Noted." I cleared my throat. "We should have a wedding."

She wrinkled her nose. "Is that really necessary?"

"For appearances." I shrugged and she started pacing again. "The horse community is small and people talk. We're not breaking any rules, but if competitors find out, we won't have any friends left, and you won't have any clients."

She stopped pacing and looked at me. "Oh."

"We don't have to do this, you know. I can ride. Not at level four, but I could make a decent showing at level two."

Essie's stare was withering. "This is Pirate's future we're talking about. I didn't steal him from that asshole's backyard just so you could make a *decent showing* at level two." I couldn't hide my grin. My hellion was nothing if not competitive. "I want to ride him. I want to win. We can do this. We *are* doing this."

"You're sure?" I asked.

"Stop making this seem like a big deal. It's *not*. People get married and divorced all the time."

"Alright, then. I guess that means I have a question

to ask you." I stood, came around the desk, and took her hand. She eyed me with deep suspicion. "Essie Louise Price, will you marry me?"

She looked to the ceiling, as though awaiting deliverance in the form of fifty thousand dollars landing at her feet. When that failed to happen, she sighed deeply and gave me her answer.

"I guess so."

14

ESSIE

"Ready to cause a ruckus?" I asked as I flipped down the sun visor to check the mirror. It was a brisk September day full of glorious sunshine and I hadn't been able to resist rolling down the window. My reflection showed I was a little windblown, but still appropriate for Sunday dinner with my soon-to-be in-laws.

"Hellion," Brax warned. He had opened the passenger door for me to get out, but now he leaned into the triangle of space, one hand on the door, the other on the frame of the truck above my head. His large body blocked out the blue sky—and my exit.

"What?" I asked, blinking up at him innocently.

"I thought we were going to tell them the truth."

"That's exactly what we're going to do. Truth makes a

bigger commotion than a lie, in my experience. And when the truth is we're going to commit to a whole-ass marriage just for the chance to win a hundred grand and get Pirate a championship trophy? Yeah. That's going to be a big ruckus. Your family is going to think you've lost your mind. Steady, dependable Brax in a sham marriage?" A slow grin spread across my face and I shook my head. "No fucking way."

He stepped back to let me out. "My family isn't the one I'm worried about. Your mom is going to crack my balls like walnuts."

"Can you crack balls?" I tilted my head considering. "I guess if you squeeze tight enough, something is bound to pop, at least. Maybe—"

"Don't," Brax cut me off. He did look a little green. "Not another word."

I laughed. "This was your idea, remember."

"It was Zack's idea, actually. He gets the blame—I mean, credit."

"Zack was high on painkillers. Guess we better call the whole thing off." My tone was breezy and teasing, but I felt a little shiver of anxiety go through me. Did he *want* to call it off?

Brax smirked and captured my hand in his, tugging me along behind him past the bare-branched rosebushes and up the porch steps. "Don't tell me you're getting cold feet already."

"My toes are toasty warm, thank you very much. Are yours? You're the one with something to lose."

He stopped so fast I nearly smashed my nose against his back. My toes teetered on the top step as I fought for balance. I grasped for his shirt—because goddamn it, if I was going down, I was taking him with me—but he looped one arm around my waist, hauled me flush against his body and up off my feet, and moved me back from the edge.

And I fucking *giggled*.

I couldn't help it. I was a tall girl and solidly built. I had curves *and* muscles. Men did not simply lift me by a single arm and toss me around. Except for Brax Hale, apparently. Hence the giggle. For once, I felt small. In a good way. I loved my height, my curves, my muscles. But I also liked this. The feeling of someone else being bigger and stronger and in control of where he put my body. The knowledge of what he could *do* with my body, if he put his mind to it.

The thought of it sent a quiver of...*something*...deep inside me. Something hungry and a little wistful. I refused to call it lust. This man was going to be my husband. My *fake* husband. I would have to share a roof with him, if not a bed. There might be times when I had to actually hold his hand in public. I couldn't be getting all *quivery* about him. I fucking refused.

He crossed his arms over his chest, studying me. "What is it you think I have to lose?"

The question caught me off guard. Partly because I was still irrationally quivery, but also because I didn't have an answer. On the face of it, I was the one with more skin in the game. My reputation, my career, my mom's livelihood. If this went south, Brax wouldn't get his fifty thousand dollars, but the money was never guaranteed to begin with. He wanted the money, but he didn't need it. I doubted whether money was truly why he was doing this at all.

I looked up at the house. It was a big, rambling thing of solid pine beams. A house built to last, with an eye to the future. Prior generations of Hales had all added their own touch, leaving something behind for the generations still to come. One day Adam would, too. Ted had moved to one of the smaller cabins on the property, leaving the main house to Adam, Ben, and James. Someday, hopefully a long time from now, Lodestar Ranch would be inherited by all three brothers.

But the house would be Adam's. Where he would raise his family.

I knew Brax was fine with that. Happy, even. He had always made it clear that the ranching life wasn't for him. He loved the animals and was happy to help out when it was needed, but mostly he took care of the taxes and legal paperwork and left the day-to-day operations to his dad and brother.

Brax cared about Lodestar, for sure. And if Pirate was the winner we believed him to be, the stallion could make the ranch one of the foremost quarter horse breeders in the country. That was why he was doing this sham marriage, wasn't it? For the ranch. For his family.

He had everything to gain and nothing to lose.

So why did it feel like he was the one risking it all?

I shook my head. "I don't know," I said, as much to myself as to his question.

"It's going to be fine." He moved toward the door. "I promise."

"There you go again. Always making promises you can't keep."

He looked at me, his expression inscrutable. "I think I've kept my promises pretty damn well, actually."

"What promises—" I began, but he had already reached around me, opened the door, and nudged me through it before I could get another word out.

Voices and the scent of garlic and tomatoes wafted from the kitchen. That meant Ted was making his old standby of spaghetti, meatballs, and garlic bread. My stomach growled as we walked down the hall.

Everyone else was already there. Adam, James, and Ben laughing as they threw together a salad. Zack on a barstool, his crutches resting against the counter. My Mom—who was not a regular attendee of Sunday dinner at Lodestar, but didn't seem at all suspicious when I told her we were invited—spread a thick smear of garlic butter to a loaf of French bread while Ted stirred a large pot of bubbling pasta sauce. Over the clank and clatter of dishes was the constant hum of people chatting and teasing.

My mom looked up. "You two came together?"

My mouth went dry.

Because this...*this* was what Brax had to lose. This was what he wanted. He had probably imagined this moment in his mind. Imagined what it would feel like to bring a woman to Sunday dinner and give them the good news that she was going to be family. Hale men took marriage seriously. Ted had raised his sons in the legend of his own love story with their mother. Of course he had imagined this.

He sure as fuck never imagined it would be *me*.

And there was no fucking way anyone in that room was going to think it was *good* news that it was.

I looked at Brax. His gaze slid over my face, searching. The corner of his mouth hitched in a quick half smile. And then he took my hand, threading our fingers together, and turned to face the room.

"We're getting married," he said, like it was the easiest thing in the world.

The hum and clatter promptly ended on an audible whoosh as if they had collectively sucked up all the oxygen in the room. I felt a little lightheaded from it.

And then everyone talked at once.

"Oh, my *god*!" James shrieked as she rushed at us. "Congratulations!"

Mom pressed her hands to her cheeks. "My baby. Oh, my goodness."

Oh, shit. They thought this was real? Never in a million years would that have occurred to me. "*Brax*," I hissed.

He lifted our linked hands to his mouth and pressed a kiss to my knuckles, his blue eyes laughing at me. "It was your idea to tell them all together. I suggested a group text from the top of a mountain, remember?"

"Because it never occurred to me they would think it was real." Panick squeezed my voice into a squeak. How the hell was I supposed to know they'd entertain the possibility we were in love? I tried to reclaim my hand but he held on tight.

"This isn't real?" Mom demanded. Her hands went to her hips as she split a glare between us. "Is this some kind of joke?"

"Oh, it's real," Brax assured her. "We'll say our vows before a judge. It will be a legally binding marriage."

"For a few months, at least," I added.

Mom's glare intensified. "That's not funny, young lady."

Now we were back on familiar ground. My mother loved me with every cell in her body, but she absolutely believed she knew best how my life should be run and wished I would step aside and let her handle it. "Mom —" I started.

But Brax squeezed my hand hard enough to silence

me. "No one is taking this more seriously than Essie. In all fairness, this was my idea, and she took a fair amount of convincing." He went on to explain the rules of the competition, and what winning would mean to Pirate's career...and mine. "But even so, Essie had one condition. That if we win, the money goes to you for the purchase of Sweetie Pie."

My mom made a shocked sound of protest. "I couldn't—"

"Let me be clear," Brax said. "This isn't a gift. It's an investment. We believe in you and the restaurant. And, selfishly, I happen to like your pies and don't want to see it change hands or, god forbid, shut down. This is the chance of a lifetime for Pirate and Essie, but she won't do it if you don't agree."

"Oh, honey." Mom's eyes were suspiciously shiny as she pulled me into a hug.

I stared, slack jawed, at Brax's smirking face over her shoulder. I had been prepared to argue, to fight, to hold my ground. Then he had swept in and made me look like a hero. I didn't know how to feel about that. Grateful? Annoyed? Both?

"I love you, Mom," I said. "So much. Please let us do this. For you and for me and for Pirate."

She pulled back and wiped her eyes. "All right, baby. All right."

"Essie," Ted said.

I turned to face Brax's father with a nervous gulp.

But he looked at me with a kind smile and more than a hint of mischief in his bright blue eyes.

"I can't say I saw this coming." His large hand engulfed my shoulder and gave it a fatherly squeeze. His gaze shifted to his son over my shoulder and then back to me. "But I can't say I'm disappointed, either. Welcome to the family, darlin'."

15

BRAX

Essie's bedroom was like a time capsule. It was the smallest of the three bedrooms in the bungalow she still shared with her mom. Even though Jack was rarely home, she had never swapped to the bigger room. Little of it had changed since I had last set foot here fifteen years ago. Same four-poster, twin-sized bed. Same Ikea dresser. Photos of friends and horses lined the walls, held up with scotch tape. If I looked closely, I could tell which ones she cut me out of.

I wondered what she did with the bodies. Burned them in effigy? Used them for dart practice?

One of them caught my eye and I leaned closer to investigate. I knew that photo, because I was the one who had taken it. We had hiked to a lake the summer before our junior year, Essie, Jack, and me. The water had been freezing, hence Essie's and Jack's purple lips as they grinned for the camera. Behind them, the lake shimmered like Essie's eyes. And on the left edge, so small a person might not notice it, was a blurry peach half circle. The tip of my index finger over the lens.

I grinned.

She hadn't cut me out of all of them.

"I don't have much." Essie stood at the foot of the bed, hands on hips, and turned in a slow circle, taking stock of it all. "My clothes, of course. The winter stuff, anyway. I'll probably be back before summer."

Her blunt reference to our eventual divorce when we weren't even married yet sent a fissure of annoyance down my spine. We hadn't discussed an end date, other than tacit acknowledgment that it would be after the holidays. Filing for divorce the day after the competition would look mighty suspicious, and right after that was Christmas. No one filed for divorce during the holiday season unless they couldn't stand being married for a single second more. That wouldn't look good, either.

I knew it was going to happen. But it felt wrong to admit it out loud before we had even our vows.

I rubbed my chest, frowning. "What about the photos? You want those, right?"

She squinted at the photos and pursed her lips. "I don't know. Where would I put them? It seems silly to recreate my bedroom in your guest room. I should probably just leave them here."

"So, what? You're going to live like it's a hotel for the

next six months? Come on. I know you don't want to be there, but at least you can make it a place you don't hate coming home to. There's space for whatever you want to bring."

"Thank you. I appreciate that, I really do. But it doesn't make sense to take all the pictures down, hang them up at your place, and then take them all down again. They might get damaged. Plus, it's a lot of work." She moved to the dresser and picked up the Bell jar of matchbooks from her dad. She held it for a moment, turning it in her hand. Then she shrugged and set it down again. "I honestly don't need more than a bed and somewhere to put my clothes. I've lived with my mom my whole life, so I don't own any furniture or decorations or anything like that. It's fine, really."

She handed me a large black trash bag. "Here. For the shoes. I also have a pair of muck boots in the mudroom, so remind me to grab those on our way out."

"Sure." I didn't like the idea of packing Essie's stuff in a goddamn trash bag, but it was efficient, and we weren't going far.

Essie flipped the suitcase open on the bed. I took care of the shoes while she emptied the dresser of sweaters, jeans, and underwear. I tried not to linger on the silk and lace things she tossed into the suitcase, but hell. She wasn't bothering to hide anything. That purple thing made my mind flood with images I would never see in real life.

With my stomach clenched tight, I tied up the bag of shoes and stalked to the bedside table, figuring I could dump the contents in her duffle bag.

"No—" she yelped.

But it was too late. I had the drawer open and was staring inside. A bottle of ibuprofen. A paperback that I would hazard a guess was a romance, with a woman being embraced by a blue alien. A purple vibrator with bunny ears that I was familiar with. A palm-sized, rose-shaped thing that I was not.

"My toys are clean, so if you can say the same for your hands, go ahead and put everything in the duffle bag."

Feeling like my head was stuffed full of cotton, I turned slowly. She stared back at me, arms crossed over her chest, a defiant tilt to her chin despite her flushed cheeks.

"Be careful with the book. It's Hannah's. I don't want it to be bent or folded when I return it."

I set the book aside, figuring it would be safer in my hands than in the bag, and picked up the pills and bunny vibrator and gently placed them in the bag. The back of my neck felt hot and prickly from her watchful stare.

The rose was next, and I paused, studying it. She made a sound of dismay, but it was too late now. We were in it, this was happening, and I had questions.

"What," I said, peering at the small opening in the center, "is this?"

"It's a vibrator, Brax." There was a sardonic edge to her voice and I looked up. "Not every vibe is shaped like a dick. It's not all about penetration, you know." She shook her head. "See, there's this thing called a clitoris—"

"I mean, what does it do? Just vibrate, or—"

"It sucks." She cleared the raspiness from her voice.

My dick twitched, making it known that it was very interested in this option. That it might be a nice experiment to tie each of her limbs to a bedpost and use that rose until she begged for my mouth. Just to see which she preferred.

I added the rose to the bag. Her gaze dipped to the obvious swelling in my jeans as I turned to face her and she rolled her lips together. That was interesting. Maybe we were both imagining things we shouldn't.

"Anything else you want?" I asked gruffly.

There was the slightest hesitation before she shook her head no.

And I smirked, knowing it was a lie.

With Essie's bags stowed in the backseat of my SUV, we headed out. We had already moved Buckley to Lodestar, where he would live out the rest of his happy life, because there was no way Cat could take care of him given her long hours at the bakery. Essie was at the ranch more than she was home anyway, so it worked out for the best. The only thing we had left to do was get her settled at my place.

But instead of turning left off Columbine Street, I turned right and headed for First Street.

"Where are we going?" she asked, her forehead wrinkling with confusion.

"Just a couple errands to run. Is that okay?"

She shrugged. "I'm in no hurry."

To move in with me. That's what she meant. And it annoyed me all over again. If she could fake a marriage, then she could damn well fake being happy about it, too.

Except I didn't want her to fake it. I wanted her to actually *be* happy. Even though I knew that was too much to ask for.

I pulled into the parking lot and cut the engine. Essie looked up from her phone and glanced around. Directly in front of us was Sal's Home Furnishings. She looked at me.

"You need a lamp?" she asked.

"I need whatever you say I need." I swiveled my body to face her. "Listen up, hellion. Maybe some of this is fake, but not all of it. Here's what's true. The marriage itself. We're signing our names to a legal document. We're making promises out loud. That's real."

Her mouth opened like she was going to argue, but then she thought better of it and pressed her lips together with a short nod.

"Here's another thing that's true," I continued. "We are going to live together in *our* house. That's what it is for the duration of our marriage, whether it's ten weeks or ten years. *Ours.* So we're going inside, and you're picking something that isn't for the guestroom. I don't care if it's a lamp. I don't care if it's a brand-new couch. New dining room table? Fine. But it has to be something you like, something that gives you a little bit of happiness. Something that feels like home to you. Got it?"

Surprise and confusion swirled in her eyes, but one corner of her mouth tipped up in a hesitant half smile. "Got it."

"And when we're done here, we're going to the jewelry store to get you a ring, because here's the thing, hellion, and it's a very real part of being married to me. Even if your heart isn't taken, your body sure as fuck is, the same as mine, and you better remember that. While we're married, it's me or the vibrator. There are no other options, understand? And we're putting rings on our fingers so there's no confusion."

Her bottom lip fell open on a soft gasp and she stared at me with wide eyes.

"Essie," I said. It wasn't often I could render her speechless, and a small part of me wondered if I had gone too far. But she had to know she couldn't be my wife in name and give someone else her body. It was about more than appearances for me, and I knew she felt differently about it, but I wasn't asking for more than I was willing to give.

She blinked, swallowed, and shifted in her seat, moving her thighs together in a restless sort of way. A pretty wash of pink spread down her throat.

"I…" Her gaze fell to my mouth.

She wanted to kiss me. I could see it in the flush of her cheeks, her half-lidded eyes, the way she licked her lips. And, fuck, I wanted to kiss her more than I wanted the sun to rise in the morning. But I wasn't going to do that. Not here, not like this.

"We need to be on the same page about this, Essie. It's the only way. So if this is something you can't agree to, you need to tell me now." The words came out rougher than I intended.

She pulled her gaze from my mouth to look me in the eyes. "I can live with it."

I paused a beat, waiting for her to change her mind, but she didn't. "All right, then."

Maybe she could live with it, but I knew living with it was what would damn near kill me.

16

ESSIE

Two weeks ago I moved into Brax's sweet two-bedroom bungalow.

One week ago the Denver Post published our engagement announcement.

Three days ago we drove to the courthouse to pick up our marriage license.

And at two p.m. tomorrow, I would officially be a married woman.

Jesus fucking Christ.

But I wasn't going to think about that right now. *Not* thinking about it was how I had managed to hold myself together these past two weeks.

I refused to think about promising Brax, out loud and in front of our friends and family and his smug fucking face, that I would honor, cherish, and love him for the rest of my life.

I refused to think about the way his voice deepened when he informed me in no uncertain terms that my body was his. At least, I refused to think about it unless I knew he wouldn't be home for a good hour or so, and then I thought about it a lot with my rose pressed tight to my clit. And *then* I refused to think about what it meant that I had developed a shameful habit of coming with his name on my lips.

Right now, the only thing I was going to think about was how get the L in legend to curve the way I wanted, because it was sewing circle time.

I stepped into the library and found my friends waiting with nary a needle or thread to be found.

"What's going on?" I asked, my gaze bouncing from one serious face to the next.

James, Chloe, Hannah, and Janie exchanged a look. Chloe nodded and stepped forward.

"Well, my love, this here is what we in the business like to call a good, old-fashioned intervention," Chloe drawled. "Have a seat."

I burst out laughing. "You think I'm on drugs? I promise, I'm not."

"Then explain how not five months ago, you sat in this very room and told us Braxton Hale made you want to stab something," Hannah said. "And now you're going to *marry* him? What changed? It's not that we really think you're on drugs, but at no point in the last five months have you said a single nice word about him."

I glanced at James, who was staring at the floor, her teeth digging into her bottom lip. Brax and I had decided that the fewer people who knew the truth, the better. But keeping our secret meant lying to our friends. I knew James wasn't comfortable with it.

"He's irritating, I'll admit that much," I said carefully. Trying to keep the outright lies to a minimum. "But it's like you said, Chloe. Sometimes people rub each other the wrong way because they want to rub each other the right way." Something I could unfortunately attest to, having rubbed one out last night in the shower.

Hannah eyed me doubtfully, her forehead creasing with concern. "I mean...you *do* know that you don't have to get married to have sex, right?"

"Hate fucking is a totally valid choice," Janie chimed in cheerfully.

"Oh, my god," I muttered, rubbing my temple. But I thought I saw James hide her smile behind her hand, and that made everything better. At least she didn't hate me.

And their care for my well-being was touching. Truly. But it was also...

Annoying.

Why didn't anyone think I was capable of running my own goddamn life?

"Listen, I appreciate the care. I do," I said. "But you all know Brax. You know me. Even if this doesn't look like how you think a marriage should look, you can trust that Brax isn't forcing me to marry him in some nefarious scheme to ruin my life. Right? And you can trust me to take care of myself. I'm okay. I promise."

Another look was shared among them.

"Okay," James said at last. It surprised me she was the one who spoke, given that she was the only one who knew the whole truth. "But I want you to know that just because you *can* take care of yourself doesn't mean you have to. You have us."

"Thank you," I said softly.

She smiled back, her brown eyes warm. "Any time."

Chloe clapped her hands. "And now, this intervention is officially a bachelorette party. It's time to celebrate your last day of freedom, babe. First stop, mimosas."

"ARE YOU SURE YOU WANT TO DO THIS?" JAMES ASKED quietly.

I looked from Brax's shiny black SUV to the thick pink marker in my hand and then at James. "He needs to know about the clitoris, James," I deadpanned.

She snorted. "I'm pretty sure he knows, Essie. But in case he doesn't, Hannah is drawing a very detailed diagram on the back window."

Dusk had turned the sky gray, but it wasn't dark

enough for stars yet. I could still see the shimmer of aspen leaves streaking up the mountainside like rivers of molten gold. Elks bugling pierced through the air.

"But, seriously." James lowered her voice and glanced around to make sure the others weren't listening. "You're sure you want to get married just for a horse show?"

"It's not just a horse show, and you know it. It's a hundred grand. It's the chance for my mom to have the life she deserves. Yes, I'm sure," I said firmly. "Don't worry so much. People get married and divorced every day."

Brax doesn't.

But Brax was an adult. He had his reasons for doing this, same as me.

James looked like she was about to argue, but instead she shook her head. "All right," she said. "Then let's do this."

She stepped toward the passenger window, giving the pink marker in her hand a good shake to get the liquid moving. *The clitoris is like an iceberg*, she wrote in swirling pink letters.

"Huh," I said. "You learn something new every day." I looked down at the list of facts Chloe had prepared for tonight's bachelorette prank. Then I aimed my marker at the driver's side window.

The clitoris has over ten thousand nerves.

17

BRAX

"Y**ou know that's your truck they're screwing with, right?" Adam said as he cracked open a beer and handed it to me.

"Oh, I know it." I tipped the beer in a long swallow.

It was a chilly evening, as September evenings were wont to be at this elevation, but the season hadn't yet tipped to frigid. We were enjoying the last of the light—and the last of my freedom, Zack proclaimed—on the front porch of the main house. From our vantage point, we could just make out the dark shadows of the cabins against the pines and aspens.

There were three cabins in total, originally built for Adam, Zack, and myself—a reason to come home, should the desire or need arise, was what my mom and dad always said. Zack recently had cause to do just that, so he was occupying his for the next few months until he was free of crutches. I had never lived in mine, but I was staying there tonight, on account of the wedding we'd have here tomorrow. Dad was currently residing in Adam's old cabin, but he'd stay in the main house tonight with Adam and Ben so Essie could take his. Apparently, James, Hannah, and Janie were crowding in with her on air mattresses. Cat was installed in a guest room at the main house.

I could hear the women giggling like maniacs as they wreaked their havoc on my truck. I grinned and took another swig of beer.

"Are you going to put a stop to it?" Zack asked. He was sprawled out on the lounger Dad had bought two days ago just so Zack could comfortably enjoy the porch with the rest of us.

"Nah. It's tradition to decorate the car, isn't it?" I said. "You know, a just married sign and lots of bells and flowers and whatnot. Tie some cans to the trailer hitch."

Adam snorted. "You really think that's all they're doing?"

"Hell, no."

Chloe's high-pitch shriek could rival a rutting elk's bugle. It mingled with Essie's husky chuckle and James's full-bellied laugh. The sounds reverberated against the mountains, giving squirrels heart attacks, probably. We all traded looks and shook our heads.

"When I have a wife, I'm not going to let her touch my truck." Ben gave me a look like I had disappointed him. "She can decorate her own car if she thinks it's so fun."

I leaned back enough that the front legs of my chair tipped off the ground so I could reach over and ruffle my nephew's hair. "I think when you find a woman you want to be with for the rest of your life, there's not much you won't say yes to if it makes her laugh like that."

The porch fell silent. I lowered my chair back down with a clank and found my dad and brothers staring at me. "What?"

Dad cleared his throat and raised his beer like a toast. "Good man. Already wise in the ways of keeping your wife happy."

I smirked. "In my case, it's a matter of self-defense. Have you ever seen Essie when she's pissed? She's going to be in my house for the next several months, at least. Imagine what she could do if she put her mind to it. I'm being smart, is all."

"Yeah. I'm sure that's it." Adam's tone implied the opposite was true. "Have you heard from Jack at all?"

I shifted uneasily at the mention of Essie's brother. "He emails and texts when he can. Essie figured it would be best not to tell him we're getting married until after the ink is dry. He always said he'd be the one to walk her down the aisle and, circumstances being what they are, she didn't want him moving heaven and earth trying to keep that promise."

"Huh," Adam said thoughtfully.

Dad was more direct about it. "Son, that man is going to kill you," he said bluntly.

Don't I know it.

"And he knows how," Zack added helpfully.

A fact I was not unaware of. Jack had more than a decade of training on how to unalive a person should the need arise and, judging from the number of medals he had earned, he was damn good at it.

I had promised him I would take care of her when he couldn't. Convincing her to go along with this sham marriage probably wasn't what he had in mind.

Yeah. He was going to kill me, all right.

"I have a plan," I said.

"Yeah?" Adam eyed me doubtfully over the rim of his beer. "What's that?"

"Win the futurity championship. Give Essie what she wants. Use the money to help Cat. He won't kill me if his sister and mom benefit as much as me, right?"

"Well," Zack said thoughtfully. "He might still bruise you a little. But he'll probably leave you breathing."

We fell silent again, the only sounds the occasional hoot of an owl, the bugle of an elk, or the giddy laugh of a woman.

"You sure you want to do this?" Dad asked quietly. "It seems you're making an awfully big sacrifice for the people you love. Essie, Cat, Lodestar. What do you get out of it?"

"Pirate is my horse," I reminded him. "And Lodestar

is as much mine as anyone else's. If this is how I choose to contribute to the success of the ranch, then that's my decision."

Dad digested that a moment before speaking. "All right. I've said my peace. If it feels right to you, it's not my place to say it's wrong."

"Thanks, Dad," was all I said.

When the truth was nothing had ever felt more right in my life.

18

ESSIE

I was getting married today. What the actual fuck. September was my favorite month in Colorado. The air was crisp, the sky blue, and the mountains got their first dusting of snow. The best part was the aspens, their golden leaves even more vibrant against the deep green pines. If I could choose any month for my wedding day, it would be September.

Ironic, really.

I huddled on the cabin porch in my sweats, wool socks, and shearling slippers, a steaming mug of hot coffee keeping my hands warm. It was mid-morning and still chilly. The bright Colorado sunshine would warm it up some by mid-afternoon, when Brax and I would be declared husband and wife.

James, Chloe, Hannah, and Janie were still sound

asleep on their air mattresses. I would be too, if it weren't for this infernal hum of anticipation putting me on edge. Which was so stupid, because this wasn't even a real marriage.

But somehow it felt real. Brax was real. I was real. Living under the same roof was real. Our friends and family celebrating our union was real.

And the wedding was absolutely real.

Lodestar Ranch was the natural location. For one, because it was free. But also, it was beautiful. Where else could I be surrounded by the horses, mountains, and people I loved the most? It was perfect.

It also could accommodate the guest list, which included nearly every person in Aspen Springs. Such was the way of things here, and we didn't want to arouse suspicion by going against tradition. We had an uneven ratio of groomsmen to bridesmaids, but the good thing about this being a fake marriage was that we cared less about the minutiae of wedding details that might drive another bride crazy.

I almost wished we had told Jack our plans. He would have found a way to show up for me, even knowing the truth, but that wouldn't have been fair to him. I didn't really like the idea of anyone else walking me down the aisle, but I had the feeling if I went it alone, there was a high possibility I'd turn tail and run. So, Mom would walk with me.

A local magistrate would do the honors. Mom was in favor of a minister, but that was a no for me. I could lie to a judge all day without a qualm, but I drew a line at lying to God. I wasn't even sure I believed in a higher being, but better safe than sorry.

"Hey." James stumbled onto the porch with a wide yawn. "How's the most beautiful bride in the world?"

"I'm not beautiful yet," I laughed, pointing to the hot rollers in my hair. "You're going to help me fix that, right?"

"You're gorgeous just as you are, no makeup or fancy hairdo required." James booped me on the nose. "But I will absolutely help you get ready. That's what we're here for." She flicked a hand over her shoulder toward the door. "The others are getting breakfast going."

We took our time with cinnamon rolls, bacon, and orange juice. There was no need to rush. I wanted to look nice, of course, since all eyes would be on me, but I had no interest in a big poofy dress. That wasn't me at all. I had opted for a white sundress of eyelet lace that hit at my knee, and I was pairing that with cowboy boots. I was doing my own makeup, too.

It didn't take long to get ready once we cleaned up from breakfast. I took extra care with my makeup. I filled in my eyebrows and added false eyelashes, which wasn't my usual look for a day at the ranch, but other than that, I looked exactly like myself, only prettier. The last step was the deep red lipstick I had been loyal to since high school, but I was waiting until the last minute for that.

I stared at myself in the mirror as my friends gushed about my hair, my eyes, my dress. All I could think was, *would Brax like it?*

Why did I even care? Asking my ex-best friend to like *anything* about me was a good way to hurt my own feelings. How the hell was I going to marry someone who thought I was a walking catastrophe when my feelings for him were...complicated. So fucking complicated.

My face felt hot. My hands were shaking.

I needed to get out of here.

Abruptly, I turned from the mirror and grabbed my jacket. "I need a minute."

"Are you alright?" Chloe asked. "It's okay if you're not. My car is right outside."

I laughed. "I appreciate the offer, but I'm fine. Really. I just need some air. I'm going to check on Pirate."

James nodded like this made perfect sense. To her, it probably did. Horses were a refuge for both of us. "All right." She checked her phone. "You have thirty minutes until it's go time."

Guests were already milling about when I quietly sneaked past the main house and up to the barn. Pirate greeted me with a head bob. He let me rest my cheek against his white face for approximately two seconds before he started snuffling my jacket pockets for treats.

"Yeah, yeah," I grumbled. "I didn't come empty handed. I'll trade you a carrot for a little affection. Seems fair."

"Is that all it takes?" an amused voice asked behind me.

I spun around, my hand on my heart. "Jesus, Brax. You scared me. What are you doing here?"

"Marrying you, supposedly," he said on an extended drawl. "Hopefully I didn't get the date wrong."

I tried to give him an exasperated look, but it was hard to summon the requisite emotion when he looked so ridiculously good in that suit. His blue eyes rivaled the cloudless sky for brightness, his shoulders were broader than ever, and his chiseled jaw and cheekbones looked like he'd had the bones sharpened even further just for today.

I suddenly felt a little awkward about myself. A little self-conscious. Like maybe I wasn't fancy enough for Suit Brax. I should have made more of an effort, done the big white dress and all that.

"Fuck, you're pretty," he whispered.

I grinned, feeling much better about the whole thing. "Thank you. But you're not supposed to see me before the wedding. What are you doing here?" I asked again.

"Looking for you."

"Well, you found me."

"Yeah, I did."

I stared at him, waiting. His gaze dipped from mine, and he rubbed the back of his neck. Was Brax...nervous? That couldn't be right. Brax was never nervous. He was always so *sure*. Sure of himself, of his surroundings, of how things should be. Sometimes he was wrong, but even then, he was sure of how to fix it.

"Here's the thing, Essie. In twenty minutes, the magistrate is going to say *you may now kiss the bride*, and I don't think that's something we should do for the first time in front of an audience."

"Oh." I blinked. Somehow that had not occurred to me. "I guess we could tell him to skip that part?"

His head snapped up on a low growl. "No, we are not going to skip that part."

"Braxton Hale, are you saying you want to kiss me?" I put my hands to my hips and studied him through narrowed eyes. "What happened to *too much, and not enough*? Hmm?"

He glared right back. "Get your ass over here, hellion."

I took a step, but apparently it wasn't fast enough for his liking, because he hooked an arm around my waist and brought me flush against his chest. Now I was the nervous one, breathless from the heat and strength of his body.

This close, it was hard to get my bearings. I looked at

him and saw my past, present, and future swirled together. The best friend I had adored, the jackass who irritated the life out of me, the man who in approximately twenty minutes would be my husband—he was all of it. He was everything.

He rubbed his thumb over my bottom lip. "You're not wearing lipstick."

"Not yet. I didn't want to risk smearing it." My words came out soft and breathless.

"Good." His face came so close all I could see was the blue of his eye. "Because this might get messy."

The words ghosted against my lips and I shivered.

And then his mouth was firmly on mine and all I felt was heat.

For a moment, we simply stood there, mouth against mouth, chest against chest. And then he made a low sort of noise and he moved. I found myself shifted against the wall, his strong arm around my back tethering me to his body, and he licked his way into my mouth.

I had feelings about that, strong feelings, but I couldn't seem to anchor myself to a single one. They all rioted inside me like a summer storm. Hunger and rage, joy and sadness, need and longing.

His fingers tangled in my hair, digging into my scalp. He tasted like honey and strawberry jam from the biscuits he'd had for breakfast. I let it all consume me, the feel of him, the taste of him, the familiar scent of him that made my eyes sting with tears.

It was too much.

I couldn't get enough.

Damn him.

I nipped his lip. Maybe to punish him, maybe because it felt good.

He chuckled quietly against my mouth. "Behave, hellion, or we're not going to make it to our own wedding."

"I don't care." I clung to him, rocking my body against him, feeling the evidence of what I did to him wedged hard against my belly.

"Fuck!" He tore his mouth away on a rough, ravaged groan.

We stared at each other. He looked stunned...shattered. His hands flexed against my back, my scalp, like he was considering going in for more.

But then he released me and stepped back. And I hated that. Hated that he always let go first. Hated that I was always the one who wanted more.

"Let's go get married," he said.

And all I could do was nod.

WHEN THE MAGISTRATE TRULY SAID "YOU MAY NOW KISS the bride," I looked at Brax and straight-up panicked.

Because now I knew what it was like to have Braxton

Hale's mouth on mine and hell, no, that couldn't happen again. I wouldn't survive it.

Maybe something of this was on my face, because the glint in his eyes turned downright mischievous. Before I could do something smart—like run—he wrapped one arm around my waist and cupped the back of my head with his other hand.

"I've got you," he whispered so quietly that only I could hear.

And then he dipped me low and kissed me while the crowd whooped and hollered their approval. Despite his dramatics, the kiss itself was almost chaste. Sweet and light, and solicitous of my cherry red lipstick.

When he brought me right side up again, we linked hands and raised our arms overhead in victory, like we had accomplished something to be proud of, when all we had done was trick everyone here into believing they were witnessing true love.

Maybe I should feel bad about that, but I didn't. Look how happy it made them, to believe love conquered all. I had lost count of the number of folks who had approached me the last two weeks just to tell me they had always known it would be me and Brax in the end, that we were meant to be. I didn't want to take that away from them too soon. There would be time enough for that later.

"I now present, Mr. and Mrs. Braxton Hale!" the magistrate announced.

Brax and I looked at each other. I wrinkled my nose and gave an almost imperceptible shake of my head. I had no intention of changing my name. He smirked a little and nodded.

And then it was done.

We were married.

19

BRAX

All things considered, married life was not what I had expected, and I'd had pretty vague expectations to begin with. I hadn't put much thought into the day-to-day merging of our lives, but I had figured that, at the very least, life would be different.

So it came as a bit of a surprise that it wasn't.

One week after we had pledged to cherish each other every day for the rest of our lives, we had barely spoken a handful of words to each other.

Part of that could be blamed on our schedules. Essie was up and out of the house a good three hours before me, since days started early at the ranch. Whereas I had the luxury of making my own schedule, and I had decided early on that that schedule would never start before nine a.m. One of the benefits of being the only attorney in a farming town was that my clients were unavailable before noon.

But that also meant I tended to stay late at the office. Most nights, Essie had eaten dinner and was already headed to her room for the night by the time I got home. We lived like ships passing in the night—or roommates passing in the hallway—more than husband and wife.

The only thing that had changed was the reading chair by the fireplace. That was new. It was the thing Essie had picked out at the furniture store. It was a deep green, made of soft corduroy material, big enough for her to curl up with a book, even with her long legs. One morning, I noticed a plaid throw blanket draped over the back. She was making use of her chair, even though I never saw her do it.

Because I never really saw her at all.

Still, I was glad to see evidence that she wasn't just holing up in the guest room during the few hours she spent home every day. She had taken me at my word that this was her home, too.

I stopped by Jo's before work on Wednesday. It was my ritual because I happened to like lattes, and I refused to get one of those stupid espresso machines that created mountains of extra trash one tiny plastic pod at a time. I would rather pay the five dollars and keep Colorado beautiful.

Chloe looked up as I entered with a jangle of the bells tied to the door. "The usual?"

I nodded. "Thanks."

She plonked a white porcelain cup under the nozzle. I never got my latte to go, preferring to hang out a few minutes and get the local gossip. It wasn't a business tactic—being the only lawyer in sixty miles meant Aspen Springs folks had little choice in the matter—but I found it helped me to remember the human side of my business. These were real people with real problems that I wanted to help solve.

"How's married life, Brax?" Chloe asked as deep brown liquid streamed into the cup.

"Can't complain." I studied the glass case of pastries. Several varieties of muffins, including blueberry, pumpkin, and apple. Scones and biscuits. They served hot breakfasts here, too, but I wasn't much for big breakfasts.

"No," Chloe agreed. The corner of her mouth hitched up. "I suppose you couldn't."

What did she mean by that? James knew the truth— if we hadn't told her along with our families, then Adam would have spilled it himself, so there wasn't any point in hiding it. I was sure Essie hadn't shared our secret with Chloe or her other friends.

But that didn't mean Essie hadn't said other things about me.

And just because we were supposedly happily married didn't mean she couldn't complain about me.

I glanced up from the pastries and found Chloe

watching me while a knowing smile played on her lips. Like she knew exactly what I was wondering.

Chloe pushed a metal pitcher of milk under another nozzle and flipped the switch. Instantly steam hissed and she raised and circled the pitcher, heating the milk inside. When it was half milk, half froth, she poured it over the espresso, using a large spoon to hold back the froth until the cup was nearly full. Then she finished it off with a frothy aspen leaf.

"Nice," I said.

She nodded, looking pleased. "I'm getting pretty good at foam art. Nothing super fancy yet, though."

"I almost hate to ruin it," I said, before taking a sip and doing exactly that. I wiped the milky froth from my upper lip. "But it has to be done."

"Not all art is meant to be permanent. Maybe that's what makes us appreciate it more." She tilted her head. "Like love."

I had the feeling she was leading me somewhere. Might as well go along with it. For now. "Isn't love supposed to be permanent? The good kind, anyway."

She shrugged. "Everyone dies, Brax."

I held very, very still, my grip on the coffee mug so tight that my knuckles matched the white porcelain. And suddenly I was back there again, on the edge of the cliff, screaming Essie's name. And I was next to my mother's bed, her paper-thin skin nearly translucent as she fell into her last sleep. Watching my dad fall apart and knowing I would have done the same.

"Eventually," I said, my voice rough. "Everyone dies *eventually*."

"Exactly. Everyone dies." She said it so matter-of-factly. I wanted to throttle her. "I would have thought, growing up on a ranch, death wouldn't be a squeamish topic for you."

She wasn't wrong. I had witnessed the end of life for many animals, including ones we intended to eat. "Death doesn't make me squeamish," I said. "I have a perfectly normal, healthy dislike for it, that's all."

"Hm," she said. "I suppose anyone would dislike death after losing their mom so young, like you did."

"I didn't lose her young. I was a grown man when she died. Four years ago, now," I corrected. I was surprised she didn't know that. She wasn't born and raised in Aspen Springs like most of the people here, but she'd been here for nearly a decade now. "She was nearly seventy when she passed. Cancer isn't pleasant no matter when it happens, but she'd had a good life and we were able to keep her mostly comfortable at home in the end."

"I'm glad she didn't suffer." She pulled an apple muffin from the case and slid it across the counter to me on a plate. "Here, try this. I want to see how the flavor goes with that espresso."

I broke off a piece and popped it into my mouth, then washed it down with a swig of latte. "It's good."

"Right?" She busied herself with cleaning the nozzles on the espresso machine. "It must have been hard on your family when your mom passed, even though you weren't children anymore. Your dad..." Her voice trailed off. She bit her lip and rubbed harder at the nozzle, until the metal gleamed.

"It hit him bad," I acknowledged, because there wasn't any hiding it. The whole town witnessed him drown his grief in a bottle of whiskey. "It took him a year or so to pull himself together." I took another bite of muffin, another sip of latte. "It was hard on all of us, of course, because we loved her. But he took it hardest. You grow up kind of expecting your parents will pass on before you do, in the natural way of things. It's different, losing a wife. The day Essie almost died scarred me, even though she survived it. I suppose it was the shock of nearly losing someone when I wasn't expecting it. That puts a fear in a person."

Chloe had been nodding along, but suddenly she stopped and tilted her head thoughtfully. "Well, isn't that funny," she murmured.

"I'd say there isn't a damn thing funny about any of it," I said, narrowing my eyes.

"Funny isn't the right word, you're right. Strange is what I meant. The day she almost died? Was that in high school?" she asked.

I nodded. "Did she tell you about it?"

"Only in passing. She never shared the details. The strange thing, though, is that she never said she almost died. She said *you* did."

I took that in. Turned the words over in my mind. Trying and failing to make sense of them.

"What happened that day, if you don't mind my asking?" Chloe's keen green eyes were locked on me.

"I don't mind you asking, but it's a story for another day," I said. "I have to get to work."

"Maybe I'll ask Essie to meet me for lunch. She can tell me herself."

"Essie's out at Lodestar, so I doubt she'll have the time to drive all the way to town." I stuffed a dollar in the tip jar. "Thanks for the muffin."

Chloe grinned like the Cheshire cat. "Oh, she's home today. Wednesday is her day off. Didn't she tell you?"

Essie was home? I'd taken to parking on the street to give her the garage spot, so I hadn't noticed her SUV was still there when I left this morning. There hadn't been a sign of her in the kitchen, either. She must have slept in.

A day off might be nice.

Before I could second guess myself, I had my phone out of my pocket and was texting Sylvia, my secretary, to clear my schedule as I was heading for the door.

"Have a good day!" Chloe called after me, her words laced with laughter.

Something occurred to me, and I paused at the door. "You were at my mom's funeral. The whole town was."

"I remember."

My gaze narrowed. "Then why'd you act like you didn't know how old I was when she died?"

She laughed. "Because I knew you'd correct me. There are lots of ways to get someone talking, Brax. That one happens to be yours."

FLEETWOOD MAC WAS PLAYING AS I WALKED IN THE DOOR. I was used to coming home to a quiet house. Empty, before Essie, and it might as well have been empty after Essie for all the noise she made. This was different. A good kind of different.

A *very* good kind of different, I realized as I rounded the corner into the kitchen, because there was Essie, her back to me as she leaned over the countertop, scrolling her phone and eating cereal, the hem of her tee shirt riding up far enough to reveal a tiny pair of underwear cut to reveal the undercurve of her glorious ass.

God*damn*, that was a fine sight.

A strangled groan escaped me. She dropped her spoon and it clattered in the bowl as she whirled to face me.

That's when I realized she was wearing my University of Colorado tee shirt. It was a little loose on her and hit right below her hip. And fuck, it looked good on her. Her face was bare, and while I loved the red lipstick she wore like armor, there was something about seeing her like this that made me ache.

"Hello, wife," I said, and if I intended the words to sound ironic, I knew I'd failed. I sounded hungry.

"You're home," she squawked.

"You're in my shirt," I replied.

She glanced down at herself. "Oh, right. Laundry day. I'm out of clean clothes."

"I told you to bring everything," I couldn't resist pointing out. Maybe I was still annoyed that she'd left things behind on the assumption of how quickly we'd divorce. "We can swing by your mom's house later today and get the rest of it."

She shifted, tugging at the hem of my shirt like maybe it could miraculously grow an extra inch. It bounced right up again. "You don't have to work?"

"I take a day off every now and then," I said, like I had intended today to be one of those days all along. Like I hadn't cancelled meetings on the off chance I could convince my wife to give me more than five minutes of her time.

"Well, that would be great, then," she said. "How about now?"

"Now?" My gaze drifted down her bare legs and back up again. "I feel like this is the kind of errand that requires pants, hellion." I was in no hurry for her to make that happen.

She made an exasperated face at me and I grinned. "Yes, prig, I know. Do you have something I can borrow?"

We settled on an old pair of sweatpants. She was tall for a woman, but I was tall for a man, which meant the bottoms bunched up around her ankles. Even with an elastic waistband, the pants hung low on her waist, saved from plunging down her thighs by her curvy hips and ass. With her hair piled in a messy bun that showcased the rainbow colors on top of her head, she looked ready for a day off spent on the couch, watching reruns of shows without really paying attention.

It did things to me, seeing her in my college shirt and worn-in sweatpants. It made me want to scoop her up and...and *cuddle*, of all fucking things.

I watched as she tugged on her sneakers. "Ready?"

She nodded. "Let's go."

Cat wasn't there when we arrived, which was no surprise since she worked six days a week at Sweetie Pie, but Essie still had the keys. She let us in, and we headed for her old room.

"Take everything," I ordered as Essie opened a dresser drawer. "Just in case."

Her crisp salute was undermined by an exaggerated eyeroll. "Yes, *sir.*"

But she did as I said despite giving me attitude about it. *Brat.* She emptied a drawer of tee shirts and shorts into the suitcase and then moved on to the next one.

I took another look around the room while she worked. Again my gaze landed on the photo of Essie and Jack at the lake, and the barest smudge of my finger.

"Are you sure you don't want to take any photos?" I asked.

"I'm sure." She closed the suitcase with a grunt. "Too much work."

I glanced at our reflection in the mirror over the dresser. She was too busy fighting the suitcase closed to pay me any mind.

"Okay," she said. "I'm ready."

"You have *everything*?" I asked, adding the emphasis just to piss her off.

She hefted the suitcase onto the floor. "Don't worry. I won't ask to borrow your precious old sweats ever again. I have enough clothes to last a month even if your washing machine breaks down."

Well, shit. Now I wanted to set all her clothes on fire. Leave her nothing *but* my sweats to wear.

I followed behind as she rolled the suitcase down the hallway. She stopped at the dining room table to flip through a stack of mail.

"Should I change my address?" she asked. "I probably should, right? For appearances. I have to put my address on the competition entrance form. Seems like a hassle, though."

"You can do it online. It only takes a minute," I told her.

"Hm. I suppose—" She stopped rifling through the envelopes and magazines, her face completely blank as she picked up a postcard. She studied it for a moment, then flipped it over. Her expression didn't change as she read it.

She set it down again. "Let's go."

With that, I knew exactly who it was from. A helpless fury washed over me as I strode to the table. Because Essie? Expressionless was the last thing she was. Anger, joy, sorrow, fear, desire, they all showed up on her face. She never tried to hide who she was or what she was feeling.

Except when it came to the pathetic excuse for a man who was her father.

She didn't stop me when I picked up the postcard. *Hey, baby girl. Congratulations! Wish I could be there for the wedding, but I'm in Greece. This place is magic when the summer tourists are gone. Wish you were here! Love, Dad.*

I set the postcard down with purpose, afraid I would crumple it in my fist like the trash it was if I kept holding it, and looked at Essie. "It's just because of our circumstances. He'd be here for the real thing." I knew it was a lie even as I said it.

"I didn't tell him it was fake," she said neutrally. "Come on, let's go."

I didn't budge. "Why didn't you tell him?"

Her gaze flicked to mine and then she looked away again, shrugging. "I figured...he wasn't going to come, anyway. But someday, maybe I'll get married for real, and even though I know he won't show up, I'll hope he will, and when he doesn't, it will crush me. Better to get it out of the way now, when it doesn't actually hurt. So that I *know*."

"Essie." My chest felt tight. I had the crazy idea that it might be worth flying out to Greece tomorrow and flying back the very next day, just for the pleasure of kicking this man's ass into the Aegean Sea.

"It's fine. I'm fine," she said, her tone still flat, which meant she was not fine at all.

So I ignored her words and put my arms around her. It was like hugging a rock. Her arms hung at her sides, not returning my hug. There was no give to her rigid muscles. No crack in the shields she had up.

"Okay, that's enough, thank you. Can we go now?" she said.

But still I held on.

She didn't fight me. I wondered if maybe that was her way of proving how little she cared about the whole thing.

I kept holding on.

And then suddenly everything changed. She didn't melt. She didn't relent.

She turned *fierce*.

Her arms scooped under my shoulder blades, and she grabbed me by the shoulders. She dug her fingers into my muscles, into my bones. I didn't doubt there would be ten little bruises there tomorrow, but I didn't care. Dampness spread across my shirt where she pressed her face. Her hoarse breath sawed in and out.

Still I held on.

"Why do I *care*?" she raged and her fingers dug in even harder. "It's so stupid."

"It's not stupid to care, honey," I whispered against her hair. "He's the dumbass here, not you. The best thing about you is that you care. You're all heart, Essie Price. And that...Do you know how amazing you are? You stole a horse to keep him safe. You married me to help your mom."

"Then why doesn't he think I'm amazing?" she asked damply.

"Because he's small, honey. He's so fucking small. And you...you're bigger than the whole sky."

She inhaled sharply. And when she slowly let it go, I felt her tension go with it. Her fingers relaxed their death grip on my shoulders. But I didn't stop holding her.

"Imagine being the kind of person who goes to Greece as a tourist and then complains about all the tourists," I said. "Imagine being that particular breed of asshole."

She snorted a laugh against my chest.

After another long breath, she sighed and pulled away. "Can we go home now?"

"Yeah, honey. I'll take you home."

20

ESSIE

For once, I let go first.

Maybe because for the first time in my life, someone gave me exactly what I needed. Not what they thought I should have. Not something less than I wanted. For the first time, I wasn't left wondering why I always asked for too much, why I tried to *give* too much.

Brax didn't make me feel like too much. He made me feel like it was *enough*.

I felt...full.

And that terrified the ever-living bejeezus out of me.

Because I knew what it was like to be empty. I remembered how it felt when Brax shut me out fifteen years ago. He would do it again. He would remember I was too much. It was just a matter of time.

I might as well prove it.

I figured I wouldn't even have to try very hard. Just be myself, but turn it up a notch.

I was all the more determined because he was being so goddamned sweet to me after the postcard incident with my dad. And that was unacceptable. One thing I could not ever tolerate was pity, and coming from Brax, it was even more galling. Sometimes girls had shitty fathers. So what? It wasn't like I was seeking male attention at strip clubs to validate my self-worth. I was *fine*.

I had *years* of experience getting under Brax's skin. *Years* of learning which buttons to push to yield maximum aggravation. It should have been a piece of cake.

When he came home one evening to find me on the couch watching one of my favorite movies and plopped down beside me, I took the opportunity to provide a running commentary of every single thought I had ever possessed about this movie and anything remotely relevant to it. That kind of thing had driven him crazy in high school. He used to threaten to stuff one of his dirty hiking socks in my mouth if I couldn't shut up.

But he fucking *smiled* at me and asked if I wanted popcorn.

Popcorn!

And then somehow, I found my legs on his lap while he worked out the knots in my calves that came from hours in the saddle, while I bit the palm of my hand to hold back my screams because his strong thumbs digging into my tight muscles was a pleasure that mingled with pain, and unfortunately, that was exactly how I liked it.

The next morning, he offered me a ride to Lodestar, since he needed to head out there anyway to take care of some ranch paperwork.

"But then I have to leave when you leave," I protested. "I was planning on putting in a long day."

"It's fine. I'm bringing my laptop, so I can just work from there. I'll stay as long as you need me to."

I scowled. Why was he being so dang nice?

"I guess that's okay," I said.

He grinned. "Much obliged to you for finding it in your heart to allow me to drive you to work. Mighty kind of you."

It was our usual back-and-forth. But now it felt different. We had always teased each other, even when we were best friends. Back then, it was all good-natured. After the day he almost died, he stopped it all together, and anytime I tried to poke fun at him, he simply walked away. It wasn't long after I stopped trying to get a reaction from him that he started needling me again, but there was a rougher edge to the teasing.

Now that edge was gone again.

I didn't know what to make of it. If he kept this shit up, I might start to wonder if he actually liked me. I didn't want to wonder. Wonder led to hope, and hope led to heartbreak.

Around noon Brax poked his head into Pirate's stall, where I was giving him a rubdown after our morning session. "You hungry? Dad's making sandwiches at the main house for lunch."

I wasn't in the mood to play one big happy family with Brax's dad and brothers. I was in a shitty mood, and the nicer Brax was to me, the more on edge I felt. "I'm good here."

My stomach growled because I was starving. Ted made awesome sandwiches and it annoyed me that I had to turn it down. Closing Pirate's stall behind me, I headed for the breakroom. There might be a leftover donut or something. James and the ranch hands tended to bring in a lot of treats to share.

Brax followed me. "I could go get the sandwiches and we could eat them outside. It's a nice day."

"I'm having a donut." To prove my point, I flipped open the box, selected a glazed, and took a big bite.

The muscle in his jaw tweaked. "You can't just eat a donut for lunch, Essie. You're going to be working, what, another five or six hours? You'll bonk."

He was right. I knew he was right. But I couldn't back down now.

I took another bite.

The muscle in his cheek popped even harder. With an aggravated grunt, he grabbed an apple from the bin, rinsed it off, and handed it to me. "At least eat an apple with it."

"Thanks, Mom," I muttered, taking the apple and brushing past him.

He followed me, which was a problem because the only place I was going was away from him. I headed out of the barn and wandered aimlessly toward the pasture. Maple, a pretty chestnut mare, greeted me at the fence. I gave her the apple and she lipped it up.

Behind me, Brax growled.

"Why the hell are you so ornery?" he demanded. "You've been in a bad mood for a week."

"My mood is fine when you're not around," I snapped.

Annoyance darkened his blue eyes, and for a moment I thought I had finally broken him. This was the moment he was going to walk away. But then his expression shifted and he scrubbed a hand over his face. "All right. Tell me what I did so I can fix it."

Goddammit. Now I felt bad.

"Why?" I asked. "What's the point?"

The look on his face suggested I was in serious danger of being throttled. "Happy wife, happy life, right?" he said with a sardonic edge to his voice.

"You wouldn't know how to make a woman happy even if she was sitting on your face," I muttered.

He stilled. "What did you say?"

"I said..." My voice trailed off as I realized that there was no way in hell I could repeat myself. Self-preservation lodged the words deep in my throat. *You're in danger, girl.*

"I know what you said."

His words were both a promise and a threat and I shivered in the Colorado sunshine.

For a moment we simply stared at each other.

And then—

"Fuck it," he growled.

He came right at me. I backed up and kept backing up until my back hit the fence post, and still he kept coming, not stopping until he was so close I had to tilt my head back to meet his eyes.

And promptly wished I hadn't.

Good lord, this man was going to eat me alive. And I was going to let him do it.

"You've put me in an awkward position, hellion." He dropped to his knees right there in the tall brown grass. "You know how much I love being right. But you love proving me wrong. So if I eat this pussy until you scream my name, will you be happy? Or will you be mad that I'm right? It's a paradox."

I could feel the heat of his hands through the thin material of my leggings as he glided his wide palms up my legs, stopping at the crease of my pelvis. His hands were so broad that his thumbs could graze the cleft of my pussy if he put his mind to it. But he wouldn't. Not here, not out in the open like this. Would he? "I guess we'll never know, will we?"

His lips quirked. "Oh, we'll know."

And then he caught hold of the waistband and dragged my leggings down to my ankles. Goose bumps broke out on my bare legs as I stared down at him, dumbfounded. He had really done it.

His hands swept up my thighs, under my sweater. "You're not wearing underwear." He sounded almost angry, and a whole lot desperate.

"I hate panty lines," I admitted. "I never wear underwear with leggings."

He muttered something under his breath about never letting me leave the house like that again. His thumb swiped the cleft of my pussy. "Fuck, you're wet."

"I'll wear what I want," I said, breathless from what his hands were doing to me, but still not too breathless to argue. "Anyway, who cares? No one will know if I have underwear on or not."

His hands stopped and I wanted to kill him. His blue eyes glittered up at me like shards of ice. "*I'll* know."

Goodness. My hips bucked, demanding more attention from his clever fingers.

He had the audacity to laugh. "Do you know what I think, hellion?"

I frowned down at him. "No, but I'm sure you're about to bore me with the details."

He laughed again, deeper this time. "I think you like this. I think you get off on fighting with me." He slipped a finger inside me and my pussy clenched around him.

"Because you keep running your mouth, but your pussy keeps getting wetter. You're fucking soaked, hellion."

Oh, god. He wasn't wrong. "Stop talking," I ground out. "You're ruining it."

His smug grin flashed up at me. "The only thing I'm going to ruin is this perfect pussy for other men. Grab the fence, honey."

And before I could think of anything smart to say—and it would have been a long, long time before anything came to mind—he wrapped his hands around the back of my bare thighs and hoisted me in the air, tossed my legs over his shoulders, and wedged himself between my body and my leggings. Because apparently uptight Brax didn't care about things like grass stains on the knees of his jeans or muddy heel marks on the back of his clean shirt.

Well, damn. I was already impressed, and he hadn't even put his mouth on me yet.

But he was going to.

Out here. Where anyone could find us.

A breeze lifted my hair and swirled it around my shoulders. The wood fence rail bit into my shoulder blades. Suddenly it was all too real.

"Brax," I said uncertainly.

"No," he bit out. "Don't...don't tell me to stop. I've waited so long. Tell me yes. Just this once, say yes to me."

I looked at the man kneeling in front of me, the man

who had broken my heart and held me together, and gave him the only answer I could.

"Yes," I breathed.

His teeth nipped the sensitive skin of my inner thigh and I nearly lost my hold on the fence. I whimpered and shifted my hips, worried that I was going to go tumbling to the ground.

"Hush," he whispered. "I've got you."

Then he pressed his face against me, he made a sound of pure contentment, and he *breathed*.

And I breathed with him.

It was like the world expanded in that moment. The jagged mountain peaks in the distance. The wide open sky above us, brilliant with sharp sunlight. The sting of cold on my cheeks and the encompassing warmth of his body. The hum of the breeze rustling the grass. I was part of all of it. I *felt* all of it.

Then he licked me, the world contracted, and all I felt was him.

His breath, his mouth, his tongue, his teeth.

My pleasure.

Because, sweet mother of all things holy, his *mouth*.

His goddamn mouth.

It was like I was being consumed by him. Completely devoured. Like he couldn't get enough. His hands dug into my butt cheeks, cupping me to his hungry mouth like a chalice.

I ground against him, needing more, and then

immediately pulled back, worried that I had asked for too much. But he made an encouraging, eager sound and sucked harder at my clit. Sweet heavens, the pleasure was unrelenting.

My head tipped back on a moan, my hands gripping the fence rail so tightly I could feel it start to give, and I came in wave after wave.

And it was the stupidest thing.

Because as he gently set me back down to earth on shaky legs, I swiped my cheeks with the back of my hand, and it came away wet.

I was crying.

21

BRAX

I took one look at Essie's damp face and fled.

I didn't run, precisely, but it wasn't a casual stroll, either. It was more like a brisk speed-walk, interspersed with bouts of jogging.

I had never considered myself a coward, but standing there with Essie's taste on my tongue, that stricken look on her face, I knew I had reached my limit. She had come apart for me, my name on her lips, and I was not going to stand there and listen to her say she regretted it. It would kill me.

So I speed-walked my cowardly ass right on out of there.

I was halfway to my truck before I remembered I was her ride. It didn't matter how I felt, how terrified I was that I had just fucked everything up, I couldn't leave her stranded at Lodestar Ranch. She'd kill me. And if she didn't, my dad sure would, and then my mom would rise up from the grave and kill me a second time for good measure.

I groaned, jangling the keys in my hand.

Which reminded me that one of those keys happened to unlock the door to my old cabin, where Essie had spent the night before our wedding. I changed direction, sending a text to Essie as I went.

> Have to take care of something. Meet you at my truck in an hour?

An hour should be enough time to get my head on straight. Or at least pull myself together enough to fake it.

I buried my face in my hands and made a sound of extreme self-loathing. Fucking hell. What had I done?

I didn't have anywhere near an hour to ponder that question, because about three minutes after I closed the cabin door behind me, it banged open again, and there was Essie.

Shit.

"You have to take care of something?" she demanded. Her cheeks were bright pink from the cold and also a healthy amount of rage, I would hazard to guess. "The only thing you have to take care of is removing my foot from your ass, because I'm about to put it there."

"Listen," I started, and then stopped because I hadn't

gotten so far as figuring out what it was I wanted her to listen *to*.

"I don't want to listen," she growled. "I want you to fuck me."

That drew me up quick. "Come again?" I asked, just to be sure I heard her correctly.

"Yes," she said. "That is exactly what I'm trying to accomplish."

"But you cried," I said, like an idiot.

"So what?" She scowled at me. "It was a lot, okay? Sometimes I cry when I'm overwhelmed. Doesn't matter if it's a good thing or a bad thing. I cry. Is that too much for you?"

I laughed and grabbed a handful of that oversized sweater she was wearing, using it to pull her to me. "Hellion, you've always been too much for me."

Her face did something awful and she struggled, trying to get away from me without ruining her sweater. But I had her now, and I wasn't letting go.

I lowered my face closer to hers until she had nowhere to look but me. "So I guess I'll have to become more, so I can be enough for you."

She leaned back and her eyebrows furrowed with confusion as she scanned my face. "What?"

"I told you, honey. You're bigger than the whole damn sky. How could I ever hope to hold on to the sky?"

But she still looked at me with confusion, like she

couldn't make sense of my words. That was fine. Maybe it was even better that she didn't.

I wrapped a chunk of rainbow striped hair around my fist and gave it a tug. "You want to fuck, hellion? Let's fuck."

Her hands were already on my belt buckle before I even finished that sentence.

With a rough tug, she had it open. The snap was next and then the zipper. I loved that she wasn't gentle or shy about it. Her eyes looked right into mine as she slid her hand into my boxers, nothing demure about it, just desire. I gave a single, sharp inhale as she wrapped her hand around my dick.

And for the first time, she faltered. Her eyes lowered to where her hand disappeared beneath the cotton paisley fabric.

"Don't even think about stopping this now." I knew I sounded desperate, and I didn't fucking care. I would beg if I had to. Get right back on my knees and convince her with my mouth.

"Oh, I'm not changing my mind." Air hissed between my teeth as she ran her palm up and down my dick like she was taking its measurement. "I'm just wondering how much of your cock I can stuff in my mouth before it hits the back of my throat."

My eyes crossed. My dick twitched.

Essie smiled. "I'm thinking, not all of it, but enough

that with my hand on the rest of it, you might not notice a difference."

Jesus. Fucking. Christ.

"Wait, you just got bigger." She stroked me again, thoughtfully. Up and down, up and down. *Squeeze.* "Okay, I can fit a little less than I thought, then. We'll just have to find out, won't we?"

"No," I choked out.

She didn't listen—of fucking course, she didn't listen—but before her knees could hit the floor, I scooped her under the armpits and put her back on her feet again.

"Why not?" she demanded, sounding angry.

"You got me all worked up. I won't last with your mouth on me. The first time I come with you is going to be inside you." I whipped her sweater over her head and groaned at the sight of her breasts wrapped up in a sports bra. "But just so you know, that's going to go quick, too."

"Oh," she said dryly. "How lucky for me."

"You came on my mouth ten minutes ago. You're going to come on my fingers next. Before we leave this cabin, you *will* come on my dick. Do you still want to complain?" I asked, unzipping her bra and freeing her breasts into my waiting hands. I rubbed my thumbs back and forth over her nipples until they formed tight buds.

"I'll save my comments until the end," she said in a husky voice that thickened my dick even more.

I huffed a laugh as I lowered my head to her breast. "Not all of them, I hope. I'm a big fan of positive reinforcement."

"You have to earn it first."

I grazed my teeth over her nipple before giving it a hard suck. Her hand clamped down on the back of my skull.

"Good boy," she gasped out.

And fuck if that didn't have me almost blow in my jeans like a goddamn virgin.

I let go of her nipple with a loud pop. "Take your clothes off and get on the bed."

She arched a sardonic brow at me, but shimmied her sports bra off her shoulders, tugged off her boots, and peeled her leggings down before kicking them aside. And then she sauntered past me with a little smirk, like she knew exactly how much I was going to enjoy watching her pert ass go by.

And I very much did.

"Spread your legs, honey," I said. "I want to see."

She opened her legs maybe half an inch. From the teasing expression in her eyes, I had the feeling she wasn't being shy. *Brat*.

I pulled my henley off over my head and heard her suck in a sharp breath. My jeans and boots followed. She had propped herself up on her elbows to watch, so I gave her something to look at, wrapping my hand around my aching dick and giving it a long, slow pull. She licked her lips and that was nearly the end of me.

"Wider," I gritted out. "Show me where you want me to touch you."

This time, she obeyed. Her thighs parted, revealing her pretty pussy. She dragged her index finger up the seam and tapped her clit. "Right...*there*."

But she didn't stop touching, and she moaned a little. In two strides I was next to her, then over her. I grabbed her wrist and captured her finger in my mouth, sucking the taste of her pussy.

"Tastes like mine," I murmured.

"Then make it happy," she demanded.

My fingers touched where she had touched, tracing small, delicate circles over her clit that had her hips bucking into my hand.

"Harder," she pleaded.

I wanted to resist, to tease her the way she teased me, but I couldn't stop myself from doing exactly what she demanded. There wasn't a damn thing in this world Essie could ask of me that I wouldn't give her.

My fingers rubbed harder. It was almost too intense, the way she watched me, her gaze pinned to my face like what she saw there was even more important than what I was doing with my hand. Like I might disappear if she blinked.

I slid a finger inside her soaked pussy, then added a second. Her muscles tensed around my fingers and my dick leaked pre-cum out of pure jealousy. "Tell me," I rasped.

"Yes." She arched into my hand. "Exactly like that. You're doing such a good job, baby."

And then she came, her inner muscles gripping my fingers in rhythmic spasms. "Fuck," I hissed. "*Yes.* God, you're so fucking beautiful." It bordered on pain, watching her release like that while struggling to keep my own need in check.

I reached for my jeans, and the wallet I kept in my back pocket—and shit—

"I don't have a condom," I remembered out loud.

I had never been a one-night-stand kind of guy, but I generally kept a condom in my wallet for spontaneity. After I parted ways with my last girlfriend a little over a year ago—around the same time Essie retired from barrel racing—I hadn't bothered to replace it.

Essie looked at my dick and then up to my face. "I have an IUD, because periods are kind of a bummer when it comes to riding horses. And I got tested after my last encounter nine months ago. No diseases."

"It's been a little over a year for me. All clear."

If she noticed the timeline coincided with her permanent return to Aspen Springs, she didn't acknowledge it. "Fuck me, Brax," she ordered.

She pushed my shoulders until I rolled onto my back, then hiked one leg over my waist, straddling me while my hands settled on the curve of her hips. She wiggled a little, gliding her pussy over my aching shaft until I was soaked from her wetness. And then she paused, staring down at my chest.

"What is this?" Her fingertips trailed the red mark guarding my heart and she squinted in the dim light. "You have a tattoo?"

I grabbed her hand, stilling her. My heart thumped hard underneath our palms. "That's not important right now. What's important is getting my dick inside you."

"All right, then," she purred, and swiveled her body against me.

My hands dug into her hips. "Are you sure?" I asked, my voice more than a little desperate.

She laughed, soft and husky. "I'm sure," she said.

I swallowed hard. God. I was about to fuck my wife for the first time, and I was going to do that bare.

I shot up to capture her mouth in a kiss. "Then take my cock and put it inside you. I want to watch you fuck me."

With one hand splayed on my chest, she rose onto her knees and reached between us and wrapped her hand around my length. When she notched my crown against her entrance, we both groaned in unison.

My hips bucked up and she sank down, meeting each other half way. The fit was exquisitely tight, so goddamn perfect.

My voice was all gravel when I asked, "Are you

okay?" Because she hadn't moved in a few seconds, and I was only halfway inside her.

"Yes," she said, her voice strained. "Just going to take this slow so you don't split me in two."

She slid down another inch, and then another, both of us riveted to the sight of her body stretching to take me.

"Fuck, honey, you take me so well," I encouraged.

Her hands slid to my shoulders and she used the leverage to take the last couple inches. With her fully seated on my cock, the last thread of my control snapped so sharply I could almost hear the *ping*.

"Sorry, honey. I told you this was going to go quick." My hands clenched her hips with almost bruising force as I lifted her off my dick and slammed her back down again. Over and over, her tits bouncing, her nails digging into my shoulders, as she whispered filthy things into my ear.

And then it really was too much, and I rolled her onto her back, twined our fingers together, and pounded into her until white lights exploded behind my eyes and I came harder than I'd ever come in my life.

We didn't make it back to our house in town that night. Each time one of us sat up and made some move to put clothes back on, the other would put a stop to that right quick. We explored each other thoroughly, reaching for each other again and again in between drowsy half-naps. Her mouth on me, my mouth on her, my dick driving into her from behind, her riding me slow and deep until my eyes crossed.

But no matter how we started, we always ended the same. Face to face, Essie flat on her back, our hands intertwined over her head, my body pleading for what I could never say out loud.

Stay with me.

BRAX

JACK

You want to explain the letter I got from Mom?

BRAX

Shit. I was going to tell you.

JACK

Is this a joke? Because I'm not laughing.

BRAX

Listen, I know you're mad. Give me a chance to explain.

JACK

You don't have a fucking clue what I am. But you're about to find out.

ell, fuck.

That was ominous.

I stared at Jack's last text. Where was he right now? Somewhere in eastern Europe, I was pretty sure. That was a long way from Aspen Springs, Colorado. And not even Jack could kick my ass from five thousand miles away.

I was pretty sure, anyway.

But that was a worry for another day, because today was Wednesday, and I had more important things to do. Like stare at his sister's ass as she bopped and shimmied to the music in her headphones while she folded laundry.

I had taken to working from home on Wednesdays, setting up my makeshift office at the kitchen table, where I had a good view of most of the house, with the exception of the bedrooms. Essie tended to sleep in until eight or nine, when she emerged from her bedroom in my sweatpants and college tee shirt, which she had apparently commandeered as her own, despite her promise to return them.

I wasn't mad about it.

But I scowled at her as if I were.

Generally, that led to her taking them off, which led to my clothes coming off, too.

We had sex a lot on Wednesdays, maybe because we didn't get to see much of each other the rest of the week. Sometimes I saw her eyes narrow in on the tattoo on my heart, and her lips would flatten in a frown. But she didn't ask me about it again. And she still slept in the guestroom.

We had been married for a month now, and in some ways, we were getting to know each other all over again. Sometimes I caught her watching me with a befuddled expression, like she was wondering how we got here from where we were.

I was more interested in figuring out where we were going.

The doorbell rang.

I glanced up at Essie, who was holding a sweatshirt under her chin, her lips moving to words I couldn't hear. Then I closed my laptop—I doubted Essie would go snooping, but I took my clients' privacy seriously—and got up to see who was at the door.

A package delivery, probably, though I wasn't expecting anything.

But I didn't get a chance to see, because the second I opened the door, something hit me right in the gut, knocking the wind clean out of me. I doubled over, my hands on my knees, as the corners of my vision went black.

"Take a slow breath, not too deep," a voice rumbled from far away.

And shit, I knew that voice.

My gaze locked on the black army boots on my front porch. I followed those up to the fatigues and then, finally, to his face.

"Jack," I heaved. "You asshole."

He thumped my shoulder. "You're fine. Walk it off."

I was about to tell him what he could do with that advice when I was interrupted by an ear-splitting shriek, followed by the slap of bare feet on wooden floors, and a flurry of color as Essie raced by me and hurled herself into her brother's arms.

"Jack!" she shrieked. "You're home!"

He twirled her around, making her laugh, before setting her down again. "I had some vacation days to burn. Mom said you went and got yourself married to this jackass." He jerked a thumb in my direction. "Is that true?"

Essie looked at me and blinked slowly, apparently noticing for the first time that I was not looking my best. She turned back to her brother with a frown. "What did you do, Jack?"

Jack looked beyond her to meet my gaze head on. "Nothing he shouldn't have seen coming."

I couldn't argue with that.

"Jack!" Essie slapped his bicep, then slapped his other arm for good measure. "Don't hurt my husband."

My husband.

I straightened up so fast I nearly went light-headed again.

She had never called me that, not once in our four weeks of marriage. She had never called me anything *ever* except Brax or prig, or Braxton if I was really getting under her skin. It might piss Essie off to know that I was actually quite fond of her little nickname for me. But this...this might be my favorite.

My husband.

I grinned at Jack and his eyes narrowed.

"Why don't you go back inside, Essie, and give Brax and me a chance to catch up?" he suggested, his eyes never leaving my face.

Essie folded her arms under her chest. "Seeing as this isn't 1950, no. I don't think I will."

They looked at each other in that way twins had. Essie and Jack had always been able to have entire conversations without saying a single word out loud. I had the feeling if this was an argument, Jack was about to lose.

Sure enough, ten seconds later, he shook his head. "Fine. We'll all go inside."

But when Essie stomped by me, I caught her by the elbow. "You mind if I have a word with your brother first? I owe him a conversation."

Her head tilted as she considered. "Fine. I'll allow it. But don't be dumb, Brax." Then she tossed a smirk over her shoulder. "Nothing below the belt, Jack. I'm particularly fond of that area." With a wink at me, she sashayed into the house.

I swallowed a chuckle at Jack's stricken expression.

He scrubbed a hand over his face. "She's fucking with me."

"Of course she is," I agreed. We both lowered ourselves to the top step and sat down shoulder to shoulder. "She wanted to piss you off and she knew exactly how to do that. But..." I hesitated. There was no polite way to say *I'm railing your sister every chance I get, and she fucking loves it.*

Jack whipped to face me. "Mom said it was because of a horse. You two got hitched so Essie could ride some horse you own in a competition?"

I nodded slowly. "That's right."

"Why didn't you just sell her the horse? Or make her a part owner?" he asked.

"That's a good question." I rubbed my chest.

"Is it one you have an answer to?"

"No," I said after a long pause, during which I studied the paint peeling off the porch rail like there would be a test on it tomorrow. "I can't say that I do." Not one he would like hearing, at any rate.

Jack grunted at that.

"Essie wanted this," I said. "No one made the choice for her."

He squinted into the distance. "She wanted to marry you, or she wanted to ride?"

I didn't have a good answer to that, either.

"Yeah. That's what I thought." He got to his feet, unfolding his body slowly. It looked lazy, the way he moved. I wasn't fooled. "You made me a promise."

I pushed to stand, too. "We were seventeen. Things were different then. You had a reason, and we both knew it was right. That reason doesn't exist anymore."

"Some things don't change, Brax. I reckon your feelings for Essie are one of them."

He wasn't looking at me when he said this, but once again, I wasn't fooled. Back then, when we were kids, it was easy to think he wasn't paying attention simply because it never seemed like he was. Now I knew better. Jack Price saw everything. It wasn't that he never showed his hand. It was that he never showed he had a hand to begin with. All the time I thought we were playing dice, he was playing poker.

And winning.

I leaned against the porch rail, mirroring his position. "I don't see what that has to do with anything," I said. "As Essie pointed out not ten minutes ago, this isn't 1950. She can file for divorce any time she wants. I won't stop her."

But shit.

I didn't say that out loud, but my face must have said it for me.

He laughed and shook his head. "You poor dumb fuck. You know you can't keep this from her."

"I'm telling you, it doesn't matter," I bit out. "She's an adult. She can make her own choices regardless of how I feel about it."

"Then why haven't you told her yet?" he challenged.

It would be real great if he'd stop asking questions he knew I didn't want to answer.

"Chickenshit. About emotions, of all things. Jesus Christ, man." Jack made a disgusted sound. "I didn't come cross an ocean to punch you in the stomach because you married her. I punched you because you didn't tell her why. When I read Mom's letter, I knew you hadn't told her. Because Mom said it was because of a horse." He snorted. "It was never about the fucking horse. I know that and you know that. The only person who doesn't know that is Essie."

I grunted, which was as much an admission as I would ever give him.

"You have to tell her, Brax," Jack said quietly. "It's the only way she'll stay."

"I know," I said, but that wasn't true at all.

Telling her was the fastest way to make her leave.

FIFTEEN YEARS AGO

. . .

"I LOVE THE SMELL OF PETRICHOR IN THE MORNING," ESSIE said.

She lifted her face to the sky and sniffed the air like a hound dog catching the scent of prey, then flashed me a grin. Proud of herself for using one of her favorite words in combination with a quote from *Apocolypse Now*, the movie we had watched with Jack last weekend. Essie's taste in movies usually trended toward action flicks or romantic comedies, but lately she had been choosing old war movies in a not-so-subtle bid to keep Jack from enlisting in the military when we graduated.

"It's not going to work," I said. I glanced at her through the windshield to gauge her reaction as I leaned into the truck and emptied my backpack of everything but my lunch and water bottle. I lifted the bottle, testing its weight. Full enough to share, I figured. We weren't going far.

"It could work," she argued, immediately connecting the dots of our conversation. We knew each other too well.

I shook my head, slammed the door shut—not because I was mad, but because the old hinge needed convincing—and locked the truck. There was no point in arguing. Essie would do what Essie did. And so would Jack.

"You ready?" I asked, looking over her jeans, tee shirt, and sneakers.

The sneakers gave me pause. We had chosen an easy

out-and-back trail that totaled three miles. Minimal elevation gain but excellent payoff. Still, her shoes weren't known for being grippy and it had rained the night before, leaving everything slick.

"Stop worrying," she said, giving my shoulder a push to get me moving in the direction of the trailhead. "We'll be fine. I've hiked in these before."

"You've walked, you mean."

She rolled her eyes and gave me another encouraging shove. "That's what hiking is, silly."

"All right, let's go," I said. Essie was a competent hiker and she wasn't reckless. She might seem wild and rash to other people, but I knew her better. She took risks, sure, but only with careful thought.

Still, I slowed my pace once we passed the trailhead marker, letting her take the lead and set the pace. It was only polite, since my longer legs gave me an advantage, plus it meant I could keep my eyes on her.

I breathed an unwarranted sigh of relief when we reached the viewpoint. Essie had been right. She was fine. The trail was wet and sometimes slick, but it wasn't hard to safely navigate. And this was our reward. It wasn't the top of a mountain, but the view was nearly as good. The Rocky Mountain range stretched around the outcropping where we stood, pines and aspens giving way to gray peaks, some still patchy with snow.

Essie's cheeks were pink from exertion, her eyes brighter than the sky, her chest rising and falling deeply.

Looking at her made me dizzy in a way the height could never do, stole the air right from my lungs. I had to look away to steady myself.

She spread her arms wide and tilted her face to the sky, letting the wind whip her hair into a frenzy behind her. Her tee shirt tightened around her torso. It felt like torture, but I didn't think it was on purpose. Sometimes, moments like this, where I saw a little too much of her, I suspected it *was* on purpose. Like she was testing me to see if she could make me react like every other boy who couldn't resist her. But right now, I figured she just wanted to feel free. Essie loved the wind.

I took the lead on our way back down. Most of the trail was gently sloped, but there were a few steeper spots. She'd be more likely to fall forward if she slipped going down, and I'd be right there to break her fall.

"You know what, we should skip school tomorrow, too," Essie said behind me. "Say we have food poisoning, and that's why we had to leave school so suddenly today. No one will believe we were only sick for an afternoon."

I turned to face her. "Essie, we are not skipping school tomorrow. We have two weeks left of school. Suck it up, buttercup."

She grimaced. I laughed and took a step backwards.

And the earth crumbled beneath my foot. My other leg buckled and I flailed for something, anything, to hold onto. There was nothing. I was going over the edge and there wasn't a damn thing I could do to stop it.

And then suddenly Essie's face was all I could see, so close it blocked out the sky and the trees. Her blue eyes on mine with all the determination and focus she normally reserved for running barrels. It all happened so fucking fast.

The feeling of falling.

Her face.

My teeth clanking together as my body was forcefully wrenched from one place to another.

A scream.

I was back on solid ground, but Essie was no longer beside me.

"Essie!" I roared her name over the edge, my heart in my stomach. Her body lay flat against the incline, face down, maybe ten feet below where I stood on the edge.

"I'm alive." She lifted her head and slowly moved her hand to push the hair from her face.

I inhaled a shallow breath of air, suddenly aware that my lungs were burning from lack of oxygen. "Jesus fucking Christ, Essie. Don't move. I'll get you."

"No, it's not safe. Stay up there. The ground here feels pretty unstable. It's all scree. If you try to climb down, you're going to slide and all those rocks are going to come right at me. Just give me a second. My foot's wedged in these boulders."

Her prone body wiggled as she carefully pried herself free of the boulders. I nearly died a hundred times over watching her, helpless to do anything, terrified that if I tried, I might send her falling another thousand feet.

"There, I've got it," she called. "Okay, I'm coming up now."

I straight up panicked. "No! Stay there. I'll go for help."

"That could take hours. I'm not going to wait here alone for hours. I can do it."

Fuck. I roughed a hand over my head, tugging at the strands, full of nervous energy I had no release for. "Don't stand up. Crawl, okay?" I struggled to keep my voice calm. The last thing Essie needed was to worry about me falling apart. "Go slow, grab onto anything that looks safe."

She didn't answer, but she stayed on her hands and knees. Her progress was painstakingly slow as she paused between every movement, sometimes sliding back an inch or two on the loose gravel.

"Your phone better be in your pocket when I get up there," she said.

I blinked. "My phone? Are you hurt? I don't have signal out here to call for a rescue. But I'll carry you down if it comes to that."

"My ankle is a little sore, but no, I mean you better not be recording this. I don't need embarrassing video of me crawling up a mountain, covered in dust and mud, for you to show my future husband or whatever."

I stared down at her. "Are you fucking kidding, Essie? This is not the time for jokes."

"Oh, really? When would be a better time, then? After I'm dead?"

"Essie, I swear to fucking god, when you get up here, I'm going to—"

"You're going to what?"

I didn't answer. She was within reach now. I grabbed her by the elbows and hauled her the rest of the way over the ledge. She stumbled into me, her breath erratic. I wrapped my arms around her waist and backed us away from the edge.

She burrowed into me, her body vibrating. We stood there, clinging to each other, her head resting on my chest, tucked under my chin. Her lips pressed against my shirt in a damp kiss, like she was trying to reassure herself with my heartbeat. I breathed in her scent, the vanilla underneath the dirt and sweat. It felt like the first full breath I had taken since she went over the edge.

"You're going to what?" she whispered.

My mind went blank. "Hm?"

"You said, *Essie, I swear to fucking god*," she mimicked, her voice dropping to a deep husk, "*when you get up here, I'm going to*—what? What are you going to do?"

Never let you go.

My arms tightened around her.

I loved her. Fucking hell, I loved her.

"Don't you dare try to spank me," she said. "I'm warning you, I bite."

She laughed shakily. Her body still shivered against mine. She was telling jokes, but she wasn't fine at all.

"It's okay." My voice was hoarse. "You're okay."

She jerked her head back to look me in the eyes. "You almost died." The words were an accusation, her expression fierce.

I remembered the look in her eyes as she grabbed my shirt with all the strength she had in her body. She had saved my life without any consideration that it might cost hers. She'd do it again in a heartbeat. I knew that. Whatever Essie did, she did with her whole heart. That was how she lived. That was how she loved.

Fuck.

I loved her.

And the worst part was, she loved me, too.

23

ESSIE

JACK

Mom wants you to come to dinner tonight.

ESSIE

Brax too?

JACK

Hang on, I'll ask.

Yeah. According to Mom, spouses are a package deal.

ESSIE

Great, my husband and his enormous package will be there. :)

JACK

I hate you.

> Maybe I'll start dating one of your friends. See how you like it.

ESSIE

> You can try. One of them might take pity on you and lower her standards.

I was going to murder my husband and make myself a very happy widow.

My mom, who was aware that my marriage was a sham, sat at the head of the small rectangular dining table. My brother, who was aware that the marriage might be a sham, but its consummation was very real, sat at the foot. Brax and I occupied the chairs between them, facing each other. I wasn't aware of much of anything at all except that Brax kept stroking his socked foot—Mom didn't like shoes being worn inside—against mine.

And I couldn't tell him to stop without informing my mom and my brother that he was doing it in the first place.

I was on edge.

Maybe because I kept having flashbacks to all the times we had sat exactly like this, minus Brax playing footsie with me, so many years ago. Brax had been a staple at our house from fifth grade on and generally ate dinner with us once or twice a week. It went both ways, with me and Jack sometimes staying at Lodestar Ranch for dinner and even spending the night. Looking back, I suspected Jenny, Brax's mom, had done it purposefully to give my mom a break.

Or maybe because Brax kept acting like he was my goddamn husband or something.

He kept his hand on my lower back when we entered the room together. He pulled out my chair so I could sit down. He was entirely too solicitous to my mother.

Okay, maybe that was just because Mom and Brax had always gotten along well. But still. It was annoying.

"Essie, how about you help me clear the salad plates?" Mom suggested. "Brax, will you pull the Guiness pie from the oven? Jack, there's a bottle of red in the cupboard. Could you open it, please?"

We all got to our feet. I stacked the four salad plates and brought them to the sink, where I gave them a quick rinse and put them in the dishwasher. With Jack taking a corkscrew to the red wine, I pulled down four glasses and four dinner plates.

"Let me help you," Brax said, setting the Guiness pie down on a potholder in the center of the table.

"I've got it." I clustered the four glasses on top of the stack of plates. It was a little wobbly, but if I balanced the stack on one forearm, I could—

Brax swept the glasses up by their stems, two in each

of his large hands, and dropped a kiss on the top of my head.

I scowled. "What are you doing? Everyone in this room knows our marriage is fake."

"Practice." He smirked and did it again. "No one is going to believe it's real if you keep glowering like that every time I touch you."

Not every time.

I could think of some very specific times when I did not glower at his touch, and unfortunately, I thought of those times right now.

I shifted, squeezing my thighs together, and my gaze dropped to his mouth.

His beautiful, smirking mouth.

He leaned forward, his lips brushing my ear as he whispered so lowly that only I could hear, "You're wet right now, aren't you, hellion?"

Smug bastard.

I pushed past him with a growl. It would have felt good to drop the stack of plates right on his feet, but I didn't do that. I set a plate in front of each chair. Gently, so he would know he hadn't affected me.

He grinned. I wasn't fooling him at all. And from the way Jack's lips flattened into a grim line, I doubted I was fooling anyone else, either.

"Isn't this nice?" Mom beamed as she served us each a fat wedge of Guiness pie. "Just like old times."

My gaze collided with Brax's like it was pulled there

by a magnet. And the *look* on his face. I sucked in a sharp breath. Hunger and heat and something that edged unbearably close to wistfulness.

"Yeah, just like old times," Jack said, and there was something in his tone that pricked my attention. "Isn't that right, Brax?"

My gaze volleyed between my brother and my fake husband, but whatever Brax felt was hidden behind a bland smile.

"I wouldn't say *exactly* like old times," Brax said. "Some of us are going gray."

Since there wasn't a single thread of silver on Brax's dark head, and my mom was a box-dye devotee, it was obvious who his remark was intended for.

"Braxton," Mom scolded. "You boys are always ribbing each other. Pay him no mind, Jack. It looks distinguished on you. Essie, how are things at the ranch? Any special new clients you're excited about?"

"Oh. Um." I swallowed a bite of pie and took a hasty sip of wine, then wiped my mouth. Brax was back to rubbing his foot against mine under the table and I shot him a narrowed-eye glance. "I'm not training horses right now. All my time at Lodestar is focused on getting Pirate and me ready for the Futurity."

Mom frowned. "What do you mean? A horse can't train eight hours a day. Couldn't you fit in a client or two?"

"I resigned from the apprenticeship. The rules don't

allow current training activities of any kind for non-pro competitors. So." I shoveled a bit of pie into my mouth, hoping that would be the end of it.

Of course it wasn't.

"Oh, Essie, I don't like that. What are you doing for money?" Mom asked, setting down her fork to give me her full attention.

"I have savings. I'm still not paying rent, thanks to my sugar daddy over here." I jerked my head in Brax's direction. "As soon as the competition is over, I'll be back to work—*real* work, not just an apprenticeship. James wants to hire me as a full-time trainer."

"But James is coaching you and Pirate for the competition, isn't she? Don't you have to pay her for that? I can't imagine she comes cheap."

"I get the family discount for Pirate's board and training," Brax cut in. "Once he's bringing in stud fees, Lodestar will get a cut of that. It all evens out in the end."

"And I'm helping out with ranch chores, since I have some extra time on my hands," I said. "So James is coaching me free of charge."

Mom shook her head. "I still don't like it."

"Good news, Mom. You don't *have* to like it." I kept my tone breezy despite my increasing annoyance. "I'm doing it, and I'm fine."

"I know, honey. But I want you to be better than fine.

You worked so hard to get to the top of your sport. I don't understand why you threw it all away."

I took a sip of wine, not trusting myself to speak.

"She didn't throw anything away, Mrs. Price," Brax said with quiet firmness. "All the talent and skill she honed for the last twenty years? She still has that. She took it with her and she's using it now. She and Pirate have a real shot at taking home the championship this November. And that's going to launch her into a career that she's passionate about. I'd say that's better than fine."

The tension was thick. I washed down the sudden ache in my throat with a long swallow of wine. Brax had stood up for me? He hadn't approved of a single decision I'd made since the day he almost died. Or so I had thought.

Was I wrong about that?

"Brax," Mom said, and I felt his leg stiffen against mine. Her expression was so soft as she looked at him. "I told you to call me Cat."

Brax relaxed. "I'll try to remember that."

The smile she gave him was full of affection. "People are going to think it's weird if you call me Mrs. Price. I'm your mother-in-law."

"For now, anyway," Jack said, his smile just as wide as Mom's but not as nice, somehow.

Something was definitely going on between them.

Brax was still nudging my foot with his when he

smirked at Jack. I wondered if he would look so calm and smug if I teased him a little.

I decided to find out.

I ran my foot up the inside of his calf.

He looked at me across the table, one dark eyebrow raised.

I took a sip of wine. "When do you have to go back, Jack? How long do we have you?" My toes rubbed Brax's inner thigh, and he coughed.

"Another four days," Jack said. "But I'll be home again for Christmas."

"Oh, that will be nice," Mom said. "We missed you last year."

"National security doesn't believe in holidays." Jack laughed like it was a joke, but there was a weary edge to his voice. Maybe tomorrow I'd convince him to spend the day with me. Take a trail ride or something.

But right now I had a husband to torture.

I wedged the ball of my foot against Brax's bulge. His eyes narrowed on me as he finished his last bit of pie and then he smiled at my mother. "This is excellent, Cat. Thanks for cooking."

"Anything to get out of dishes," Mom said brightly. "That was an offer, wasn't it?"

"Yes, ma'am—" Brax broke off in a moan that he quickly covered with a coughing fit as I wiggled my toes.

I was all concern. "Are you okay, dear?"

The look he gave me was downright murderous. "Wonderful," he clipped.

Jack stood and started gathering the empty dishes. "I'll help clean up."

It took a moment longer and a few deep breaths before Brax slowly got to his feet.

"You'll pay for that, hellion," he warned quietly, as he joined me at the sink.

"I have no idea what you're talking about," I said blithely. "I am a perfect lady."

With the dishes done, Mom asked Brax and Jack to bring in some firewood and I took the opportunity to use the bathroom. After doing my business and washing my hands, I opened the door only to be greeted by Brax's scowling face.

"What are you—" That was as far as I got before he put a hand to my belly and nudged me back into the cramped bathroom, kicking the door shut behind us and locking it. "Brax!"

"Take a good look at yourself, hellion." He turned me by the shoulders to face the mirror over the sink. "Does that look like the face of a perfect lady?"

I smiled sweetly at our reflection. "It sure does."

"Really? Because I think it's the face of a brat." Behind me, his eyes on mine in the mirror, he traced the line of my jaw with his thumb. "You know what happens to brats, don't you?"

I could barely think straight with his voice rumbling

in my ear and his dick hardening against my ass. "What?" I asked.

"They get exactly what they deserve."

Dear god, I hope so.

My breath stuttered as he flicked open the snap of my jeans and pulled down the zipper with excruciating slowness. I spasmed as he dragged a finger across my lower belly, following the elastic of my underwear.

"I wonder if you're wet," he mused. "You were so mean to me at dinner."

He didn't wait for me to answer, which was a good thing because I couldn't formulate coherent sounds at the moment. His hand slipped into my underwear, his middle finger followed my seam to my entrance, and with no hesitation at all, he pushed inside.

"Wet. I fucking knew it." He sounded almost angry about it and he slipped his finger out again, painting my clit with my wetness. "You get so wet when you're mean, hellion."

My head fell back against his chest on a soft moan.

"Quiet." While one hand played with my pussy, his other wrapped around the base of my throat. He squeezed gently. "I had to sit there at the dinner table with you playing footsie with my dick. I had to make polite *conversation*."

I whimpered and he squeezed again, less gently this time.

"Not a damn sound, hellion," he growled.

I licked my lips, my gaze locked on his in the mirror, and nodded.

His hand cupped my pussy and this time, two fingers slid in. It was a tight fit with my thighs pressed together. I tried to widen my stance but he stopped me. He slowly pumped his fingers in and out. My hips bucked, urging him to move faster, but he refused to be rushed.

"God, you're soaked." He groaned when my inner muscles contracted around his talented fingers. "And you're so close. You want to come so badly, don't you, Essie?"

My lips parted, but he squeezed my throat again. At the reminder, I merely nodded.

He stared at me in the mirror, his eyes darkening as his gaze flicked from my eyes to my damp mouth to my chest, rising and falling with each heavy breath. "Should I let you come? Or should I leave you like this, the way you left me? Aching and frustrated."

My eyes widened as I realized what he thought I deserved and what I thought I deserved might be two very different things.

My hand grabbed his at my throat. I dug my nails in. Our gazes collided in the mirror, his feral, mine desperate. A muscle ticked in his jaw.

"I should leave you like this. But I love to watch you come, and maybe that's what *I* deserve," he said roughly.

His fingers pumped faster. My eyes closed as the pleasure built.

"Eyes open, Essie," he commanded. "Look at us."

He ground the heel of his palm against my clit and sent me flying. My eyes flew open, my fingers digging into his hand on my throat, as waves of pleasure rocked my hips into his hand again and again.

"That's it, honey," he husked, his mouth against my temple. "Just like that. Look how pretty you are when you come."

When the spasms subsided, he gently pulled his hand from my underwear and stepped around me. I slumped against the wall, panting, my jeans still undone, watching through heavy lidded eyes as he washed his hands and dried them on the towel.

He was smirking when he turned to me. "You feeling okay, dear?"

I made an incoherent sound.

He chuckled softly and squatted down so he was eye-level with my belly button. Gently, he tugged up my zipper and fastened the snap. Then he leaned forward and kissed me there, taking a deep breath.

"Come on, then," he said, straightening again. "I can still smell you and it's making me hungry for dessert."

24

BRAX

I came home from work Friday afternoon to find Essie wearing my sweats and standing in front of the fireplace, staring at the row of framed photographs lined up along the mantel. My mom and dad on their wedding day. Me and my mom. My brothers and I on horseback. Essie and I exchanging vows. And the last one...Essie, Jack, and the tip of my index finger.

"You're home early," she said, not turning around.

"Snow is coming down pretty thick," I said. "The storm is supposed to be a gnarly one. Figured it was better to be home than get caught on the road."

She nodded and picked up the photo of our wedding. "Who took this?"

It was a good question, since we hadn't hired a photographer.

"Ben," I told her.

My nephew hadn't been interested in being a groomsman alongside his dad and Zack, and we weren't doing flower girls or a ring bearer. When he'd asked if he could take photos, I'd agreed and not thought about it again until he sent me these.

"He used his phone. Can you believe that?" I asked, coming to stand next to her.

She stared down at the photo a moment longer before placing it back on the mantle. "He did a great job. I had no idea." Her voice sounded odd. Subdued. She gestured to the line of mismatched frames. "It looks nice. Like something a real couple would do."

Aha. There it was.

I wondered how she hadn't figured it out yet. Essie wasn't stupid. My guess was that she simply didn't want to know. That hurt, but not nearly as much as it would if she said those words out loud.

"That's the idea," I said. "If anyone comes over, we should look like a happily married couple, right?"

"Who's going to come over?" she challenged with a lift of her eyebrow. "I think they might notice I'm sleeping in the guestroom."

"You can invite friends over, you know. You should, actually. This is your home, too." When she blinked surprised eyes at me, I smiled. "Anyway, you don't have to sleep in the guestroom. Feel free to come join me in mine. Nude."

She laughed. "Maybe I will. Should I bring this picture you stole from my bedroom? Don't think I didn't notice." She gave me a sardonic look. "We can hang it on the wall right across from the bed. Make Jack watch us—"

A loud pop cut her off and we were plunged into sudden darkness. Essie yelped and groped blindly for me. I grabbed her hand and directed it to the mantel, letting it ground her until her eyes adjusted.

"Stay here. I'll grab the flashlights."

Power outages during storms were common enough that I kept a handful of flashlights and a stockpile of batteries in a kitchen drawer. Since I knew the layout of my home like the back of my hand, the lack of light didn't slow me down. I grabbed two, flicked them both on to make sure the batteries weren't dead, and I was back by her side in less than two minutes.

"Here you go." I handed her one and kept the other for myself. "I'm going to take a quick look outside and see what happened."

She nodded. "Be careful," she said, like a reflex.

I liked it. Three months ago, she would have suggested I drop dead instead.

It was dusk when I opened the door and stepped outside. The snow was already a couple inches deep and more came down in thick, fluffy flakes. Every house on the street was dark. A few other people were out, checking things same as I was, and we waved to each other.

I grabbed an armful of firewood and went back inside. "The whole street is out. Probably a power line down. It could be a while before the power company sends someone to fix it." I kicked the snow from my shoes.

Essie nodded. "They'll want to wait until after the storm. I guess we'll just have to eat all the ice cream before it melts."

I laughed. "Or we could stick it outside."

Essie feigned a shocked gasp.

"All right," I said. "We'll eat the ice cream."

"It's what Mom, Jack, and I always did. Eat the perishables and play cards in front of a fire. Sometimes we'd paint each other's nails if we got really desperate."

"Jack, too?" I asked, even though I suspected I knew the answer. Jack wasn't the kind of man who thought nail polish was a threat to his masculinity.

"Jack, too," Essie confirmed. "He was partial to blue. Like, the shade of cotton candy."

I could see that.

"I'll get the cards," I said. "You get the ice cream."

"Really?"

"Sure. What else are we going to do?" I loosened my tie. "I'll get a fire going and then I'll change out of my work clothes. With the power out, it's going to get chilly in here soon."

"I'll take care of the fire," Essie said. "Go ahead and change."

I took a quick, lukewarm shower and changed into a pair of gray sweatpants, a navy hoodie, and thick wool socks. When I returned, the fire was crackling and the living room was cast in a warm, golden glow. On the coffee table was a tray of hummus, cucumbers, and carrots. I could hear Essie humming in the kitchen.

"Ready?" she asked, glancing up from the bottle of wine she was opening. Her gaze traveled down my gray sweatpants and she licked her lips.

"My eyes are up here, Essie." I held up the deck of playing cards. "I don't think wine is perishable."

She grinned and handed me a glass. "Better safe than sorry. I figured we could eat dinner first, and then have the ice cream for dessert. Like real adults."

I laughed. "Is that what the hummus is? Dinner?"

"It was either that or steak tartare."

"I'm good with hummus."

We took our glasses of wine to the living room and sat cross-legged on the floor.

"Thanks for cooking, dear." I scooped a glob of hummus onto a cucumber slice and popped it in my mouth.

Essie smirked at me. "I *can* actually cook, you know. We should do that sometime. Cook dinner together, I mean."

I damn near swallowed my tongue along with my food. "Really?"

"Yeah. I like trying new recipes, but it's more fun to cook with someone. Mom is a great cook, obviously, but by the time she gets home from the bakery, the last thing she wants to do is cook more food, you know?"

"That makes sense." I took a gulp of wine to slow down my next words. To make them sound less eager than I really was. "Sure, we can do that whenever you want."

She hummed happily and bit into a carrot with a loud snap.

"Speaking of your mom, what was that about at dinner the other night?" I asked. I focused on getting the perfect amount of hummus on my cucumber slice. Maybe if I didn't look directly at her, she wouldn't spook. "She didn't seem to be very happy that you aren't barrel racing anymore. Is she still hung up on you retiring?"

"Oh, that." Essie made an annoyed sound and snapped a carrot stick in half. "She's never been a big fan of change, you know. I mean, she started working at Sweetie Pie when she was sixteen, and she's been there nearly every day since. *Don't fix what ain't broke* is probably her favorite saying ever."

I laughed. How many times had I heard Cat say that exact phrase? Too many to count. "That's true."

"She's worried for me. That's nothing new. She's been worried about Jack and me since the day she peed on a stick. Worried I'd get pregnant. Worried I'd break my neck. But now it's morphed into something different."

I watched her play with her food and took another sip of wine. "What's that?"

"I don't know. Like she's disappointed, maybe?" Her shoulders slumped a little. "Something changed when I turned thirty. People stopped worrying about me doing things too fast and started worrying I would do them too late, or not at all. Things like settle down, get married, have a baby."

"I know the feeling," I said. "Dad has hinted more than once that I was dropping the ball on his dream of having a baseball team worth of grandchildren."

"But at least people think you're a normal thirty-two-year-old, even if you aren't married with kids yet. People have different expectations of men." she said. "No one thinks I'm normal. It's like everyone else got a memo on how adults were expected to behave, and no one told me. I keep disappointing people, and I don't even know what I'm doing wrong. I mean, I'm responsible! I have a good savings account and I even put money in a Roth IRA. I have a job. But I guess none of that matters if you live with your mom or have rainbow hair."

"Or if you retire early from a career when you're still at your peak and pivot to a job where you're a lowly apprentice?" I asked gently.

She groaned. "Mom will be mad about that forever."

"Why did you quit, anyway?" I prodded.

Her chin jerked up. "I didn't quit. I was done."

I smirked a little at her fierce expression. That was my hellion, through and through. "Okay, why were you done?"

"Hm." She looked at the fire, her face thoughtful. "Do you know who Serena Williams is?"

"Best tennis player to ever live? Never heard of her," I deadpanned.

She rolled her eyes. "Okay. Well, you know she wasn't unbeatable, but she was the best. And no one else during her career was ever going to be better, even if they beat her. That's how it was for me in barrel racing. I wasn't Serena Williams. Abigail Bryson was. Sometimes I was ranked number two in the world. The year I retired, I was ranked number three. Sometimes I won against Abby, and that was always fun. Mostly, though, she beat me. And that was fine. Honestly."

The firelight flickered over her face and fuck, she was so pretty sitting there, eating hummus and drinking wine, telling me about herself. It was so quiet in here, without the hum of electricity powering the fridge and heat, the snow muffling the outdoor noises. There was just the sound of crackling fire, and Essie. I hoped the power never came back on.

I had missed this. Our friendship. I had missed this so fucking much.

"The thing is, though, I wasn't getting any better,"

she continued. "I probably could have stayed right where I was for another decade, if I wanted to. Maybe I would eventually become number one in the world, if Abby had a bad year or went on maternity leave or something. But I still wouldn't be better than I was right then. I knew that, and so I didn't actually care if I *ever* got to number one. I had more than fulfilled my dreams, and I dreamed pretty big, as you know. I didn't have anything left to work for. No new goals. I was...bored," she confessed. "I know that sounds ungrateful, but it's true. I wanted a new challenge. I was just...done."

"I don't think that sounds ungrateful," I said, and meant it.

"Well, good. Because I didn't mean it. It's what I say because so many people think that's what I am, anyway. People thought I was selfish for going after my dream, and they thought I was ungrateful for leaving it behind." She paused. "Not my mom, though. She never thought I was selfish, even though sometimes I agreed with the people who said I was. She sure thought I was crazy sometimes, though."

There was a look in her eyes when she spoke of her mom, and of sometimes feeling selfish. Like maybe she really did believe it.

I couldn't take it. I scooped her off the floor and sat down on the couch with her on my lap. "You listen to me, Essie Price. You are not selfish. She followed you to shows because that's what she wanted to do. She did things for you because she was your mom, and that's what parents do. It doesn't mean you owe her your career. You get to live your own life however you see fit, and you don't owe it to anyone to live it for *them*."

She stared at me for a long time, fiddling with the hair at the back of my neck.

"Okay?" I insisted.

She nodded, a little smile playing on those lush lips. "Okay," she said.

"Good. Because now you're going to get the ice cream, and I'm going to deal the cards. What are we playing?"

She shrugged, her blue eyes heating in the glow of the fire. "The only game I know is strip poker."

"Fuck, yes."

The power could stay off forever, for all I cared.

25

ESSIE

Three days later, the bright Colorado sun had melted most of the snow from the roads. But there were still patches here and there in the pastures, especially in the shady spots, and the mountains were completely white past the tree line and would remain so until June, at least. I didn't mind. Colorado winters were beautiful. Crisp and dry and somehow full of both sunshine and snow. I'd take a Colorado winter over a Florida summer any day of the week.

It was Jack's last day in Aspen Springs. He was leaving first thing tomorrow morning for who knows where. Mom was at the bakery until three, which meant I had my twin all to myself for a couple hours. Like I'd hoped, he was spending the day with me at Lodestar Ranch.

Five minutes into our trail ride, I could swear the

stiffness in Jack's shoulders had relaxed an inch. Fresh air and horses. There was no better medicine. With me on Ginger, a pretty chestnut mare, and Jack on Domino, a trusted paint gelding, we took the long way to a small creek that cut through one corner of the ranch property.

We didn't talk much as we went. Jack was quiet by nature and I was a chatter, and rather than meet in the middle, we took turns. I gave him space to be silent for a bit, and then he'd give me space to talk. We had never discussed it, or whose turn was when, or anything like that. It was simply what we did. As natural as breathing.

I took a deep breath as we wound between a copse of pines, inhaling the spicy scent until my nostrils tingled, and I saw Jack's chest rise and fall as he did the same. His shoulders relaxed another inch.

When we came up to the creek, we halted our horses and just *looked*. The creek was full and fast from the recent snow. The field stretched out on either side, a pale fawn color that shimmered in the sunlight. Beyond that rose the snow-peaked Rocky Mountains.

Jack leaned forward, resting his forearm on the saddle horn, and gazed out at the grandeur before us.

He didn't cry. But the look on his face...I wished he would. I wished he would scream and howl and rage and set free whatever made his face twist like that and never let it come back again.

"Do you have to go back so soon?" I asked softly. "Maybe—"

"I have to go back, Essie."

"Why?" I asked, even though I was aware that a soldier couldn't up and leave the Army. And Jack had never once given the impression there was anything he would rather do. But I'd never seen that look on his face before, either.

"Because someone has to. And I'm good at it."

I sighed. "All right. But I want a full two weeks for Christmas. No excuses."

He grinned and shook his head. "Ten days. That's all I can give you."

"I'll take it." My stomach rumbled. "Want to stop here for lunch? The view can't be beat, and I'm dying to see what concoction Ted made for us."

The second I had told Ted we were going for a trail ride, he had insisted on packing us lunch. Ted was a true genius when it came to building sandwiches, so I had the feeling we weren't going to find peanut butter and jelly.

We dismounted and tied Ginger and Domino to a low-slung branch, then found a flat enough boulder along the river bank to make a good seat. The rock was cold as hell under our butts and we both laughed about that.

I was right about the sandwiches. Ted had made us each a six-inch sub stuffed with ham, turkey, provolone, peppers both hot and sweet, shredded lettuce, and mayo.

"Oh, man," Jack moaned around an enormous bite. "This is delicious. What did he name it?"

Ted liked to name his creations. "Homecoming. In your honor, I assume."

Jack's mouth twisted. "There's a saying about that."

"Home is where the heart is?" I suggested.

He shook his head. "You can't go home again."

"I don't like it."

That look was on his face again. "I fucking hate it."

I didn't know what to say after that. I knew not to press. Jack would talk when he was ready—if he was even allowed to, which wasn't very likely. So I did the only thing I could. I scooched closer until our shoulders bumped against each other and I let him be silent for a while.

We finished our sandwiches. There was also a container with four chocolate chip cookies, which I suspected came from James, since Ted wasn't much of a baker. James made a batch every week for the ranch hands.

"So, you really went and married that jackass, huh?" Jack said, indicating that quiet time was over.

I raised a sardonic eyebrow. "If by *that jackass*, you mean your childhood best friend, then yes. Yes, I really went and married him."

Jack paused long enough that I wondered if he had decided to cut talking time short, but then he said quietly, "He was your friend, too."

"Was he?" Damn, that came out more bitter than I intended. "I thought we were at the time. But we couldn't have been that close, right? Because when he decided he was done with me, it came as a huge surprise. We never even had a fight. He just...wasn't my friend anymore. He never even told me why. That's not what real friends do."

Jack took a swig of water and wiped his mouth on the back of his hand. "I'm sure he had his reasons."

"Don't defend him!" I tickled his rib and he laughed, swerving to defend himself. "He might be your best friend, but I'm your twin sister. You have to take my side." I was laughing, too, but I was serious.

"I am *always* on your side," he said in a tone that nearly vibrated with intensity. "No matter what."

"Good. Because at the very least, he should have explained it to me. He should have had the courage to say to my face that we couldn't be friends anymore, and he should have explained why. He owed me that much."

Jack removed his ball cap and roughed a palm over his close-cropped hair. "Well, that's the problem, Essie. He couldn't have told you even if he wanted to."

"What are you talking about?" I stared at my brother in utter confusion. "Why not?"

He paused for a beat, and then another one, twisting the brim of his hat in his hands while my heart twisted in my chest. Finally he looked me square in the eyes.

"Because he made me a promise."

26

ESSIE

rax was already home from work by the time I pulled my SUV into the garage. I glared at his truck parked on the curb, as though it were the source of all my rage, when really it was its owner. Normally I got home a couple hours before him, but he had taken to coming home early on Friday nights, in addition to working from home on Wednesdays.

I found him inside, sprawled on the couch, reading the book Hannah had lent me. I had feelings about that, but I would deal with that later. He was still in jeans, but barefoot, and he had traded his button-down and tie for a gray henley. Perfectly relaxed.

I put a stop to that immediately.

"What did you promise my brother, Brax?" I demanded, hands on hips.

He shot up like the couch was on fire, the book

tumbling from his hands. "Essie, now, wait a minute, okay? Before you go off half-cocked, let me explain."

"That's exactly what I'm telling you to do." I narrowed my eyes as he took a step closer. He froze. "Go on, then. Explain."

He stared at me, his eyes pleading. "I don't...I don't know how."

"You...don't...know...*how*?" I repeated incredulously. "Gee, Brax, it's almost like you didn't have *fifteen fucking years* to contemplate that question." He winced at the venom in my voice. "Tell me what you promised my brother."

He looked away, his jaw ticking. "Essie...fuck." He pinched the bridge of his nose and shook his head, like he was trying to focus his thoughts. "Do you know what the statistics are for Aspen Springs?"

My forehead wrinkled. "What statistics?"

"The statistics for getting out. Towns like Aspen Springs, with maybe two thousand people, in the middle of nowhere? People don't leave here, Essie. And when they do, they don't go far. They go to Fort Collins and Aurora because they can't afford Denver or Boulder on a fast food salary."

"Okay, so? Who wants to leave?"

"*You* do." He threw up his hands, exasperated. "You did. Don't you remember what it was like back then? How badly you wanted to see the world? You wanted to be a rodeo star. The next Charmayne James. Remember?"

"Of course I remember. I was still living that dream until a year ago. I *am* a rodeo star. Girls still ask me to sign their boots when they see me out. I got everything I wanted, but, Brax..." I couldn't believe I had to explain this to him. I thought he understood. "I never wanted to leave Aspen Springs. It's my home. I love it. I was running *toward* my dreams, not away from home."

"I know you love it here. That was the problem. To make those dreams come true, you had to leave some things behind. Like me."

The way he said that, so soft, so aching. Like it broke his heart.

"No." I sucked in a sharp breath. "No. *You* left *me*. That's what happened. We were friends, and then one day, we suddenly weren't. And you never told me why. You..." I shook my head. "You didn't leave Aspen Springs. You didn't even leave Jack. You just left *me*. Why?"

He reached for me but I stepped back, evading his touch. "Please, honey. Try to understand. That day changed everything."

I knew which day he meant. I had always known. But I still didn't know why. "I apologized, Brax. I apologized so many fucking times." My voice cracked, but I forged ahead. "I know it was my fault. I convinced you to skip school. I convinced you to go hiking even though the trail was slick. We shouldn't have been there, and it was my fault we were. It was my fault you almost died—" My eyes squeezed shut, like I could block out the memory.

"Fuck, Essie—" His rough hands cupped my face so gently. "Look at me, honey. It wasn't your fault. I wanted to be there with you. I never blamed you for what happened that day. But I wasn't the one who almost died. *You* went over that cliff, not me."

"Oh." I blinked at him. "Right. I know. I remember. But I wasn't even very hurt. A little bruised, that's all."

His laugh came out strangled. "You saved my life. That's how you fell off that fucking cliff. Do you remember *that*?"

"What was I supposed to do? Stand there and watch you die?" I demanded. I blinked rapidly against the stinging wetness in my eyes.

Because I did remember.

I remembered the split second when he flailed between safety and danger, how he reached for a tree but not for me, like he would rather die than risk taking me with him, how all I could think was *no*. No, I was not going to live in a world without Braxton Hale. There had been no option *but* to save him.

"Here's what I remember," he said quietly. His thumbs gently traced my cheekbones. "I remember the look on your face when you pulled me back from the edge. I remember you put everything you had into hauling me back. You didn't save anything for yourself. I knew...fuck, Essie. I had always been in love with you, but that day, I realized you loved me, too."

"Then why..." My brows pushed together as I worked through what he was trying to tell me. "You pushed me away. You stopped talking to me. Why would you do that if you loved me?"

He dropped his hands from my face. Stepped back. "It had to be that way, Essie. Don't you get it? Us being together was the worst thing that could have happened to you."

"Says who?" I stared at him, an awful feeling twisting in my gut. "Answer me. What promise did you make to my brother that was so important we couldn't be friends anymore?"

He looked at me and shook his head.

"Brax," I said. "Fucking *answer me*."

A muscle popped in his jaw as he turned away, rubbing his chest. "I promised him I wouldn't give you a reason to stay."

My brow furrowed. "I don't understand. Why would he—why would you—"

But Brax didn't stick around to explain. He opened the door and walked through it, shutting it firmly in my face.

I couldn't believe he did that. He just...walked away. In the middle of a conversation.

My stomach twisted and my heart ached. Holy fuck, I was so tired of the men in my life walking away from me. Like how I felt about it didn't matter to them at all, not even a little bit. I was so damn tired of it.

Tired...and *mad*.

My phone buzzed with a voice message from Chloe. "Hey, babe. I'm at the Painted Cat. Janie is working tonight. Say hi, Janie. Come hang out with us!"

I wasn't in the mood to go out. I was in the mood to chase Brax down and force him to have an honest, open conversation with me. But I wasn't going to do that. I wasn't going to chase a man down and beg him to care about me. I would shave my head clean bald before I did that.

Before I could talk myself out of it, I had changed into a sparkly top that showed plenty of cleavage, the jeans that made my ass look phenomenal, and my favorite pair of going-out boots. The next thing I knew, I was down at the Painted Cat, and Janie was serving me my first shot of tequila.

Maybe if I occupied myself with enough bad choices tonight, I wouldn't make the worst one of all. I wouldn't pick up the phone and beg Brax to talk to me.

"Miss Essie Price, as I live and breathe," a deep voice drawled out.

I looked up into the grinning face of Bobby Waters.

"Bobby? What are you doing in Aspen Springs?" Rodeo season was long over, and his home base was Oklahoma.

"Just passing through, darlin'. I forgot this town was yours, or I would have let you know I was here." His gaze travelled down my body, taking the scenic route. "But I sure am glad I found you."

Couldn't say I felt the same. I had never left this man's bed feeling anything but kind of regretful.

I held up my left hand like a shield and wiggled my ring finger. "I'm married," I blurted out.

He grinned, but the edges were sharper this time. "Well, congratulations. Is the lucky man here now?"

I shook my head, feeling irritated at Brax all over again.

"Well, then, there's no reason two old friends can't catch up, is there? What are you having?"

I rolled my lips together, weighing my options. I didn't particularly want to reminisce about old times with Bobby Waters. But a small, petty part of me remembered Brax's reaction when I said his name.

"A beer. Whatever's on tap. Thanks."

Then I sent Brax a pin with my location, and a text.

> Come get your wife before someone else does.

27

BRAX

I broke the speed limit.

I ran the only traffic light in this goddamn town.

If I could have broken the laws of physics, I would have done that, too.

Fucking Essie.

Gravel sprayed in a dusty cloud as I slammed on the brake in front of the Painted Cat. It would have been prudent to take a minute to pull myself together. Maybe take a few deep breaths until my fury dissipated enough that I could see straight.

But I wasn't going to do that.

She had sent me that text to provoke a response, and by god, she was going to face the consequences of that now. Because I was fucking *provoked*.

I yanked open the wooden door and stormed inside. It took a second for me to find her in the dim yellow light, but when I did, my rage only intensified. Because she was standing there in skin-tight jeans and a sparkly top with a plunging neckline, fucking *smiling* up at a man who was aiming his own smile back at her chest.

Not just any man.

Bobby Waters.

How many times had I heard her name coupled with his on rodeo gossip sites? Too fucking many. It had killed me every time. Not because I had anything against the guy. I barely knew him. But it had happened often enough that I began to wonder if this asshole intended to stick around permanently. That maybe she might be serious about him.

A mistake, she had called him. Well, she was fucking right about that. And she was about to find out just how much of a mistake he was.

I was barely aware of moving people aside as I strode toward my wife. She caught sight of me and for a brief moment she looked like she had regrets. But it was too late for that. She nodded like she was paying attention to what Bobby was saying, but her gaze never left mine. Something he might have noticed if he had bothered to look up from her chest for a second.

I got right between them like he wasn't there and took hold of her elbow. "We're leaving."

She stepped back. "No. I want to dance."

"We're not dancing," I said.

"I didn't ask you." She tipped her glass to her lips and a flash of blue glinted. Her wedding ring. She hadn't taken it off.

Something settled inside me. Relief, maybe. But the adrenaline still pumping through my veins demanded a release. She started this fucking game, but it was one I was more than willing to play.

"You'll dance with me, won't you, Bobby?" she asked, smiling up at him.

Bobby glanced warily at me. "Uh—"

"You know, I always took you for a man who enjoyed having two unbroken legs," I said conversationally. "Was I wrong about that?"

He didn't need to think long about that. "I think this isn't something I need to be in the middle of." He tipped his hat to Essie. "Ma'am."

She rolled her eyes as he disappeared into the throng. "Really? Violence isn't the answer, Brax."

"Then don't pose questions where violence is the only reasonable choice, hellion. Now, get your purse. We're leaving."

"We are *not* leaving." She slammed her glass onto the bar top. Her dark hair swirled around her shoulders from the motion. "I want to dance."

I glanced around. No one danced at the Painted Cat, despite the music blaring over the speakers. People came here to drink and find someone to bring home. That was all. "This isn't a honkytonk, Essie."

But she ignored me, looped her arms around my neck, and tipped her head back to look at me. Her cheeks were flushed pink, her eyes sparkling. So fucking pretty. "Don't you want to dance with your wife, Brax?" she asked in that husky voice of hers that went straight to my dick.

"I don't know how," I admitted.

She laughed softly against my neck. "Don't worry, baby. I'll do all the work."

Fuck, I liked that, her calling me baby. I was such a sucker for this woman, even when I was pissed as hell. My hands settled on her hips. She pushed her body to mine, pelvis to pelvis, chest to chest. She gyrated her hips in time to the old Guns N Roses song playing and turned us in a slow, lazy circle.

There was something so intimate about this. Our dance. My fury. Her teasing. All of our emotions on display right out in the open for people to see and interpret however they wanted to. I never did this. My past relationships with women—the handful I'd had, all lasting less than a year—had been even-keeled, even sedate. Maybe we'd hold hands in public, but nothing more than that. I wasn't one for public displays, either of affection or anger.

But Essie wore her emotions like a second skin.

And I didn't care who was watching. All I cared

about was my wife's body pressed against mine with a look in her eyes that promised more.

"Is this so bad?" she asked, her breath sliding across my throat.

"No," I grunted out. Having my wife's body grind against me when my blood was already hot wasn't what I would call *bad*. Risky, maybe. This place had a filthy bathroom, and I had half a mind to drag her into it. As the last notes died out, I said, "*Now* we're leaving."

"But I'm having fun," she pouted, her bottom lip jutting out in a way I couldn't resist.

"This fucking mouth." I dragged my thumb down her lower lip. "I want to see this red lipstick smeared all over my cock, and it's either going to happen here or at home. Your choice. And, hellion?" I leaned down so the tips of our noses almost brushed. "You are in so much trouble, honey."

She blinked rapidly. And then she grabbed her purse.

I HAD SEEN ESSIE BE A LOT OF THINGS.

Happy, for example. I loved seeing her happy. Irritated, at me more often than not. Focused, before a big race, when the only thing on her mind was the horse beneath her and the barrels in front of her.

But I had never seen her nervous.

Until now.

She flitted around the house, putting things away, babbling. It was cute.

But being cute wasn't going to save her.

I followed her into her bedroom.

"Essie," I said.

She froze and stared at me with wide blue eyes.

"Come here, Essie." My tone was no less commanding for its softness.

Head tilted, she studied me, gaze assessing. I wondered if she'd refuse, and what I'd do about it. It might be fun to find out. But she didn't refuse, despite the hint of trepidation in the way her fingers fidgeted by her sides as she came toward me.

We were nearly toe-to-toe when she stopped. "What?" she asked, all innocence, as if she truly had no clue what her text had done to me. She knew, though. She fucking *knew*.

I traced the shell of her ear as I tucked a strand of hair behind it. Then I leaned down to whisper, "You've been bad, hellion. So fucking naughty. Letting other men think they have a shot with what's mine. Flirting with them while I watched. You wanted to make me angry? You wanted me jealous?"

A shivery exhale escaped her, and she grabbed my biceps like she needed the support to keep from sliding to the ground.

I nipped her earlobe, and she gasped. "Well, congratulations, honey. It worked. Now take off your clothes and get on your fucking knees."

For a moment, she didn't move. Just breathed ragged little breaths that made me even more desperate.

Then she let go of my arms and took a step back, then another, her gaze never wavering from mine. Her shirt went first, followed by those goddamn jeans, leaving her standing there in nothing but tiny scraps of black lace.

I flipped open the snap of my jeans and unzipped. "Everything," I said as I took my dick out, thick and hard and pulsing with need. She watched me stroke myself as she shimmied out of her bra and underwear, a pink flush darkening her cheekbones.

Then with a little smirk, she dropped to her knees.

I groaned at the sight of my beautiful hellion, kneeling so prim and proper with her thighs squeezed together, her hands folded demurely on her lap. But there was nothing demure about the look in her eyes. The way she stared at my dick was fucking carnal.

"Suck me," I ordered.

Her blue eyes flicked up at me from beneath her thick, dark eyelashes. "Oh, no," she murmured as she ran her palm under the length of my dick, guiding it to her luscious mouth. "What a horrible punishment."

I took a step back.

She frowned. "Why—"

"Beg me."

Her gaze went to mine. "You want me to beg you to suck your cock?" she said in utter disbelief. I could see her point, considering how talented she was with her mouth.

"Tell me how much you want it." When she kept staring at me, I started to turn away, my jaw clenched so hard it was lucky I didn't crack my teeth, because saying no when her mouth was this close to my dick? Fucking agony. "Suit yourself."

Her hands shot to my hips, holding me in place. "Wait," she whispered. She licked her lips. "Please, baby. Please let me suck your cock. I'll make you feel so good, I promise." There was a hungry desperation in her voice that had a bead of precum leak from my dick.

"Fuck," I hissed. "Yes. Open your mouth, honey."

She took me into her mouth with a hard suck. My eyes damn near rolled to the back of my head. She hummed, the sound vibrating against my dick.

And then proceeded to give me the best blow job of my fucking life. Her mouth was so hot, so wet, so greedy, that I could barely hold myself together. Red lipstick painted my length, her mouth making a mess of my dick, my dick making a mess of her mouth. She brought me right to the edge in less than two minutes.

"Stop," I gritted out.

My dick still deep in her mouth, she narrowed her eyes at me. I might be giving the orders, but with her hands on my balls, my cock in her mouth, she was the one with all the power. The only reason I was the one in control was because she allowed me to be.

With a whine, she released me. "But I want—"

My eyebrows arched, I stepped around her and headed to the bathroom. "Stay where you are. On your knees."

I didn't look behind me to see what she would do with that command. Either way, we'd have some fun.

She was still there when I returned with a damp washcloth.

"You made a mess, hellion." I tossed the washcloth into her lap. "Clean me up."

"Yes, sir," she said, lifting the cloth, but I stopped her, capturing her chin between my thumb and index finger and tilting her face to look at me.

"Not sir," I corrected. "Husband."

Those dark blue eyes of hers didn't leave mine for a second, even as I felt the movement of her throat as she swallowed hard. "Yes, *husband*."

And then she cleaned her red lipstick off my cock with gentle, thorough strokes. After, she flipped the washcloth over and wiped her mouth, leaving it a rosy pink.

My cock ached with frustration at being denied an orgasm. Was I punishing her, or punishing myself? "Get on the bed. Face down. Ass up."

She crawled to the center of the bed. It was a damn

fine view, but she wasn't where I wanted her. After shucking my clothes, I grabbed her hips and tugged her back to the edge. I stood behind her and ran my palms over the rounded contours of her backside, then slipped between her thighs. I groaned at what I found there.

"You're soaked, hellion." I slid my fingers up her seam, spreading her wetness as I went. Whimpering, she pushed back against my hand. Immediately I withdrew. She looked at me over her shoulder, frowning. "You've been bad, Essie. Letting another man think he could have this. What should I do about it?"

Her eyes were dark and desperate as she met my gaze. "Spank me."

My palm came down on the silky globe of her ass with a resounding crack. Once, twice, three times. She cried out, a sound of mingled pleasure and pain, and dropped her forehead to the mattress, twisting the quilt in her fists.

I kissed the red bloom, felt the heat of it against my lips. "You won't do that again, will you? You won't make another man think he can take what's mine." When she hesitated a little too long, I nipped at her silky skin. "Hellion," I warned.

"I won't," she said, but I heard the lie of it in her voice. She would. She liked this game too much to resist.

But I rewarded her anyway. Because I liked it, too.

I flipped her over and pushed her knees wide. Her pussy was pink and swollen from arousal, glistening with wetness. I bent down and gave her clit one hard suck. Her hips lifted on a hoarse cry. She was so close. It would only take a second and she'd come. Another lick, another suck. And fuck, I wanted it as badly as she did.

But I didn't fold.

I straightened despite her protests, despite how much I wanted to bury my mouth in her sweet pussy. I dragged my aching cock through her wetness and teased her entrance. Her hips tilted.

"Please," she moaned.

"Please what?" I asked.

"Please…" Her eyes darted back and forth in confusion. "Please fuck me?"

"Please fuck me, *husband*." I growled the correction. "That's what you call me. Me, and no one else. Not fucking ever, do you understand? I belong to you. I've *always* belonged to you." I caught her hand and dragged it to my chest. To my heart, and the tattoo that claimed it. "This is your mouth, Essie. Your kiss. The one you put there the day you went over the cliff. I have always kept you right here on my heart."

"Brax," she whispered.

"I can't be satisfied with anything less than everything. Not when it comes to you. Back then, I knew we couldn't keep on like nothing had changed, because *everything* had changed. If I didn't walk away from you then, I never would have. I would have tied you to me the first chance I got. I'd do it now, if you let me. Fill you up again and again with my cum until your belly is round with our baby."

I splayed my palm beneath her belly button, imagining it. Craving it. "All you ever had to do is just say when."

28

ESSIE

All this time.

All this fucking time.

What was I supposed to do with that information? I couldn't process it. Couldn't begin to understand what it meant for us then, and what it meant for us now. His chest heaved as he watched me, waiting, his expression a little unsure. My body was strung taut, demanding the release he had repeatedly denied me, and I…I couldn't think. Only feel.

My fingertips traced the familiar lines of the tattoo. The sharp peaks of the cupid's bow. The full lower lip that dipped into a pout. My mouth. My kiss.

On this man.

My god, this man. My best friend. My husband. I was so deeply in love with him that I couldn't find the begin-ning or the end of it. It had simply always been a part of me, and even when I tried to cut him out, I hadn't been able to.

And now I knew that I had been a part of him, too.

All this fucking time.

"Please fuck me, husband." It was half command, half plea.

With a groan of relief, he ran the fat crown of his dick up and down my slit, pressing it hard against my clit with each pass. Teasing me until I was soaking wet again. Pushing in an inch, both of us watching my body stretch for him, before pulling it back out.

My desperation grew. "*Please*, Brax. I can't take any more."

He chuckled darkly. "Yes, you can."

Sweat glistened on his forehead and a muscle ticked in his jaw. I wasn't the only one he was torturing. That might have made me feel better, if I wasn't out of my damn mind with lust.

"You want me to fuck you, wife?" he rasped.

"Yes," I begged.

For a moment, I thought he might refuse me again and I would be forced to murder him. Shoot flames out of my eyeballs and incinerate him on the spot, until there was nothing left but a pile of ash.

Maybe he sensed that I had really and truly come to the end of my rope, because this time he slid inside me all the way to the hilt, until his pelvis met mine.

And then he moved. Slowly.

So fucking slowly.

Apparently, he wasn't done torturing me, after all.

I could feel every part of him stuffed inside of me. Every ridge, every vein, every time he pulsed when I squeezed my internal muscles around his thick cock. The slow, relentless thrusts turned me wild. I wrapped my legs around his hips, dug my heels into his ass. Scratched my nails down his veined forearms.

On and on, the pressure built.

I lifted my hips to meet his thrusts, trying to convince him to go faster. He responded and snapped his hips forward faster and harder. Kissed me hard on the mouth. His hips slammed roughly against mine with a slapping noise before he eased off again, returning to the slow, deep thrusts.

"Brax!" I sobbed. "Please."

His hips stilled, his chest heaving, perspiration dotting his muscular torso. His eyes found mine with a laser-like intensity that felt magnetic. I couldn't look away if I wanted to.

I didn't want to. I never wanted to.

"Tell me you're mine, Essie." He bent forward, capturing my left hand. His thumb rubbed the metal band. "Say it."

I didn't hesitate, even though it hurt to say it out loud. "I'm yours. Always yours."

Satisfaction flared in his blue eyes, and finally he let go. One hand slipped between our bodies to find my clit and he rubbed hard as he fucked me hard enough to make the bedposts scrape against the wooden floor with every thrust of his hips.

"Mine," he said roughly as we fell apart in each other's arms and he spilled inside me.

It hurt how true that was. It hurt even more that he had always *known* it was true. I was his, now. I was his, way back then.

That was why he had left.

And that hurt most of all.

I SLEPT. IT HAD BEEN AN EMOTIONAL ROLLERCOASTER OF A day, and that combined with the epic orgasm had wrung me out. The second Brax tucked me up against his hard, warm body and pulled the quilt up over us, I was dead to the world.

He was still there when I opened my eyes to darkness. It was the first time we had spent the whole night together. Usually, we started the night on the couch and ended up in his bed, before I would eventually untangle myself from his arms and go back to the guestroom.

I lay there for a moment, listening to his quiet snores. It was too dark to see, but my fingers found their way to the tattoo on his chest just the same. I traced it there, in the darkness, my heart doing uncomfortable things in my chest.

All this time.

With a sigh, I slid out of the bed, careful not to disturb him. It was Saturday, the one day we both had off. My body was so attuned to rising early that I woke up at 5 a.m. every day of the week, whether I had to work or not. Of course, on my days off, I simply rolled over and went back to sleep. I had the feeling that wasn't going to be possible today.

My brain was wide awake.

I pulled on Brax's sweats that I had commandeered and headed to the kitchen to make coffee. I wasn't hungry yet, so I wrapped a throw blanket around my shoulders, shoved my bare feet into shearling slippers, and took my coffee onto the porch to greet the sunrise and sort out my messy mind.

The sky was a grayish purple, still dark enough that a few stars still twinkled. I didn't know any constellations except the Big Dipper, because it was obvious, and Orion's Belt, because it looked like an upside-down frying pan, but I loved to look at the stars. When I was a kid, I couldn't wrap my mind around the fact that they were always there, regardless of whether I could see them or not.

Love was supposed to be like that. Immutable and true even when you couldn't see it.

But I was still that child staring at the blue sky, searching for proof.

It had been there all along. The tattoo. My kiss on his heart. And he had hidden it from me. He had hidden his heart from me. It felt like a betrayal, but maybe one that neither of us could have understood at the time.

The door opened, and Brax stepped out, looking adorably rumpled.

"Hey." His voice was gravelly from sleep. "Is there space for me on that swing?"

Silently, I scooched over a couple inches and opened the blanket. He sat down, then rearranged my body so I was facing him sideways, my legs draped over his lap, the blanket wrapped around us both.

"You didn't want coffee?" I asked, noting the lack of mug in his hands.

He shook his head. "I didn't know where you were. If you had gone to Lodestar without saying goodbye, or—" He broke off and shrugged.

His feet were bare, I realized. It was twenty-three degrees out here and he was fucking barefoot. My chest ached as I realized his first thoughts had been of me this morning, that he had been in such a hurry to find me that he hadn't stopped to take care of himself first.

I pulled off my slippers and dropped them at his feet. "Here. They'll be tight on you, but it's better than nothing."

"You'll be cold," he protested.

"I have the blanket. I'm fine." I was already tucking my toes into the flannel.

He hesitated. "Essie—"

That's when I lost my shit.

"Put your goddamn feet in the goddamn slippers, Brax," I said softly.

It might have been the quiet that tipped him off. I was never quiet. He eyed me warily as he shoved his feet into the slippers.

"I am an adult. I have been in charge of my own feet for at least twenty-eight years now. The only person who gets to decide if my feet are too cold is *me*. Do you understand?" I kept my voice pleasant, but inside I was seething.

"Then isn't that the same for me, too?" he asked reasonably. "I get to decide for myself."

"No, Brax. You don't. Because you're a jackass who would freeze his own feet off rather than take something from me that I am freely offering, because you don't have any faith in my ability to take care of myself. Therefore, you forfeit all slipper-decision autonomy until you can pull your head out of your ass." I blew on my coffee, sending the steam curling into his face.

He paused. "This isn't really about the slippers, is it?"

"No," I said. "It's not."

He sighed and scrubbed a hand over his eyes, wiping away the last vestiges of sleep. Silently, I handed him the mug. He took a sip, then handed it back to me.

"Come on, Essie. What would you have done back then if I had told you I was in love with you? We were seventeen. We were way too young to handle how we felt about each other. Your mom was right about that. That kind of love, at that age? It takes over your brain. Overrides all common sense."

I squinted at him in the shadows. My mom made no secret of the fact that her greatest fear was that I'd end up a teen mom like her. "Is that what this is about? My mom? Because I did, in fact, lose my virginity my senior year of high school. And *you* lost yours the year before."

To Valerie Kensey, a girl Brax had dated for six months. Damn, I had hated her. Now she taught fifth grade at the local elementary school and had a husband and two sweet little girls. She was actually pretty nice. But back then, she had something I couldn't admit I wanted, and I hated her for it.

"Fucking Connor McRae," Brax muttered, and it occurred to me that he had similar thoughts of the boys I had dated.

"He's nice," I said sweetly, enjoying my husband's caveman side. "I saw him at the grocery store the other day. He's the manager now, you know."

Brax glared at me.

I gave him another sip of coffee. "My point is that there weren't any unwanted pregnancies for either of us, as far as I know." I gave him a questioning look, and he nodded. "So if you're going to sit here and tell me you made that promise to my brother because you were worried you'd knock me up, I'm going to remind you that condoms are a thing, something you were aware of even back then."

"It wasn't about sex. Not entirely, anyway. It was *you*." His hands squeezed my thighs under the blanket. "Think about it. If we had gotten together that summer, would you still have travelled all over the country for barrel racing competitions? Or would you have been more selective, choosing smaller, local rodeos so you could stay close to me?"

I frowned. The pull to be near him had been so strong back then. If we had been *together*? With kissing and promises and touching each other naked? "I...I don't know."

"And then we would have kept dating through our senior year," he continued. "Because what we had wasn't a short-term thing, and I knew it even then. What then? Would you have put your dreams on hold a little longer? Compete part-time so you could follow me to college?"

"I don't know," I said again.

He was relentless. "By the time I graduated college, we would have been together for five years. What would we have done then? Marriage? Babies? That's what people do after five years together. What would have happened to your dreams?"

"*I don't know.*" I blew out a frustrated sigh. "That's a whole lot of questions I don't have answers for because

I'm not omnipotent. The thing is, neither are you. But you still tried to answer those questions for the both of us. That's not fair. We should have worked through those issues together."

"I didn't want to be the thing that held you back," he said quietly. "The way you pulled me from the cliff? I wanted to do that for you. I couldn't stand the thought of you giving up *anything* to be with me, much less everything."

"Brax, I—" I leaned over and carefully set my mug on the porch railing, then shifted so I was fully straddling his lap. With my hands on either side of his face, I held his gaze. "That's something we need to decide *together*. This marriage won't work otherwise. If we're in it, we have to be in it *together*. There's no other way."

He blinked slowly. "What—what did you say?"

"I said we need to decide together," I repeated.

"No, the other part."

I wrinkled my nose. "This relationship won't work otherwise?"

"You said marriage." His throat worked as he stared at me. "Does that mean this is real?"

"Of course it's real," I said tartly, like my insides weren't turning to mush from the heartbreaking vulnerability in his eyes. I took my hands from his face and folded them behind his neck. "A marriage is a legally binding contract, remember?"

"Essie." He touched his forehead to mine. "I don't

mean on paper. I mean in your heart. Is it a real marriage in your heart?"

I closed my eyes. "Maybe it always was."

Abruptly, Brax pushed to his feet, with me clinging to him like a monkey.

"Brax!" I laughed. "What are you doing?"

"Taking you inside. I want to make love to my wife."

29

BRAX

We took two days to haul Pirate from Aspen Springs to Oklahoma City, where the National Reining Futurity Championships were held. James and Adam elected to fly to minimize the time they spent away from Ben. Ben, of course, was more upset about missing the show than missing his dad and James. I had the feeling his granddad would spoil him rotten while we were away.

I had never been all that fond of road trips, but now I saw the appeal. Six hours of nothing but open road, the occasional patch of red brake lights, and uninterrupted time with Essie. I had never had this much time with her, awake and out of bed, and I was fucking greedy for it.

We talked about Pirate, and my plans for reviving the breeding program at Lodestar Ranch, if we could find someone to run it. We talked about Essie's mom, and how hard she worked. We talked about Zack, and his slow road to recovery. We gossiped about our friends, and the people we had grown up with, and random people we saw at the hotel diner.

There was nothing special about any of it, and that's what made it so special. The conversation wasn't heavy. It wasn't loaded with double meanings and old pains. Two months ago, this wouldn't have been possible.

Now, it felt like a marriage.

A *real* marriage.

We stopped in Dalmart, Texas, for the night, at a place designed for people traveling with horses. It was slightly more than halfway to Oklahoma City. I never slept well in strange beds, but with Essie's body curled against mine in a perfect fit, it felt like home.

At some point during the night, I half-woke with my dick hard and Essie's fingers tracing the tattoo on my chest. Without opening my eyes, I rolled her sleep-warm body—still naked from the evening's earlier activities—on top of mine and slid inside her. She hummed softly and pressed a kiss to my neck. We had slow, sleepy sex and then promptly fell asleep again exactly as we were, Essie draped over my torso, my dick still inside her.

Before the sun rose, we woke up and did it all over again.

"You know what we need," I said, as she slowly

merged us onto the highway for the final leg of our journey.

She barely glanced at me, all her attention focused on the road. "What?"

"A honeymoon."

That got her attention. "Really?"

I couldn't blame her for being surprised. Honeymoons weren't common in Aspen Springs. Most people couldn't afford the vacation, moneywise or time-wise. Ranch work didn't stop for births, deaths, or weddings.

"What made you think of a honeymoon?" she asked.

"This." I gestured to her and me and the truck. "I like it. No annoying brothers. No meddlesome friends. Just you and me, making up for lost time. I think we deserve that, don't you?"

"Yes." She flashed me a small, quick smile. "Could you take the time off?"

"I could, with a little planning. January and April are out because I do a lot of tax work then. I figure summer wouldn't be great, either, because you'll want to be showing and training." I wanted her to know I under-stood this. That her career was just as important as mine.

I had meant what I said, when I told her I didn't want her to give up anything for me. I still felt that way about it. Back then, she couldn't have the life she wanted, unless I wasn't in it. I was always the thing that held her back, even when she didn't understand it.

Things were different now. Some dreams she had already accomplished. Other dreams had grown and changed. But Essie living exactly the life she wanted to live, that was as important to me as ever.

I couldn't be something holding her back. I wanted to give her everything.

She checked her mirrors and nibbled her lip, thinking. "Spring, then?"

"Spring," I agreed.

And had the pleasure of making my wife smile.

THE THING THAT SEPARATED PRO AND NON-PRO competitors in the Level 4 futurity championship wasn't skill. Some of these non-pros—riders who owned the horse themselves rather than being paid to ride by the owner—devoted their entire lives to the sport of reining and competed in the arena year after year. Many of them were quarter horse breeders by trade.

Their spins were just as compact as the pros. Their sliding stops every bit as fancy. Essie and Pirate had their work cut out for them, a fact I was very much aware of as I stared down at the dirt arena, clenching and unclenching the fairgrounds map in my fist until it was damp with my sweat.

She wasn't outmatched, though. Neither was Pirate. But it would be a real fight.

A hard knot of anticipation twisted my stomach as I sat through the next two riders. They were good. Very fucking good. But Essie was better, and I didn't think it was the fact that I was head-over-heels in love with that woman that made me think so.

"Pirate has them all beat," Adam said next to me. He sprawled on the bench, his long legs spread out in front of him and crossed at the ankle. Looking like he didn't have a care in the world.

As opposed to me, hunched over my knees, both legs bouncing with nerves.

Every competition mattered, but so long as the horse and rider made it through healthy and safe, no single ride could ruin a career. There was always another chance to win, another ribbon to earn. The Futurity Championship was no different. It could make Essie's career, but it couldn't break it.

But somehow, I couldn't convince myself of that today.

Maybe it was that mean little voice in my head that whispered Essie had married me to be here today, and if she lost, she might have regrets about that.

Big regrets.

I could accept losing. But I couldn't accept that.

"Our next competitor is Ms. Essie Price on Pirate," the announcer's voice boomed over the speakers.

"Here we go," Adam said, straightening in his seat.

I took a breath, trying to calm the storm inside my chest, but it was impossible. I couldn't have been more nervous if it was me out there on Pirate.

The crowd cheered as Essie entered the arena on Pirate. I didn't think it was my imagination that the applause was louder and longer than for previous competitors. I had lost count of the number of girls who had caught sight of Essie as we explored the fairgrounds and begged for an autograph or a picture. It was incredible to witness her in her element, and damned humbling to be the lucky bastard who got to take the photos.

Fuck, she was beautiful, sitting so tall and proud on Pirate. They made a gorgeous pair. The white patches of Pirate's coat gleamed like moonlight against the midnight-black patches. The competition was more about skill than looks, but looks sure didn't hurt, and Pirate was truly something special to look at.

But then they began, and all I could see was *her*.

My wife.

Her dark hair lifted as they loped around the ring, revealing a glimpse of rainbow. She looked determined, but more than that, she looked at ease. Like she was having the ride of her life. All her hard work, all the hours spent in Pirate's saddle, all the hours spent out of the saddle, building their bond? It all led to this moment, where it didn't look like work at all.

It looked like joy.

The audience seemed to know they were witnessing something special. Watching Essie and Pirate together was like watching a dance. They moved in perfect synchrony, a fluid blend of strength and grace that drew a smattering of applause every time they executed a move. Essie's body melded seamlessly with Pirate's as she guided him through circles and flying lead changes with nearly invisible cues.

They were a team. A partnership.

As Essie and Pirate executed perfect spins, the crowd cheered. And then it was time for the showstopper, the move that could be dangerous but never failed to draw gasps from the crowd.

My girl didn't even hesitate. She nudged Pirate into a lope and then a gallop before bringing him to an abrupt halt in the center of the ring. Pirate did exactly what he was supposed to, dropping his hindquarters on the ground and with his legs stretched out in front of him in a spray of golden sand. After a pause, the stallion was back on his feet and doing a rapid rollback.

Holy shit.

It was perfect.

And Essie? Essie was magnificent.

The crowd erupted into cheers and applause that only got louder as the judges' score flashed on the screen, putting Essie and Pirate in first place. Essie leaned down and gave Pirate an enthusiastic pat on the neck. And then she looked up to the stands and waved to the crowd, turning this way and that like she was looking for something.

For some*one*.

I was on my feet, cheering and whistling like everyone else, but my calls were swallowed up by the raucous crowd.

But still, she found me.

Her gaze hit mine like it was pulled there by a tractor beam.

She grinned, happiness radiating from her like a rainbow.

"I'm going down there." I was already making my way down the stands when I tossed the words over my shoulder.

"There are still two more riders," Adam reminded me.

But I didn't care. Even if both competitors scored higher than Essie and Pirate, that would put them in third place. That ride deserved to be celebrated, no matter how points shook out in the end.

Apparently, James agreed, because I found Essie and James wrapped in a hug, swaying side to side as they laughed giddily.

"Brax!" Essie pulled free of James and rushed into my open arms.

I picked her up, lifting her off her toes, and then set her back down again. "Congratulations, hellion," I murmured against her hair. "That was a hell of a ride."

"Right? Pirate was amazing!" Her eyes sparkled with joy and adrenaline.

"*You* were amazing," I said, rubbing a bit of dust from her cheekbone with my thumb.

She gave me an impish look beneath her lashes. "I was, wasn't I? And you know, even if we take third, that's still a hefty chunk of cash for Mom to buy Sweetie Pie. Plus, Pirate is still young. He's only going to get better from here. He's going to be a brilliant sire, I just know it."

I shouldn't have been surprised that Essie was thinking about how her ride could benefit her mom and Lodestar Ranch right now, and really, I guess I wasn't. I was in awe of her and her big, beautiful heart, but surprised? Nah.

That was Essie, through and through. She wasn't selfless, and she wasn't a pushover. But she cared. She cared so damn much.

God, I was so in love with this woman.

"Essie, you did good," Adam said, coming up behind us.

"Thank you," she said. "We couldn't have done it without James. I don't know if anyone else could have brought Pirate along as fast as she did. When you think about where he was six months ago, it's honestly a miracle."

"No miracle," Adam said, looking at James with that way he had. Like she hung the moon, and the sun and stars to boot. "Just talent and hard work."

"Maybe," James said, even though her cheeks turned pink from Adam's praise. "But I think a lot of his success today was you, Essie. The bond you share…it's special. I think you know that. He wanted to win for you."

Essie's eyes looked suspiciously shiny as she nodded rapidly.

We were so busy feeling good that we almost missed the announcement.

"And in first place, Essie Price on Pirate! Winners, please come to the arena for your victory lap."

Essie stared at me with wide, shocked eyes. And then the most gorgeous smile split her face from ear to ear.

My wife had just made another dream come true. And there was nowhere I would rather be than by her side when it happened.

30

ESSIE

Everyone decided to meet up at the Painted Cat to celebrate the day we got home to Aspen Springs. James and Adam arrived with Zack on his crutches. Chloe and Hannah were there, as well. Janie had the night off, so for once she got to drink with us instead of serving us.

But she still snuck behind the bar to make me a special cocktail. "It's a black and white, in honor of Pirate."

She poured white rum, coconut rum, simple syrup, and cream over ice, then topped it with cocoa-infused dark rum. The result was a stunning black-and-white layered drink that made us all gasp in appreciation.

It tasted good, too.

"Yum." I wiped the froth from my upper lip.

Brax took a sip from my glass and his eyebrows shot up. "If you drink more than one of these, I'll have to carry you out. Not that I'm opposed to that."

I laughed. "This is going to be my only drink tonight. Five a.m. comes early."

Brax smirked in the knowledge that he could sleep in until eight. "Mind if I go keep Zack company?"

I glanced past him to where Zack was sitting sideways in a booth, his cast stretched out on the bench. "He looks like he could use some cheering up."

Brax ordered two beers, pecked me on the lips, and nodded to my friends. "Ladies."

"Hm," James said thoughtfully, and I realized she was watching me.

And I was watching him.

I blushed. Seriously blushed. There wasn't much that could embarrass me, but apparently, swooning over my husband was one of those things. "What?" I said defensively. "He's got a nice ass."

"Oh, for sure," James agreed. "But I'm more interested in that sweet little kiss he gave you. It sure didn't look like a kiss between mortal enemies. It didn't look like it was for show, either. The competition is over, anyway. What would be the point?"

"Whatever," I mumbled into my glass.

James considered me with her head tilted. "Anything you want to share with me, Essie?"

"Fine." I took a long swallow of my drink and let the alcohol give me courage. "Maybe our marriage isn't so fake anymore."

"Oh, Essie." James cupped my face, squishing my cheeks in her palms. "Maybe it never was."

"Rude," I said through my smushed lips.

"What's going on?" Chloe asked, pulling herself from a side conversation with Hannah and Janie.

"Nothing," I said quickly. "James is congratulating me again, that's all."

"Oh, is she congratulating you because your sham marriage is actually the real thing and now you don't have to lie to your best friends anymore?" Chloe asked. She leaned her elbow on the bar, cupped her chin on her palm, and stared at us with those green cat eyes of hers.

James let go of my face and my jaw flapped open. "How did you know?"

"Essie." Hannah pushed her glasses up the bridge of her nose, all the better to stare me down. "You happened to get engaged right after Zack is too injured to ride a horse you love so much you literally stole him, and immediately sign up to ride in the owner division? Come on, now. We all knew."

"All of you?" I looked to Janie for confirmation.

She nodded. "We were going to take bets on your divorce date, but that didn't work out."

"Why?" I asked. "Did you think it would end in murder instead?"

"No." James snorted. "Because not a single one of us thought you would get divorced."

"There's still time," I said flippantly, but my stomach cramped from the mere thought of it.

People get divorced all the time. That's what I had said to Brax, that day in his office. It was true, there was no denying that. But I didn't want it to be true for us.

And that mean little voice kept reminding me that he had walked away from me before, and there was nothing I could do to stop him from doing it again.

"Need to hit the ladies' room," I muttered. When James took a step behind me, I added, "I'll be back in a minute."

She nodded and settled back on her barstool.

I didn't do anything silly like ruin my makeup by splashing water on my face, but after a few deep breaths while staring my reflection dead in the eyes and reminding myself that I was Essie Fucking Price, with or without a man, I was ready to return to celebrating.

Until a rough hand clamped down on my wrist. "I want my money."

I stared at his weathered hand, shocked by his audacity to actually touch me, and then slowly raised my eyes to Alan Gaffney's leering face. "We all want things, Alan, but if you don't remove your hand from my arm, the only thing you're going to want is an ambulance ride to the hospital."

It wasn't an idle threat. Jack had taught me how to fight. Not just how to fight—how to fight like a girl. He had shown me how to take down someone bigger and stronger than myself, on the reasonable assumption that my attacker would be male. With Alan, it wouldn't even be that hard. He was taller, but he had all the muscle mass of a man who spent his life on a barstool.

"Pirate is my horse," Alan said. "When he wins, I get paid."

"Pirate belongs to Braxton Hale," I reminded him. "Or are you too drunk to remember selling him?"

"I remember, girlie. I remember that Brax and me are co-owners. I have just as much a right to that horse and his winnings as Brax does."

I froze. "What?"

Alan's fingers dug into my tendons, but I didn't wince. "He owes me my share. And if he doesn't pay it in a timely manner, maybe I'll take my horse back home where he belongs."

My gaze shot to where Brax was sitting in a booth with Adam and Zack. He wouldn't let that happen, would he? But then again, he had allowed Alan, the very man who had left Pirate to wilt in his own filth, to still own him, if what Alan said was true.

I couldn't make sense of it. How could Brax have done this?

And how could he have kept it from me?

"Excuse me, I need to borrow my husband for a minute." I rested my palm on his shoulder and smiled wide at Adam and Zack.

"What's—" Brax's voice cut off as he got a good look at my face. My smile might have fooled the others, but it didn't fool him. His eyebrows pushed together in a dark frown and he got to his feet. "I'll be back in a minute."

I took his elbow and maneuvered him to an unoccupied corner of the bar.

"Hey." Brax tilted my chin, eyes scanning my face. "What's going on?"

"I just had an interesting conversation with Alan Gaffney." My grip tightened on his elbow. "Please tell me it's not true."

The ensuing pause sent my heart right into my stomach. "Brax," I said.

"I can't tell you it's not true when I don't know what he said." He stepped closer. "Tell me."

"He said I owe him money." My gaze dropped to his chest. I had an awful feeling that Brax wasn't going to be able to refute Alan's claim. "He said he was a part-owner of Pirate and is entitled to his share of his winnings. Is that true?"

His frown deepened. "He had no business talking about that with you. His contract is with me. Whatever he earns, it doesn't come out of your share, so don't worry about that. Where is he? I'm going to—"

I pushed away from him. "So it *is* true?" My voice was shrill. "How could you keep this from me? Why didn't you tell me?"

I didn't wait for an answer. I whirled away, but only made it half a step before Brax caught me by the belt loop of my jeans and hauled me back.

"Oh, no, you don't, hellion," he said as I fell backward against his torso. With one hand on my hip, he wrapped his other arm across my chest, keeping me in place. "You're not running away from me all mad like that without giving me a chance to explain. Okay?"

I nodded stiffly.

"The day you stole Pirate, I realized the only way to make everything turn out okay was to buy the horse. But you know Alan. He didn't want to sell. He wasn't making a dime off that horse, but he sure did like to brag about the millions he would earn from Pirate's sperm someday."

I wrinkled my nose. I remembered. That was exactly why Alan had refused to sell Pirate to me in the first place.

"So I made him a more palatable offer. He would be a part-owner and get a percentage of Pirate's earnings in the ring and at stud. That way, Alan could keep right on doing what he loved best. Bragging."

I squeezed my eyes shut. Fuck. Alan was a part owner? I hated that. He had nearly killed Pirate from neglect. He didn't deserve that horse. But even more importantly, what did that mean for Pirate? "He said if he doesn't get his money, he's taking Pirate back to his place. I can't let him, Brax. I—"

"What?" Brax let out a startled laugh. He turned me around in his arms to face him. "Essie, *no*. In the first place, I'll pay him. Alan will get his precious money. In the second place, do you really believe I'd let an asshole like Alan have any say whatsoever in the care of an animal I own? We have a contract. He's a one-percent owner. He gets absolutely no say in Pirate's life, and he sure as hell can't take him away."

"Really?" I let his words sink in. Alan had made it sound so much worse. "Why didn't you tell me, then?"

"Because I—" He looked away and blew out a breath. "Because I knew you'd hate it. *I* hate it. Just on principle. That trash doesn't deserve Pirate, not even one percent of him. I knew you'd feel that ten times more than I did. I figured it didn't matter in the long run, since I'd pay Alan from my share of Pirate's earnings. You never had to know. I wanted...I wanted you to be happy, Essie."

"That is a terrible reason, Brax," I said sternly, even

though my heart was melting my anger into nothing. "You should have told me. I would have understood."

"I know," he said softly, but there was a hint of uncertainty in his eyes. Like maybe he *didn't* know.

It hurt my feelings, this constant belief that I must be protected at all costs. That people had to do things for me or keep things from me because I was too wild and impulsive to act in my own best interest.

Which was absolute bullshit.

I could take care of myself just fine.

"What's wrong with your wrist?" Brax asked, interrupting the silent argument I was having with him. "Why are you rubbing it like that?"

I hadn't even realized that's what I was doing. I glanced down. My wrist was a little achy and red, and a bruise the size of Alan's thumbprint was forming on the pale underside. "It's nothing. Alan and I had a little disagreement, that's all."

Brax's eyes are black as night in the dimly lit bar. "Alan did this to you?" he asked, quiet rage simmering in his voice.

"He thought we weren't done talking. I informed him we were." I glared at the bruise. "I would have laid him flat if I hadn't been so worried he could use that to take Pirate from me."

A muscle flickered in his cheek. "Where is he?"

"Don't," I warned, and I meant it. "I don't need you to fight my battles for me. Had I known he was only a one-percent owner, he'd be out back looking for his teeth right about now. But the moment is over. You can't go chasing him down now because that's not self-defense. That's assault."

For some reason, that didn't seem to amuse him the way it should have.

"It's a lawyer joke," I explained. "Because you're a lawyer."

He stared at me, his jaw locked tight, his eyes fathomless. Not finding me funny in the slightest, apparently.

I sighed and glanced around. James and Adam were making an early exit to get home to Ben, and they were taking Zack with them. He was healing pretty well, but with his leg in a cast, he didn't stay out late, and he didn't drive.

"Don't worry about Alan. I can handle him myself. Can we go home now?" I linked my elbow with Brax's and tugged him along. "It's been a long week, and I don't want to end a celebration on a bad note. Let's go get naked."

He allowed me to pull him out of the Painted Cat. We met up with James, Adam, and Zack in the parking lot and said our goodbyes.

"See you bright and early tomorrow morning, Essie!" James said with a shit-eating grin.

I grinned right back. I couldn't wait to get back to work.

"Actually, could you give Essie a ride home?" Brax asked. "There's something I need to take care of."

My gaze shot to his. "Brax—"

"I'm going to pay him, okay? Don't worry."

I hesitated. "I could wait for you."

"You have an early morning. Get some rest." He pressed a quick, sweet kiss to my lips. "I'll see you at home. Thirty minutes, tops."

I nodded. "Okay."

But all the way home, I couldn't shake the feeling that I should have stayed.

BRAX

I had fucked up.

I stared into the dark night as the red taillights disappeared around a bend, taking my wife with them. Seeing nothing but that devastated look of betrayal on her face when I told her the truth.

She could have defended herself from Alan. I knew Jack had taught her well, having been used as her practice dummy on more than one occasion. She could have driven her knee between his legs or punched him right in the solar plexus.

Hell, if she wasn't in the mood for violence, she could simply have hollered. The bar was packed, and not a single person here tonight would have thought twice about putting Alan on the floor. Janie knew I kept a shotgun behind the bar, and she knew how to use it.

Though, she wouldn't have had to use it, because if

Essie had screamed, I would have torn Alan apart with my bare hands.

But she hadn't screamed. She hadn't fought him off herself, and she sure as hell hadn't called for my help. So I had sat there, laughing with my brothers, enjoying my beer, while Alan Gaffney put his filthy hand on *my wife* and bruised her fucking wrist.

She had allowed it to happen.

Because of me.

And that was unbearable.

Shameful.

I found Alan inside, his fist wrapped around a bottle of beer. "You and I need to have a little chat," I said, pulling up next to him.

He grunted. "I want my money."

"So you told my wife."

He grunted again.

"That was a mistake, Alan." I said this pleasantly enough, despite the fury building in my gut.

He glared at me. "I want my money," he repeated.

"You will get your money," I gritted out. "Read the fucking contract. Whatever you're owed, you get a check for on a quarterly basis, along with a statement of account. March, June, September, December. Understand? The money didn't magically appear in my bank account the second Pirate won. It doesn't work that way."

"Oh." Alan blinked slowly as he considered that.

Then he gave me a sloppy grin. "Well, in that case, you can tell Essie no hard feelings."

My rage boiled over.

I grabbed him by his flannel shirt and hauled him to his feet. "I won't be telling Essie shit, and neither will you. Keep her name out of your mouth, and your hands off my wife."

Alan sputtered incoherent sounds of surprise.

"Say you understand." I shook him, hard. "Say it."

"I understand," he whined.

"Good." I released my hold on his shirt and took a step back, not remotely sorry when he crumpled on the floor. "Now get the fuck out of my bar. Men who put hands on my wife aren't welcome here."

That's when the little fucker grabbed me by the leg and before I could shake him off, he had my jeans pushed up and sank his filthy teeth into my shin like a goddamn chihuahua. I kicked him in the ribs with my other foot and he let go with a howl of pain.

"Fucking hell!" I roared. "If I have to get a goddamn rabies shot, I swear to god—" And I kicked him again.

"I'm calling the cops!" Alan wailed as three men jumped in to pull me away. "You Hale boys think you're so high and mighty. Well, this time you made a mistake."

"We'll see about that," I seethed.

I HAD FUCKED UP AGAIN.

"Can't say I ever thought I'd see you on that side of the bars," Mike Bailey said, shaking his head as he slid the door into place with a metallic clang and locked it.

Mike and I had graduated Aspen Springs High School the same year and our paths had crossed a handful of times in the ensuing years. Mostly when he arrested my clients. Taxes and divorce made up the bulk of my work, but every now and then I had a criminal case. Drunk driving or nuisance charges, generally.

"I get a phone call," I reminded him.

"Yeah, I know, you can't bail yourself out. Unless you have five hundred cash in your wallet right now?" Mike looked hopeful. I shook my head. "I figured as much. We only take cash. No cards or checks. Want me to give Essie a ring? Tell her to come get you?"

My chest clenched at the sound of her name. Essie was the very last person I'd want to see me here. She had to be up at five a.m. to get to Lodestar. No way was I going to drag her down here to bail out her dumbass of a husband. Especially not when the whole thing was my fault.

Zack would have been my first choice, since I'd done the same for him on more than one occasion. But he wasn't driving anywhere with that leg in a cast. My dad was out of the question, too. I didn't think I could stand his look of disappointment when I was already this disappointed with myself.

That left Adam.

Fucking hell.

He was never going to let me live this down.

And of course he'd have to tell James why he was leaving in the middle of the night, and she'd call Essie immediately. Fuck. Not that I planned on keeping this from her—I'd caused a fucking cascade of problems from keeping secrets already—but damn. I would rather explain it tomorrow, in the bright light of day. Maybe I could bring her lunch at Lodestar and we could discuss it then.

After I had fixed everything.

That was the important part.

"Give me the phone," I grunted. "I'm calling my brother."

Mike sucked in air through his teeth with a low whistle. "Suit yourself, but in my experience wives—"

I cut him off with a glare. "Give. Me. The. Phone."

After the phone call was made, I went back to slouching on the lone bench in my empty cell. It was a slow night, though I suspected Tuesdays usually were. Thank God for small favors, or whatever.

Twenty minutes later, the station door opened. I couldn't see the entrance from my cell, but I got to my feet, even though there was no way in hell Adam could have driven all the way here from the ranch in that time.

Mike bellowed a laugh. "Well, this is a surprise! How have you been, Essie?"

No.

Please, no.

"Well," came that husky voice I loved so much, "I was doing much better before I got called down here."

Fuck.

"I should say so," Mike said cheerfully. "Come right this way, Essie." He came into view and grinned at me. "See anything that belongs to you?"

I felt sick as he stepped aside and Essie saw me behind the bars. There was nowhere I could hide.

"Yes, that one's mine, all right." One dark brow arched, and her eyes bore straight into mine. "Hello, husband dear."

32

ESSIE

For once, I didn't want to fight.

Are you okay? I had asked as we buckled in.

Fine, was his perfunctory response. We didn't say anything at all after that. I dropped him off at the Painted Cat to collect his truck, since he had gotten a ride down to the station in the back of a cop car, and met him at home.

"How's your wrist?" he asked gruffly as we changed for bed, his gaze on the floor. He hadn't met my eyes since Mike unlocked his cell door.

"Tender." I shrugged. "I took an ibuprofen for the swelling. It will be fine."

The look on Brax's face suggested he didn't believe there was anything fine about this at all.

There was so much to say. So many emotions

tumbling in my stomach. So many questions swirling in my brain.

Such as, *what the fuck, Brax, didn't I tell you to leave it alone?*

Or, *what the fuck, Brax, why do you keep fighting my battles for me?*

Most importantly, *what the fuck, Brax, how could you call Adam instead of me?*

And then some good, old-fashioned screaming.

But I didn't want to say any of that. I didn't want to fight.

I just wanted to hold him.

So that's what I did, when we crawled into bed together and he rolled onto his side, facing away from me. I snuggled up against his broad back and wrapped my arm around his middle. He stiffened and for a terrible moment I thought he might actually push me away. But then his muscles relaxed on a heavy sigh, and he covered my hand with his.

We slept like that.

When Adam had called to inform me that my formerly uptight, rule-stickler husband had somehow landed himself in jail, I had told him not to expect me at Lodestar until noon. That would give Brax and me some time to talk things through before he had to work.

That was the plan, anyway.

But when I finally pried my eyelids open, his side of the bed was empty.

Brax was gone.

I bolted out of bed and ran to the window, but I already knew what I'd find. Sure enough, his truck was gone.

He had walked away...again.

That fucking coward.

WITH NOTHING BETTER TO DO SINCE BRAX BAILED ON ME, I showered and headed to Lodestar Ranch, with a quick detour at Sweetie Pie. Because while I wasn't one of those people who believed pie could solve all the problems, I did believe my problems would still be there without pie, so I might as well suffer and have pie, too.

Anyway, I knew Mom would be working because Mom was always working, and right now, I really wanted my mother.

Mom looked up from a conversation with a customer as I walked in. After she finished helping her, Mom pulled a cherry pie from the glass case, removed a slice, and slid it onto a porcelain plate. Cherry pie was my favorite.

"To go, Mom," I said, even though all I wanted was to cry in her arms. God, being an adult sucked. "I have to be at Lodestar."

She sank her fists onto her hips and frowned at me.

"Esther Louise Price, you did not come in here the morning after you had to bail your husband out of jail just to take a slice of pie to go. Now, you go park your butt at that table over there, and I'll be over with your coffee in a minute."

"Mom!" I protested. I looked around, but no one seemed at all shocked to hear Braxton Hale, formerly an upright citizen, had spent some time behind bars last night.

"What? Everyone knows already. Three people told me before eight a.m. Now, sit."

"Yes, ma'am," I muttered. I took my pie and sheepishly slunk to the table in the corner.

I took a bite of pie, ignoring the curious looks of other customers. Occasionally, someone stared a little too long and I gave them my best *go ahead, I dare you* expression. They always looked away quickly after that.

"Here we are," Mom said, placing two steaming mugs of coffee on the table and sitting down across from me. "Cream and a little sugar."

Exactly how I liked it.

I took a careful sip, knowing Sweetie Pie tended to serve coffee piping hot, and let the warmth spread through me. I took another bite of pie, then had another sip.

"Now," Mom said. "What happened?"

I told her everything I knew, which wasn't a whole lot. Adam hadn't shared any of the gory details. All I knew was that Brax and Alan had exchanged words, Brax had attacked Alan, and then Alan had called the cops. Alan, to my understanding, had been able to walk away on his own two legs without assistance, which meant Brax had been holding back. He wouldn't have murder charges in his future. That was something, at least.

Mom's gaze fell to my wrist and her eyes narrowed. "Alan Gaffney did that to you?"

I groaned. "Not you, too, Mom. It barely even hurts anymore." I huffed an annoyed sigh and leaned back in my chair. "You...Brax...*argh*. I'm not saying Alan should get away with it. I just...I can handle it myself. I don't need people babying me."

"*Caring* for you." Mom took a slow sip of coffee. "That's what we're doing, honey. We're caring for you. And I'll tell you something, Essie. You might as well try to hold back the ocean as tell Braxton Hale not to care for you. That man would move mountains for you."

"I never asked him to!" I exploded. Frustrated, I stabbed my pie with my fork.

"No, you never asked him to," Mom agreed. "How do you think he feels about that?"

I frowned. "What do you mean?"

"Well." Her head tilted as she considered. "Do you remember when you were twelve and decided to build yourself a barn out back? It was the only way we'd be able to afford keeping a horse, if we didn't have to pay to board him somewhere, and there was enough space to set up some barrels for practice, too. You worked on that for two months and got nowhere. You wouldn't let Brax help. You wouldn't let Jack help. You kept saying you could do it yourself, until Brax finally said he didn't know what else to get you for your thirteenth birthday, so you had to let him do it as a present. Do you remember that?"

"Of course I remember." I almost smiled, remembering how hard Brax had pleaded. Then I shook my head. "I still could have done it myself."

"Honey, no. You couldn't have," Mom said matter-of-factly. "No one can build a barn by themselves, especially not when they're all of twelve years old. Not you. Not Brax. That's why he got Jack, his brothers, and his dad to help, too." She paused, then leaned forward. "*He asked for help* to get it done. That's my point."

"Subtle, Mom. Real subtle." I raised my eyebrows. "Are you saying I should have asked my husband to beat up a man for me? Because I don't think that's a lesson you want me to learn."

"Essie, honestly." Mom sounded stern, but I caught the smirk she tried to hide behind her coffee cup.

"I'm not weak, Mom," I said. "I'm not fragile. And I am so tired of people treating me like I am. I made it to the top of a very competitive sport. I'm now successfully starting a new career from scratch. I mostly make good decisions, and when I don't, I find a way forward, anyway. I don't need anyone fighting my battles for me."

Mom touched my hand. "Honey, no one thinks you're weak. Especially not Brax. Has it ever occurred to you that he's not trying to fight your battles *for* you, he's trying to fight them *with* you? Why won't you let him?"

I opened my mouth to argue, but nothing came out.

Why wouldn't I let Brax help me?

She was right. I always told him no. I was determined to prove I could do it myself. I didn't need anyone. Especially not him.

"You're the one who told me not to depend on a man. And you were right. Dad never kept a promise." I wiped furiously at my eyes. "And Brax...what if he does the same thing? He walked away before. He walked away this morning. What if I come to depend on him, and then he's not there anymore?"

"Oh, honey," Mom said softly. "Brax isn't your father. He's not going to let you down like that."

"But what if he *does*?" I insisted.

Mom made a face. A sympathetic, heartbroken, determined face. "You know exactly what you'd do about that, Essie, so don't you sit there and pretend otherwise. Because you're damn right. You're not weak. You're not fragile. So you'd cry about it and then you'd get right back on your feet and move forward." Her eyes glimmered, with tears and a little mischief. "And you'd come tell your momma all about it, because she knows how to bury a body."

I burst out laughing despite myself. "Mom!"

She shrugged. "I'm just saying. Jack has lots of knowledge to impart."

I shoveled another bite of pie into my mouth. It didn't change my problems. Brax and I had some things to work out, for sure.

But I knew what I wanted.

I just hoped Brax wanted it, too.

33

BRAX

I was at the office by seven a.m. By nine a.m. the paperwork was completed and ready to file.

I figured Essie had already left for Lodestar. She hadn't texted to let me know or ask where I was. That stung more than it should have, considering I hadn't texted her either.

Just in case she was home waiting for me, I swung by the house. After verifying that her car wasn't in the garage, I headed straight for Lodestar.

I was going to fix this. I was going to make this right for her.

Her cherry-red SUV was parked right out front of the stables. I didn't see any sign of her in the training ring, but Pirate's stall was empty, so maybe she had taken him for a trail ride to stretch his legs. At least I knew she was here and not off plotting Alan's demise without me.

"About time you showed up here," Adam said behind me.

I turned slowly to face my brother. He leaned a hip against the stall door. Smug bastard.

"You." I jabbed my index finger into his chest for emphasis. "You are a fucking traitor."

"Look, I was going to get you," Adam protested. "Of course I was. But James wanted the story, and once I told her what was happening, she insisted we call Essie right away. I told her I had promised, but she said if I took one step toward that door, I'd be on the couch tomorrow night."

"You." I jabbed my index finger into his chest again. "Are fucking whipped."

"That I am," Adam said cheerfully. "Come on. Essie's out with James, and they won't be back for a bit. We've got some stalls that need mucking."

"I don't think so," I said.

Adam shrugged. "Suit yourself. Dad said you were to go up to the main house the second you showed your face, so feel free to mosey on over there and see what he wants to chat about."

I didn't have to think long about that.

"Hand me that pitchfork," I grumbled.

Adam grinned.

We started at the far end, tag teaming each stall

rather than working separately. For the first couple minutes, we worked in blessed silence, focusing our efforts—if not our minds—on shoveling shit and spreading clean hay.

But that didn't last long.

Not that I had expected it to.

"Sure was surprised to get your call last night," Adam said conversationally. "I never thought I'd see the day when my rule-loving, law-abiding brother spent time behind bars. You want to talk about that?"

"No," I said. "I do not."

Adam gave me a long look that clearly said, *too bad*. I shrugged wearily. "Say it, then."

"Come on, man." He shook his head like he was actually disappointed in me. "What the hell were you thinking? Alan Gaffney is trash. Pathetic, drunk trash. You use your brain on someone like that. You ruin their life. What you don't do is assault them physically. And if you do, you sure as hell don't send your brothers home first."

"I'll tell you what I was thinking," I growled as I scooped up a steaming pile of shit. "I was thinking, *that motherfucker just bit me*."

Adam blinked. "What?"

"I wasn't going to fight him. You're right. He's too pathetic for that. Anyway, Essie was against me smashing my fist into his face. I just wanted to talk to him. Set a boundary."

"The kind of boundary I set with Steven MacAllister?" Adam asked drily.

About a year ago, Steven had purposefully spooked a horse James was riding. She had been bucked off and bruised her ribs. She was lucky she hadn't been hurt worse. Adam had fired Steven—and let him understand that if he ever set foot near James again, he'd be in a body cast.

"Something like that," I admitted. "But then he bit me on the goddamn shin, and I kicked him. He's lucky I aimed for his ribs and not his head."

"He *bit* you." Adam's lip curled in disgust. "That is vile."

"Still have the teeth marks." I grimaced and Adam shuddered. "He can press whatever charges he wants, but they won't stick. I'm not worried about a criminal case." A civil case might be a different story, but I had a plan for that, too.

We didn't talk for a couple minutes as I maneuvered the full wheelbarrow outside and dumped it in the manure pile. I paused and looked past the pasture to the copse of trees in the distance. My breath came out in thick puffs of steam in the cold air and I wiped the sweat from my forehead with my sleeve.

Still no sign of Essie.

With a sigh, I turned back to the barn, where more shit awaited me.

"I want to know something, Brax." Adam rested his

hands on the end of the pitchfork and leaned his weight into it.

"Yeah?" I grunted.

"Why did you call me instead of Essie?"

I lowered the pitchfork and looked at him. "Why the hell do you think?"

"I think you're chickenshit."

"Well, I'd say that's about right." I went back to shoveling.

"She loves you." Adam spoke quietly. Carefully. "You know that, right?"

I paused. *Did* I know that? Was it even true? She hadn't said she loved me. *Maybe it's real* was nice to hear, but it wasn't the same as love. She *had* loved me, once. Even if she hadn't fully recognized it then for what it was. I had wrecked that up good.

I was *still* wrecking things now.

"You remember how close Essie and I were in high school?" I asked. "And then one day we weren't."

Adam straightened and his gaze sharpened. "I remember."

"Essie and I went hiking. We weren't supposed to. We cut school, even though I promised Jack we wouldn't. She wasn't dressed for it. Fucking sneakers with no traction. I *warned* her." I shook my head. Hubris. "She was fine. I was the one who screwed up. I was walking backward like an idiot. Not paying attention. I stepped in a sketchy area, too close to the cliff. The ground crumbled beneath me."

Adam didn't move. Didn't speak. Just listened.

I swallowed hard. "I should have died. Should have fallen to my death and gotten one of those posthumous Darwin Awards. But she grabbed me and yanked me back. She grabbed me so hard that the momentum of it sent her over. She went over the fucking cliff, Adam." My voice cracked. All these years later, I could still feel that moment like I was still right there, screaming her name.

"It was my fault," I said. "My fault she fell. I knew better than to break a rule, but I did it anyway, and that's what happened."

Adam was quiet, watching me.

I looked at him, waiting for his condemnation.

"And then?" he asked.

I frowned. "What do you mean?"

"I mean, Essie isn't dead. I just saw her this morning. And you're not dead, either. So finish the story."

I barked a laugh. "She survived. She wasn't even really hurt. She didn't fall that far before her foot caught on a boulder. The cliff was mostly scree, so it was slippery, but she crawled her ass right back up the cliff. I realized then that it didn't matter that we were only sixteen. I loved her, she loved me, and it wasn't the kind of thing that would end when we graduated. But Essie had plans. Big dreams. I couldn't stand in the way of that. And if I had tried, Jack would have tossed me right over that cliff anyway."

Adam snorted at that, but he didn't disagree. He knew Jack.

"I told him I wouldn't hold her back. I promised him I wouldn't give her a reason to stay. That's why we stopped being friends. I couldn't be around her without telling her how I felt, and if I did that, she wouldn't have wanted to leave Aspen Springs." I leaned on my pitchfork. "Fuck."

"That wasn't the end, either, because now you're married," Adam said. "Finish the story."

"You know that story. The story is, I fucked up again." I wanted to kick something, but instead I shoveled another forkful of manure into the wheelbarrow.

"That's just where you are now. The story isn't over yet. You keep getting hung up on all the crappy parts. The imperfect parts. And I get it, because I get *you*, and you've always been like this as long as I've known you. So damn good, it's annoying. But everyone messes up sometimes, and you have a damn hard time coming to terms with that for yourself."

I shrugged. I knew that was true, and there was no sense in denying it. Nothing had *made* me this way. It was simply who I was. It didn't matter that I could forgive mistakes in others. I could never forgive them in myself.

"You're still alive, Brax," Adam said. "Essie is still

alive. And the two of you love each other so damn much, it's kind of gross to look at, honestly."

I choked out a laugh. It sure as fuck wasn't a sob.

My brother had the decency to look away, give me some privacy. "I thought my story was done. James made me realize how ridiculous that was. I learned the hard way that your story, whatever it might be, doesn't end until you draw your last breath. Even my first marriage... I thought I knew that story, but it wasn't until years after Emily died that I understood the full truth of it. Your story changes you, but it also changes *with* you."

Adam pulled off his work gloves and squeezed my shoulder. "I'm sorry you had to watch Essie go over a cliff. That's an awful thing to have witnessed, and I can only imagine how you felt when you didn't know if she was going to live or die. But don't get stuck there, in that memory. It wasn't the end. *This* isn't the end. You have fucking *decades* left to finish the story. So what are you going to do?"

34

ESSIE

I stared at the dropped pin, and the text message attached to it.

Come get your husband.

I didn't hesitate to do exactly that. I hit the directions button and followed the path out of the barn, past the main house, and down the trail to Brax's cabin. I found him sitting on the front stoop, a roll of papers in his hand.

He pushed to his feet when he saw me coming, relief washing over his face. "Essie."

He said my name like it was the answer to every-thing. Suddenly waiting even five seconds longer to touch him was too much. I sprinted the last few yards and launched myself into his arms. He caught me, one arm banding around my waist, crushing the roll of papers against my back, and his other hand cupping the back of my head.

"I'm sorry, Essie. I'm so fucking sorry," he murmured against my temple.

I sniffled against his shirt. It was ridiculous how often this man moved me to tears. Good tears, at least. "You can't leave me like that, Brax. I need to know you're coming back."

"I'm *always* coming back. I just...I didn't want to talk about what happened until I had fixed it. That's what I was doing. I went to my office to figure it out, and I think I have the solution." He let go of me and smoothed out the crinkled papers.

"What are you talking about?" I asked, genuinely confused.

"Alan Gaffney."

I wrinkled my nose. "Ugh. I hate that guy."

"So let's sue him." Brax laid out his plan. "I think we have a damn good civil case. No judge worth her robes is going to think you should have a physically abusive business partner. It's a risk, but I have the feeling he won't even want to go to court. It's too expensive. Us buying him out will be the best option, especially if you agree not to press criminal charges."

I looked over the papers, then set them aside, chewing my lip.

"I know you can handle him yourself, but you

shouldn't have to. You're the most stubborn, competent, amazing person I know, and I love you. You told me you don't want me fighting your battles for you, and I get that. I do. But, here's the thing, hellion." He tipped my chin to look at him. "They're not *your* battles anymore. They're ours."

I swallowed hard. God, this man. "My mom had to give up everything to raise me and my brother. My dad gave up literally nothing. I don't know how to find the middle ground between those two extremes, you know? I'm scared I'll ask for too much."

"There's no such thing as too much when it comes to you, Essie. That's what I've been trying to tell you. I'll find a way to become enough. It's not even hard. I've been doing it since the day I met you. Whatever you needed, that's what I became. You needed a barn, I learned how to build one. Your mom needed a lawyer, I made that happen. You stole a horse, so I bought it for you. And you know what? I love my career. I love that damn horse. You've made my life better in every possible way. You made *me* better."

"Brax," I whispered. My hands twisted in his shirt. My heart lodged in my throat.

"I know you're not weak, Essie. I never thought you were. That's not why—" His voice thickened, choked. "I love you. That's all. You couldn't ask for a single thing that would change that. I'm not that fragile, and neither is my love. Tag me in, hellion. Let me help you."

I stared up at him, this man I loved with all my savage, bruised heart. "All right. Sue the shit out him. But, Brax, this goes both ways. If you're my person, then I'm yours. Your battles are mine. I'm the one you call."

He grimaced, his gaze shifting away from me. "How about you're my person unless I'm being a colossal dumbass? I fucked up last night. I should have walked away from Alan, and I knew better. You don't need to clean up my messes."

"I don't agree to that at all." My head tipped back and I stared at him with all the love I felt blazing in my eyes. "It would be the honor of my life to stand shoulder to shoulder with you when you're being a dumbass. It would be the honor of my life to be the one you call to bail you out when you took something a little too far. Because that's what love is. It's big and messy and doesn't follow rules. And you, Braxton Hale, are the love of my life."

For a moment he just looked at me, his jaw ticking and his eyes suspiciously damp. Then his throat worked as he swallowed. "All right, hellion," he said gruffly. "You've got a deal."

I smiled as he bent down to kiss me.

Because I planned to make good on that bargain for the rest of our lives.

35

BRAX

ESSIE

Laundry day! I'm down to one clean pair of pants. Guess I'll be wearing leggings today. Anything you want me to throw in the wash?

BRAX

A couple pair of jeans in the bin. Thanks.

Wait, you're wearing leggings?

ESSIE

Gotta go! Don't want to be late for work! ;)

y wife was wearing leggings.

Not just leggings. She had paired them with a cropped tee shirt that barely covered her midriff, much less her commando ass.

I knew this because the second I had read her text this morning, I had seen fit to clear the rest of my schedule and spend the day at Lodestar, and told my secretary to take the afternoon off, as well. Now I was leaning against the rail of the training ring, watching Essie work her magic with a barrel racer.

Damn. There were few things I enjoyed more than watching Essie in her element.

It was one of those glorious days of sixty-degree sunshine that made a person feel like spring was just around the corner, even though in reality we were two weeks before Christmas. Birds chirped, horses pranced, and even my grumpy older brother smiled.

And my wife was wearing leggings.

I picked up the rope I had left slung over the rail. Ben had asked me to teach him a few tricks, and I'd been happy to oblige while Essie was otherwise occupied. One day Ben was going to be a star on the rodeo circuit, I'd bet my boots on it.

Essie raised her arm to get the rider's attention, and her shirt pulled up, revealing a stretch of pale, taut stomach. My gaze snagged there on her exposed skin. I worked the length of rope through my hands, rubbing my thumb over the twisted cotton fibers, and bided my time.

"Bring him to a walk and cool him down," Essie called. "You want some water?"

"I'm good, thanks," her client, and up-and-coming barrel racer, said. She swung her right leg over the horse's back and dismounted gracefully. "I'm going to untack him and walk him in the pasture out back. It's too nice out here to cool down walking circles in the ring. Is that ok?"

"Sure, go ahead," Essie said. The rider clucked her tongue and led the horse back into the barn.

Essie sauntered over to where I stood at the fence. "Hello, husband. What brings you to the ranch on this fine day?"

"I think you know, hellion." I stroked the rope again.

She hinged at the waist and grabbed the green water jug at my feet before straightening again. "Haven't a clue." She took a sip, her wide blue eyes never leaving mine.

"Is that right?" I asked. She cocked her head. "I seem to recall telling you not to wear leggings to the ranch. Did you forget about that?"

Her eyebrows went up. "Oh, I remember. In fact, I have a little something saved just for this occasion." She held out her fist to me. "Behold, my last fuck." She opened her fingers, revealing her empty palm. "Oh, wait, it's gone. Guess I spent it somewhere else." She grinned.

"God, you're such a brat," I muttered.

She planted a smacking kiss on my cheek. "You love me."

"You're fucking right, I do." I gripped her chin and pulled her face closer to kiss her on the mouth. "So damn much."

"Mm." She smiled up at me, her eyes happy and dreamy. I had kissed the brat right out of her.

Not for long, I hoped.

"I need to take care of a couple things, but then I'm free for the next hour. I have another client coming at three," she said, turning to go.

"How about you change into these jeans first?" I suggested, nudging a paper bag with my boot.

She looked down at the bag and frowned. "You cannot be serious."

"And yet, I am."

She rolled her eyes. "Yeah, I'm not doing that. Give me fifteen minutes, okay? Then I'm yours." She ambled away, giving her hips a suggestive swing, then called back over her shoulder, "Look, daddy, no panty lines."

I grinned, knowing she couldn't see me.

The brat was back.

I ducked through the rails, my boots making no sound at all in the soft dirt. My wrist flicked in a small circle, faster and faster, until the loop at the end of the rope was wide and open. Then I sent it flying. It sailed over her head and, in the split second it encircled her waist, I tugged sharply. The rope tightened, pinning her arms to her sides.

"Hey!" she shrieked.

I pulled the rope gently but relentlessly, forcing her to walk backward unless she wanted to tumble to the ground.

"You can't lasso me like a cow, Brax!" she hollered. But she took three more steps backward, coming closer to me with each step.

"And yet, I just did," I said.

When she was close enough to grab, I loosened the rope so it fell to the ground. She stepped out of the loop, scowling at me. "Don't try to run," I warned. "You'll just make me mad."

And wouldn't you know, my hellion looked entirely too interested in that prospect.

I didn't give her a chance to try me. I squatted low, put my shoulder to her belly, and tossed her up in a fireman's hold.

"Brax!" she squealed as I strode away from the barn. "Where are you taking me?"

I didn't answer, and I didn't stop until we reached the foaling pasture, out of sight of the main house and barn. Then I set her on her feet and dropped the bag next to us.

"You recognize this stretch of fence?" I asked.

A pretty pink bloomed on her cheekbones as she took a look. "Maybe I do."

"This is where I told you not to leave the house in leggings without underwear." I pressed into her from behind and ran my hands over her hips, searching. "Are you wearing underwear, Essie?"

Her voice was a little sassy, a little breathless when she said, "You know I'm not."

"Filthy girl." I swatted her ass and bit down on the junction where her neck met her shoulder. She shivered against me. "Bend over and hold on to the fence post."

She hesitated a moment, just long enough to make me wonder if she meant to refuse, and then she did as told. I took the rope and bound her hands to the wood. Tight enough that her skin would turn pink there, but not enough to cause lasting irritation.

Then I yanked those fucking leggings down to her knees. She gasped as the air hit her skin. "Bare," I muttered. "What did I tell you about that, hellion?"

"I don't remember, so it couldn't have been that important," she said.

"Then I better remind you in a way you won't forget," I murmured, then bit her gently on that sweet, round ass. "Lift your foot."

She gave me her right foot, shifting her weight to her left, and I tugged off her boot, peeled the legging off her leg, then replaced the boot. Then I did the same with her left leg.

And then I ripped her leggings clean in half.

Essie's face whipped around on a shocked gasp at the sound of rending fabric. "What the hell, Brax?"

"I warned you," I said, completely unrepentant.

"You're an asshole," she snapped. "And you owe me a new pair of leggings. The good kind. They don't come cheap, by the way."

"You can have as many pairs as you want, as long as you don't leave the house without underwear."

Her eyes narrowed into blue slits.

Head tilted, I studied her. "How wet are you right now? Because you've got that mean look on your face that usually goes with being soaked."

Her gaze dropped to the swelling bulge in my jeans and she licked her lips. "Not wet at all."

I chuckled softly. "Little liar."

She huffed and tossed her head.

I slipped my hand between her legs to check for myself and groaned. "You're a fucking mess, honey." Not being able to resist, I squatted down and put my mouth there, eating her pussy from behind.

With a wanton little moan, she pushed her hips back against my face. I kneaded the globes of her ass as I slid my tongue deep in her pussy. When I felt her inner muscles tighten, I reluctantly withdrew.

"Oh, no, you don't. Orgasms are for good girls."

"Brax!" she whined, wiggling her hips.

I gave her one more savoring lick before I stood. "God, look at you," I muttered. Her round ass. Her muscled thighs. "So fucking desperate. So pretty." I unzipped my jeans, took my dick in hand, and ran it down the crack of her ass, making her whimper.

With one deep, hard thrust, I was inside her all the way to the hilt.

And then I needed a second to get reacquainted with my self-control. Her pussy pulsing around me didn't help with that. I held completely still and stared blankly at the sky.

"Brax," Essie gritted out. She shifted on those strong thighs, dragging her pussy down my shaft until only the crown is inside her. Then she slammed back into me, making my eyes cross. "Fucking *move*."

I moved. Hard, fast, my fingers digging into her hips to put us on the same rhythm. She gave back as much as she took. Skin slapped against skin, our panting breaths mingling with the rustling breeze.

"I need—I need—" Essie's voice ended on desperate moans.

"I know what you need." My hand rounded her belly and dipped lower. I found her clit and pressed hard, rapid little circles with two fingers.

She cried out, her pussy clenching, and we came apart at the same time. Hard and fast and relentless. When the last wave of pleasure subsided, I pulled out slowly, a trail of our cum following in my wake.

I swiped one leg of her ruined leggings of the grass and used it to wipe her clean. Her heavy breaths began to return to normal, but her legs were trembling. Quickly, I untied her.

She looked at me, rubbing her wrists. I handed her the bag with clean jeans and underwear. Huffing an annoyed laugh, she stepped into the black cotton briefs and wiggled them on.

"Think you learned your lesson this time, hellion?" I asked, watching her balance on one foot and then the other as she took off her boots to get the jeans on.

She paused and looked at me. "I suppose that depends on what lesson you intended me to learn."

"Don't leave the house without underwear."

She smirked. "Unless I want to get railed by my husband's huge cock, you mean?" She pulled up the zipper and patted my cheek. "Oh, yes. I learned."

"Good. Then we're on the same page."

This time she didn't smirk. She kissed me.

And I kissed her back.

Because we were on the same page with that, too.

One year later...

I OPENED THE FREEZER AND STARED INSIDE. IT HAD TO BE here somewhere. Unless, of course, Brax had thrown it away, not realizing what it was. I pushed aside packages of beef and chicken. There, deep in the back, I found it. A cylinder wrapped twice in tinfoil and then shoved in a storage bag that supposedly could withstand freezer burn.

"Hey," Brax said behind me.

I yelped and spun on my toes, clutching the frozen cylinder to my chest. "You've *got* to stop doing that!"

"Sorry." He didn't look repentant at all. "What are you doing?"

"Oh, just…" I waived the tinfoil package in the air like it was an answer in and of itself. "What are *you* doing, besides giving me a heart attack?"

He didn't reply immediately, and that's when I realized he was holding a package of his own. A small square, wrapped in blue-striped paper, with a darker blue bow on top. His anniversary present for me, I assumed. Jewelry, maybe?

"Is that for me?" I asked.

"Of course it is," he said, but when I reached for it, he shook his head. "Not yet. Let's go for a drive."

I bit back a groan. "A drive? I love you, but it feels like all I do is drive." The forty-minute commute each way had seemed to breeze by when I first started at Lodestar Ranch, but it got old fast. And when the weather was bad? Ugh.

"It will be worth it, I promise," he said. "Please?"

I couldn't say no when he was looking at me so hopefully. "All right. Let me grab a few things first."

I ran to our bedroom and pulled out the large box I had wrapped just this morning from under the bed. I put that in a bag along with the tinfoil package, some napkins, and a couple forks.

"Ready," I said.

It was a gorgeous evening for a drive, and with Brax doing all the work, I didn't mind being back in the car. I rolled down the window to enjoy the crisp autumn breeze. September was still my favorite month in Colorado. There was nowhere else I'd rather be than right here, my husband's hand on my thigh, the splendor of the Rockies laid out before us.

"We're going to Lodestar?" I asked as we turned on the familiar dirt road. I brushed my wind-strewn hair out of my eyes and looked at him. "Our spot?"

"That's right."

I should have known. There was a place deep in the pastures, nearly to the tree line, where we liked to go and park. It had the benefit of being a five-minute drive by four-wheeler—or fifteen minutes by horse—from the cabins and main house. Private, but convenient.

It was also, in my opinion, the prettiest piece of land on the whole property. The view was breathtaking.

Of course, the view was amazing on every corner of the ranch. It was possible the time we spent there, and *how* we spent it, made me biased.

Brax turned off the road and bumped over the field until we were far enough away that no one could see the truck. I hopped down while he grabbed our blanket from the backseat. I stood there, admiring the streaks of orange, pink, and purple left behind as the setting sun hovered over the ridgeline, and breathed. Contentment washed over me.

Nowhere else I'd rather be.

"Essie."

I turned around and saw that Brax had spread the blanket out. There was a picnic basket on the blanket and a bottle of champagne in a bucket of ice packs. I blinked. He must have snuck everything into his SUV while I was grabbing his present.

"What is all this?" I asked, stupefied.

"It's our anniversary. A full year of living under one roof and not murdering each other. Shouldn't we celebrate?" There was something in his voice that made me squint a little. An uncertainty underneath his dry humor.

I moved toward him and looped my arms around his neck. "Of course we should celebrate. I have something for you." I rolled onto my toes and kissed him.

"Thanks, I love it."

I laughed. "Not a kiss, Brax. An actual present."

I disentangled myself from his arms and grabbed the bag from the truck. "Let's sit."

We both pulled off our boots and made ourselves comfortable on the blanket.

"I have something for you, too," he said, pulling out the small box.

I handed him the present I had wrapped. "Open yours first."

He smiled and started carefully working the tape free of the wrapping paper. I rolled onto my knees and watched impatiently. Finally he slipped the box free and folded the paper up in a neat little square. I would have rolled my eyes if it weren't so darn cute. So darn *him*.

"The Tecovas?" he exclaimed as he held up an ostrich-leather boot. "You said no self-respecting cowboy could wear them."

"You're not a cowboy," I said. "You're an attorney and a part-time rancher. Every self-respecting attorney should have a pair. Anyway, I was running out of ideas of what to get you for our anniversary because when you like something, you just buy it yourself. That makes it very difficult to buy you presents, you know. I had to be proactive. Do you like them?"

"I love them. Thanks, honey." He gave me a quick peck on the lips, then slid his feet into them to check the fit. "They're perfect."

I grinned happily. "Good."

"And now, yours." He handed me the present.

I ripped open the wrapping paper with all the glee of a child on Christmas morning. I loved presents. The small white velvet box inside was a dead giveaway that I was right. It had to be jewelry.

I wasn't disappointed. Nestled inside was a gold necklace with a diamond pendant. I held it up to admire it, threading my fingers through the delicate gold chain. The diamond glinted prettily from the center of a gold disk. I squinted closer, noting the numbers etched along the perimeter of the disk.

"Is that…" My brow furrowed. "What are the numbers? They look like latitude and longitude."

"That's exactly what they are." He took the necklace from me and gently laid it over my collar bone, fastening the clasp in the back. "The latitude and longitude of this precise location. Right here, where we're sitting now."

I smirked a little, even though my throat felt suspiciously tight. "You wanted to memorialize the place where I gave you the best blow job of your life?" I teased.

He chuckled softly and bit the nape of my neck, just above the clasp. "No, hellion. I wanted to memorialize the place where we'll build a home together."

My breath stuttered. "What?" I whispered, turning to face him.

"Only if that's what you want," he said hastily. "This is something we decide together. If you want to stay in town, fine. We'll stay. But you have been so exhausted from driving back and forth, and it occurred to me that I don't need an office in town. I can work from a home office and do house calls. Hell, my clients would absolutely prefer I come to them and save them the drive into town themselves. So if you want, this can be ours. We can build our home here."

"Brax." My eyes were wet. A tear trembled on my lower lashes and I blinked frantically. "Are you sure?"

"I want as much time with you as I can possibly get. This is the way to do that. So, yeah. I'm fucking sure."

I threw my arms around his neck. "Thank you. I..." My voice clogged. "I love you."

He kissed my forehead. "I love you, too, hellion. Now, let's crack open that champagne and celebrate."

"Oh!" I brightened as I remembered what I had taken from the freezer. "And I have dessert!"

"Oh, yeah? Whaddya bring? Pie?" he asked.

I shook my head. "Cake." I handed him the still-cold-but-not-frozen package. "Specifically, our wedding cake."

He gave me a quizzical look as he unwrapped the tinfoil. "What?"

"It's a tradition," I explained. "You're supposed to save the top tier of the wedding cake to eat on your first anniversary."

Brax pulled off the last layer and there it was. White frosting over a chocolate cake. He stared at it.

"Mom wrapped it up for me. I was going to throw it away, because..." I shrugged. "You know. But I figured, why not, so I kept it. Anyway, I'm not going to promise you it's still good after a solid year in the freezer. It's a weird tradition, if you ask me, but—"

He lunged at me, swallowing my words with his mouth. After a startled second, I sank into the kiss. His mouth gentled as the kiss deepened, and when he finally pulled away, I couldn't remember what we had been talking about.

"You kept it." He held my face in his palm, his thumb

stroking my cheekbone. "Why didn't you throw it away?"

"I—" I blinked, my mind going back to that day. Our first kiss. The vows. "I didn't want to," I confessed. "I wouldn't let myself think any deeper about it than that. I just…couldn't throw it in the trash. I told myself the marriage was all fake, but I think a part of me knew I would want it today."

"Essie," he whispered. He kissed my mouth like I was something precious. "This is the best gift anyone has ever given me."

My eyes were damp all over again. "It might be disgusting," I warned him. "But go ahead and serve it up. Let's have our first meal at our new home."

He smiled at that. "The first of many."

The beginning of forever.

ABOUT THE AUTHOR

Elizabeth Bright isa USA Today best-selling author of small town romance with heart, humor, and heat. When she's not writing about fierce heroines and the men who adore them, she can be found curled up with a book, a needy dog, and a large iced coffee.

Sign up for her newsletter at
www.elizabethbrightauthor.com

Also by Elizabeth Bright

Lodestar Ranch

A Cowboy in the Streets
Just Say When

Hart's Ridge

Make Me Love You
Don't Call Me Sweetheart
Trust Me
Christmas at Hart's Ridge

www.ingramcontent.com/pod-product-compliance
Lightning Source LLC
Chambersburg PA
CBHW030102310726
48970CB00004B/1117

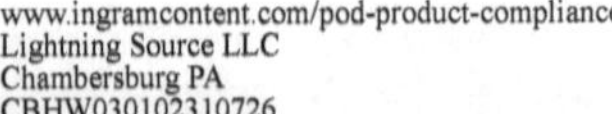